Upper Darby Public Libraries

Sellers/Main
610-789-4440
76 S. State RD

Municipal Branch
610-734-7649
501 Bywood Ave.

Primos Branch
610-622-8091
409 Ashland Ave.

Online renewals:

www.udlibraries.org
my account

Connecting you to literacy,
entertainment, and life-long learning

Before She Dies

Undersheriff Bill Gastner Mysteries by Steven F. Havill

Before She Dies
Twice Buried
Bitter Recoil
Heartshot

Before She Dies

Steven F. Havill

St. Martin's Press ☒ New York

A THOMAS DUNNE BOOK.
An imprint of St. Martin's Press

Library of Congress Cataloging-in-Publication Data

Havill, Steven.
    Before she dies / by Steven F. Havill.—1st ed.
       p.   cm.
    "A Thomas Dunne book."
    ISBN 0-312-13927-6
    1. Gastner, Bill (Fictitious character)—Fiction.   2. Sheriffs—New
Mexico—Fiction.   3. New Mexico—Fiction.   I. Title
PS3558.A785B4   1996
813'.54—dc20   95-25612
                                                                   CIP

First Edition: March 1996

10 9 8 7 6 5 4 3 2 1

For Kathleen

. . . and special thanks to Christopher P. Carusona, Max Larson, Rod Mays, H.L. McArthur, Lynda Sánchez, and Jim Stover.

099185

WHEN Salvador "Sonny" Trujillo Jr. stuck my own gun in my face and pulled the trigger, it put the cap on an otherwise rotten evening.

At least the weather was nice. There's always that. Late February in Posadas, New Mexico, is a gamble. A raging blizzard that drove cattle up against barbed wire fences and froze late winter calves was no more remarkable than a thunderstorm that filled arroyos and drowned livestock in a swirling torrent of thick, brown water.

This particular February 19th was southern New Mexico at its best. The high sun had been fading paint on cars all day with temperatures in the middle sixties. By the time the two big yellow activity buses carrying the Wittner Wildcats pulled into town, the air had softened and cooled without a stir of breeze.

My first mistake was feeling sorry enough for Deputy Howard Bishop that I agreed to cover for him at the basketball game that evening. Every member of the Bishop clan, including Howard, had the flu. Why I said yes I don't know. Dropping rocks on my feet was more fun than standing in the hot, steaming gymnasium watching five hundred fans work themselves into a rabid frenzy. The job certainly wasn't worth the thirty bucks that it paid.

High school principal Glen Archer pleaded his case. Posadas and Wittner, if not arch rivals, could at least be considered school bus window–busting enemies. Four weeks earlier, after the first season match-up between the two teams, three Posadas players had been caught locker bashing in the Wittner locker rooms. Archer fully expected some sort of payback, even though the Wittner superintendent of schools promised the sort of gentlemanly behavior that would make the fans teary-eyed with pride.

I agreed with Archer, and since I'd stiffed him enough times in the past, I foolishly gave in. I had nothing more important than a nap planned for the evening, and that could wait.

The game was scheduled to begin at eight, and I arrived at the school shortly after seven, parking 310 on the sidewalk right by the school bus entrance. I called dispatch and told Ernie Wheeler where I was and then, as an afterthought, suggested to him that he have Sergeant Robert Torrez stay central for the next couple hours in case he was needed.

"Three oh eight, PCS. Did you copy that?"

"Ten-four." Torrez's cryptic reply told me that he was about as excited as I was. I hadn't bothered to inquire whether Torrez wanted the evening off so that he could attend the game. He would have looked at me, puzzled, while he waited for the punch line to a bad joke.

I clipped the handheld radio to my belt, pulled my revolver from the holster and dumped the shells out, then reholstered the weapon and double-checked the strap. With the six hollow-point .357 magnum cartridges jingling in my pocket, I locked the patrol car and strolled into the gymnasium.

Glen Archer was in the foyer, dwarfed by the enormous trophy cases. I'd had occasion to visit many schools, and every damn one of them had the same number of trophies. Apparently no one ever lost.

"Sheriff," he said, extending a hand and looking pleased, "it's good to see you."

I shook and said something about it being a nice evening. I didn't bother to correct his impression of my rank. No one understood what the hell an undersheriff was anyway, with the exception of some of the county legislators—and they probably wondered why the office existed.

The gym was filling rapidly, and if the pregame noise level was any indication, we all would be putting our trust in the strength of the ceiling girders before the evening was finished. I fished a set of earplugs out of my shirt pocket just as Archer asked, "Is anyone else coming tonight?"

"You mean from our department? No. I understood that one of the village part-timers was going to be here."

"That's good," Archer said. I doubted that it was, since I knew the part-timer in question. Posadas couldn't afford much more than a token village department—a chief and two full-time patrolmen, along with several part-timers. They relied on the Sheriff's Department to fill the holes.

I'd seen Patrolman Tom Pasquale outside, standing with several of the coaches near the side entrance of the gym. He hadn't yet attended the police academy in Santa Fe for certification, and was still under the mistaken impression that a nightstick was the tool of choice for settling arguments. His other hobby was telling endless stories of law enforcement adventures that he'd never had.

I pushed the earplugs in tighter and realized why I loved fall football games as much as I hated dead-of-winter basketball. There were going to be no soft autumn afternoon breezes freshening this place. After two hours of sweaty scrapping between the Jaguars and the Wildcats, the gym was going to be foul enough to make me gag.

To one side of the door just inside the gym a set of wrestling mats hung against the concrete block wall. They made a convenient pad to lean against. I settled there, visible to anyone who entered. I knew most of the folks from Posadas, and exchanged pleasantries with a few as they came in. But they weren't there to talk to me.

The game excitement was explosive, and I admitted to feeling a few goose bumps myself. The roar that greeted the various cats when they sprinted out for warm-ups damn near jarred the earplugs out of my head.

I knew little about the sport other than that my eldest son had

3

wrecked his knee playing it fifteen years before and cost me several thousand in surgical bills.

The cloying smell of greasy popcorn drifted in from the foyer and my stomach rumbled in anticipation. There would be fifty pounds of the stuff scattered under the bleachers by game's end, stuck here and there in puddles of spilled soda pop. That thought killed my appetite. I sucked in my gut and paid attention to the crowd.

Late in the first quarter, a Wittner player blindsided Bucky Berman, the Jaguars' center, and Bucky slid fifteen feet on his butt before crashing into the wall under the home basket. A scuffle broke out, but the officials separated the kids and waved a technical against Wittner. The crowd loved it in a world war sort of way.

Enough popcorn blizzarded the floor that the officials called the broom out. Archer made an announcement asking for restraint, but he wasn't anywhere near as pretty as the cheerleaders. The crowd ignored him. From there on, the game went steadily downhill. Every time the decibel level touched a thousand, I cringed and thought about my snug, dark, quiet adobe house deep in the cottonwoods on the other side of town. By the third quarter, if there had been any doubt before, I knew why I never volunteered for game duty. It was for younger bloods than I.

With less than two minutes to go in the fourth quarter, the Jaguars held a thirty-two-point lead. That was when several folks in the Wittner cheering section decided it was time to show that if they couldn't play basketball at least they could fight. There'd been half a dozen scraps up to that point, none of them serious enough to warrant motion on my part.

I didn't see what started this one, but the stands emptied. For ten seconds or so I remained against the wall, arms folded across my chest. Then head coach Wayne Tuckerman went sprawling, ramming the lower bleacher skirt with his head. I pushed myself into action, hustling across the gym floor. The fight was centered just to the right of the timekeeper's table. I bulled my way through a throng of teenagers intent on seeing some blood and bruises.

4

A heavyset kid in street clothes appeared at my side and grabbed my left arm. What he wanted with it I didn't know. I pivoted and rammed my right elbow into his gut as hard as I could. I left him behind to retch on his own. Ahead of me was a sea of uniforms, perhaps half a dozen athletes from each team having a grand old time, mixing it up with spectators, officials, and a few Posadas faculty members who were probably sorrier than I was that they'd attended the game.

I saw Rod Ulibarri, the Posadas athletic director, plowing in from my right.

"Separate them out that way," I shouted, and grabbed a shoulder. It belonged to a Posadas player, and I hauled him to his feet and shoved him backward so hard he lost his balance and crashed into the arms of a group of admirers. By the time Ulibarri and I had cleared five or six flailing bodies out of the path, I could tell we were about to reach the heart of the matter.

Then two things happened at once. My left foot hit a puddle of blood fresh from someone's bashed nose and I slipped, crashing down on one knee. At the same time, someone grabbed me from behind. I weighed nearly 220, so whoever it was lost purchase, grabbing only a handful of Sam Brown belt and uniform shirt.

A hard wrench at my right side helped me regain my feet just as I realized with a stab of horror that my service revolver had been ripped from my holster. I turned and there was Sonny Trujillo, face flushed with excitement and who knew what pregame drug, holding the magnum out at arm's length, muzzle pointed at my face.

A short scream off to my left was the only sound I remember hearing. At that instant Sonny Trujillo and I were alone in our own private universe. There could have been a full-fledged riot ripping the gym apart around us and I wouldn't have noticed.

I locked eyes with Trujillo. He was a big, flabby kid whose favorite hobby was being a bully with the help of four or five friends. Now, his wide, ugly mouth was open with the delight of victory, with the realization that for once, he held all the cards.

He had reason to be delighted, of course. I, or someone in my department, had busted Sonny enough times that his rap sheet read like an index of every two-bit misdemeanor ever written . . . nothing very creative, since he and his buddies didn't have enough brains for that. But in that moment, with my .357 magnum clutched in his grimy, coke-and-popcorn sticky hand, Sonny wrote himself a new chapter.

"Don't be stupid," I barked. That was a waste of breath, since Sonny Trujillo was nothing if not stupid. I held out my right hand. "Give it to me." We became a stage show, playing in front of a live, paying audience.

"You're dead, shithead," Sonny said. He screwed up his face and pulled the trigger. The magnum's hammer clicked on the empty cylinder at the same time that someone to my right yelped in terror.

I grabbed the revolver barrel with my left hand, yanking hard and twisting at the same time. Sonny didn't release the gun in time to save his trigger finger from snapping at the knuckle. He staggered toward me and swung a clumsy fist at my head, connecting hard enough to break my glasses. Bright lights flashed and in reflex I lashed out, punching him squarely on the tip of the nose.

He collapsed in a heap, blood streaming down his face. His hand came loose from the magnum and I grabbed the revolver by the barrel like a club and spun around.

"Now the rest of you get off the floor," I roared. I heard a siren off in the distance, but backup wasn't going to be necessary. The combatants had had enough. I was sure that the sight of the crazy old cop with his blood-spattered potbelly and his handgun on the loose was enough to squelch the fun.

Arriving out of the crowd too late to do any good, Patrolman Pasquale grabbed Trujillo by the shoulders and spun him around so that the youth sprawled on his face. Trujillo howled in agony as his hands were twisted behind his back and cuffed. His mangled index finger pointed off in a direction of its own.

I tried to bend the frames of my glasses so they'd stay on my nose, then flinched as yet another blast of bright, white light filled the gym. I looked to my left and groaned. It wasn't Trujillo's blow to my thick skull that had produced lights. It was the electronic flash from reporter Linda Real's press camera.

THE sight of Sonny Trujillo, broken, bleeding, and in handcuffs, was enough to sober both sides. Glen Archer asked if I thought the game should be canceled, and I said no—hell, they might as well finish the stupid thing.

No one asked why my revolver had failed to fire. Maybe they hadn't had the muzzle-eye view I had had. Maybe they hadn't seen the hammer snap back and then forward.

By ten, the floor was clear, the teams were facing the toss, and Sonny Trujillo was in the county jail with every charge imaginable—and even some that weren't—levied against him. Patrolman Pasquale had wanted the honor of booking the woodchuck. Why he thought paperwork was exciting I didn't know, but I told him to have at it and that I'd be back in the office after the game to write up a statement.

That would give the doctor time to clean up Trujillo's messy face and make sure that he wasn't bleeding to death from my sock to his nose.

I watched the last few minutes of the game in relative peace. Posadas finally put that dog to bed, rolling up a forty-point margin.

The gym emptied at 11:05 and I breathed deeply as I walked toward 310, trying to purge popcorn fumes from my lungs. A second county car had pulled in behind mine, and Sergeant Robert Torrez got out when he saw me trudging down the sidewalk.

"How long have you been here?" I asked.

"I made sure Trujillo was bchind bars, then I came on up," he said. "I thought I should kinda stand by close."

"The next one's yours, bud." I watched as the Wittner buses rolled by. There were no heads sticking out of windows, no shouts, no errant fingers. They hadn't even stayed long enough after the game to take showers. It was going to be a delightful ride home.

"You want me to follow them out of town?" Torrez asked.

"Nah, they'll be all right. No point in encouraging all the storytellers. It's going to be bad enough as it is."

"Is it true what Pasquale said happened?"

I looked at Torrez and raised an eyebrow. "That depends on what he said."

"That Trujillo had your gun."

"That part's true."

The deputy had the good grace not to ask how I'd managed to lose the weapon in the first place.

"And he said you broke Trujillo's finger when you wrenched the gun away from him."

"That's also true. And then he took a swing at me and broke my glasses. I punched him in the face. That ended that. Except I'll probably end up being sued for fifty-million dollars by the son of a bitch's parents."

Torrez leaned against the front fender of his car. "Dang," he said, as close to cursing as he was apt to come.

"What else did Pasquale say?"

"That he didn't know as he'd have had the nerve to reach out and grab the weapon the way you did."

I gathered the six cartridges and pulled them out of my pocket. "It's pretty easy when you know the gun's not loaded, Robert."

Torrez stared at the ammunition and then a slow grin spread across his face. "Oh," he said.

"Oh, is right. Did Pasquale remember to call someone to check

9

Trujillo? To set his finger and stop up his nose?"

Torrez nodded. "Dr. Perrone was just finishing up with him when I left to come down here." He managed to keep a straight face when he added, "Pasquale said someone from the newspaper was there and photographed the whole thing."

"Yes." The last of the traffic was clearing the lot. I stepped down off the curb and unlocked 310. "We can always hope she ruins the film in processing."

Torrez grinned again. Levity wasn't one of his strong suits, and two smiles in one evening was something of a record for him. "I guess Sheriff Holman will have all kinds of strokes tomorrow, then."

"Serious ones," I said. Martin Holman was as sensitive about bad press as any politician facing an election year could be. But something in the deputy's tone made me pause. I pulled the handheld radio off my belt and tossed it on the seat of 310. "Is there something else I should know, Roberto?"

"Estelle is down at the office processing Tammy Woodruff."

"For what?"

"DWI and assault."

I settled back against the fender of 310 and folded my arms across the top of my ample belly. "You issued the DWI?"

"Yes, sir."

"And the young lady became upset?"

"Uh, yes, sir."

I leaned forward slightly and squinted. "I don't see any damage, Robert."

"A little scratch here," he said, fingering his left earlobe. "That's about it." Tammy would have had trouble reaching Torrez's earlobe, much less damaging it.

"And for that, you tacked on an assault charge?"

"Uh, no, sir. She broke one of Linda Real's cameras."

"Linda was with you?"

"Yes, sir."

"I thought she was at the game."

10

"That must have been someone else, sir. Maybe Frank Dayan."

I felt a sinking feeling in my gut. Linda Real had been with the *Posadas Register* for four years. I'd grown to like and trust her. And I'd assumed it was her behind the camera that evening. I hadn't made a point to look closely.

"Frank, huh," I said. Dayan was an unknown quantity, fresh out of the home office in Omaha, Nebraska, taking the reins after the *O&N Newspapers* chain had purchased the *Register*. It was hard to imagine anyone moving from a metro area like Omaha to dusty, brown, deserted Posadas.

"So let me get this straight. You stopped Miss Tammy for drunken driving and Linda was with you." Torrez nodded. "And Linda reared up with her camera and started snapping pictures. So Tammy flipped, not quite so drunk she couldn't imagine her little freckled face on the front page of the *Register*."

"Well, no, sir. Linda remembers what you told her about riding along on patrol just for the opportunity to take embarrassing pictures of the public, sir. While I was talking with Miss Woodruff, Linda decided to go into the Broken Spur and get a bag of chips or something. Miss Woodruff saw her, knew who she was, and off she went. She wasn't thinking too straight, sir."

I rubbed my face. It was going to take an hour to shower off the gymnasium fume residue. "You were at the Broken Spur when this happened?"

"I stopped Miss Woodruff just as she was pulling her truck out onto the highway from the saloon's parking lot."

I groaned. "You were coming in toward town, or what?"

"No, sir. I was parked. Just down the highway. I was backed into that little dirt road that leads down to Howard Packard's windmill and stock tank."

"Watching the bar."

Torrez nodded. "I can see the doorway pretty good through binoculars."

"Of course," I said wryly. Every deputy I'd ever known had his own "specialty," and worked it hard. Bob Torrez was from a fam-

11

ily of twelve, and he'd lost both a younger brother and sister one night seven years before when a car in which they were passengers missed the interstate ramp and slammed into an abutment. The driver, a sixteen-year-old neighbor, had been so soused he hadn't been able to start the car without assistance.

That had been the deputy's rookie year, and from then on, his random checks of local liquor establishments and their patrons had been unrelenting. Sheriff Holman fielded more than a few complaints, and it was to his credit that he shrugged most of them off.

"Tammy Woodruff is no juvenile, Robert," I said.

"No, but she staggered so bad she almost didn't make it to her truck. And then when she started up she backed into Gus Prescott's horse trailer."

"Any damage?"

"No, sir."

"Well, it'll sort itself out, I'm sure," I said. "Did Victor see this?"

"If he did, he didn't come out."

"That's a plus," I said and got into 310. Victor Sánchez owned the Broken Spur Saloon and Trading Post. He'd made it a point more than once to tell me that if my deputies didn't stop harassing his patrons he'd file suit. He was hot air, of course. Judging by the way most scuffles ended in the Broken Spur, he was more apt to pop somebody with a wrecking bar.

And this arrest was going to test even Martin Holman's sense of fair play. Karl Woodruff, Tammy's old man, was a nice enough guy, running his RxRite Pharmacy cleanly and professionally through good times and bad. He supported the Posadas County Sheriff's Office to the hilt, and that included keeping Sheriff Martin Holman in office.

I could imagine the headline Monday afternoon: *Republican Committee Chairman's Daughter Busted—Sheriff Fires Undersheriff and Deputy.*

Hell, I wasn't paranoid, but it was shaping into a great week.

3

I arrived back in the office shortly before midnight. A small thermonuclear cloud over the building wouldn't have surprised me, but instead, the old place was quiet. Every car we owned was in the lot beside the brick building. With everyone inside and busy, it was a hell of a good time to bust a bank or rob Wayne Feed and Ranch Supply.

I considered parking the county car, climbing into my Blazer, and going home to bed. That would have been a waste. I'd lie there and stare at the dark ceiling, mumbling to myself, and wishing I were somewhere else. I'd found over the years that the best cure for insomnia was just to keep plodding along. Eventually I'd collapse into a ten-minute nap.

The office door opened just as I reached the top step. Linda Real—her last name pronounced like the Spanish *Camino Real*—looked out, saw me, and smiled. She was pretty, with black hair cut short in a pageboy. The odd hours mixed with junk food snacks were beginning to show around her waistline. If she wasn't careful, she'd end up in ten years being as wide as she was tall. She was holding a camera in one hand and her notebook in the other.

"I thought your camera was broken," I said.

"Backup," Linda replied. Her smile was immediate and radiant—too damn radiant for the middle of the night.

13

"And I thought you had the flu," I said to Deputy Howard Bishop. He towered behind Linda, face like a big basset hound, somber and now just a little pale.

He held the door open as I shouldered past. "I was feelin' a little better, so I decided to come on in," he said.

I started to say that I wished he'd felt better about four hours before, but thought better of it. He still looked like he'd have helped more by staying home in bed. "Isn't Tony Abeyta on tonight anyway?"

"Yes sir, but he can't come in until about two," Bishop said. "And Bob's all tied up, so . . ."

"Take it slow, then," I said. "And Linda?" The young reporter had started across the parking lot toward the patrol car. She stopped and turned around. "If you get tired," I called, "don't hesitate to go home." She cheerfully waved a hand.

"Something's wrong with that girl," I muttered, and Bishop nodded solemnly.

"Yes, sir."

Linda Real spent at least fifty hours each month riding with either us, the village police, or the Fish and Game Department, and we'd long since grown accustomed to her pleasant, smiling, everpresent face. Why she did it was a mystery to me. Little ever appeared in the paper about what we did that couldn't be gleaned in five minutes each morning from the dispatcher's log. Maybe she was husband hunting.

Or maybe she and her boss were lying in wait for that perfect, Pulitzer Prize–winning photo of cops at work. I remembered punching Sonny Trujillo in full glare of somebody's flash. That wasn't the kind of publicity I wanted, no matter what the prize.

Detective Lieutenant Estelle Reyes-Guzman was waiting in my office with half a dozen file folders spread out on my desk. She looked up from one of them as I walked in. A ghost of a smile pulled at the corner of her mouth.

"What's everybody so damn happy about?" I said. "Real just went out of here like somebody's slipped her a big scoop."

14

"Busy night, sir," Estelle said. "Maybe she smells the front page."

"Just what I needed to hear," I said. I tossed my hat on a chair. "Let me find some coffee." Estelle waited patiently while I found a cup that wasn't crusted over. The coffee was just the way I liked it—about four hours old and beginning to form an oil slick on top.

I was annoyed that someone had called Estelle in the middle of the night for this nonsense. Tammy Woodruff could sleep off her intoxication like anyone else.

"Who called you down?" I asked as I walked back into the spacious clutter that was my office. I set the cup down on the edge of the desk, well away from the avalanche of paperwork on the other side.

"No one," she said, and held up a folder. "Francis took the kid down to see my mom earlier today." I grinned at the slang reference to her son. I had called little Francis Guzman Jr. *The Kid* ever since he'd been born. If I was still alive when he turned twenty-one maybe I'd try something else, but for now, the tag suited him just fine. And I didn't have trouble remembering it. Estelle glanced at her watch as I took the folder from her. "Yesterday, I mean. And then Francis is going to bring his aunt up for a visit."

"Which one of many aunts is this one?" I could keep track of Estelle's family easily enough. Her mother, tiny, wrinkled, and independent, lived across the border in Tres Santos in the same miniature adobe house that Estelle's grandfather had built nearly a hundred years before.

But Estelle's in-laws populated Old Mexico from one end to the other, an endless assortment of brothers, sisters, cousins, uncles, aunts—the entire gamut. Francis Guzman was the sole U.S. citizen in the family, but that distinction was more of an oddity for the Guzman clan than an accomplishment.

"His Aunt Sofia," Estelle said, her own accent making the simple word elegant.

"I don't know her, I guess."

Estelle shook her head. "You met her at the wedding. She lives

15

in Veracruz. Francis has always been one of her favorites. When we were married, she came to Tres Santos for the wedding. You might remember that she was the lady who spent almost the entire time sitting and talking with my mother?"

"Ah," I said. "The lawyer." I remember her vaguely, remembered how stiff and starched she'd been at first. Maybe she shared a little of the apprehension others of the Guzman clan might have felt about Francis, the successful surgeon, marrying this only daughter of an ancient Chihuahuan peasant lady. The patrician noses hadn't been out of joint for too long, as I remembered.

"Right. She's retired now. Her husband died a couple of years ago." Estelle began gathering up papers. "She spends most of her time traveling around Mexico, visiting the new generation."

"Why didn't you go down with Francis, then? What are you hanging around here for?"

"I have an exam Monday, or I would have gone along."

"An exam? In what?"

"Economics. And by the way—we need a statement from you on Sonny Trujillo."

I took the folder she held out. "Aren't you supposed to be home studying or something? I thought college students stayed up all night, cramming for exams."

Estelle grinned and got up, vacating my chair. "I'm caught up," she said. "I'll do a little review this afternoon, before the gang arrives."

Of course she was caught up. Someone who could manage a family that included an active one-year-old, a physician husband, and an aging mother living in Mexico—as well as part-time work for us—wouldn't let studying for a college class slow her down.

Her career with our department had taken its share of wild turns. Now she worked part-time, on-call in our detective division. She was our detective division. There had been a time when Martin Holman had wanted to expand the department, including at least three detectives. The county would have liked the idea if someone else

16

could have provided the money. No one ever did. Holman, ever the smooth *politico*, compromised by promoting Estelle from sergeant to lieutenant . . . with a promised increase in pay. We all knew what "promised" meant.

I sat down and opened the folder with one hand while fumbling for a cigarette with the other. I had quit smoking a year before, but the action was still automatic. I found my glasses instead and put them on. One earpiece was still crooked, and I grunted as I tried to bend it back into shape without snapping the fragile hinge.

"Need some tape?" Estelle asked.

I ignored her suggestion. "What about Tammy Woodruff?" I asked.

"Her father said to leave her in jail until morning. He'll see about it then."

"Good man."

"And Sheriff Holman called."

"I bet he did."

"He got a call from Victor Sánchez again."

"About Sergeant Torrez?" I tossed the folder on the desk and leaned back, glad for the minute to relax.

"He said that if Bob didn't quit harassing his customers, he'd take on the deputy himself." Estelle grinned. "Either that or he's going to file suit."

"Hell, same old tune. Tell him to try 'em both," I chuckled. "Why not. Victor needs something to make his life a little more interesting. Mopping up spilled beer must get pretty dull after a while."

Estelle moved toward the door. "Is there anything else you need tonight, sir?"

"Hell, no. Thanks for taking care of the Woodruff girl for us. They could have called in Aggie Bishop just as easily." Deputy Bishop's wife worked occasionally when we needed a matron.

"The flu, sir," Estelle said, and I made a face.

"Any word on your truck, by the way?"

17

"No, sir." She shrugged. "I'm sure it's long gone."

"You guys didn't even have it long enough to scratch the paint," I said.

"Oh yes," Estelle replied. "Francis backed into the fence down at mother's." She smiled ruefully. "But they stole it anyway." Even with a dent, the thieves had gotten a hell of a deal. The big two-tone blue Suburban had had less than a thousand miles on it. The Las Cruces police had been sympathetic and diligent. But the truck was gone, driven out of the mall parking lot while the family was shopping.

"Next time, maybe you should buy something about twenty-five years old," I said. "Then nobody wants it."

"I suppose," Estelle said. "If you need me for anything, I'll be home." She paused in the doorway. "Why don't you come over for dinner Sunday night?"

"What are you having?"

Estelle cocked her head and frowned at me in mock exasperation. She knew my see-food diet habits as well as anyone. "Seven o'clock. We'll expect you."

I waved a hand. "Give your aunt my regards if something comes up," I said.

"Sir . . ." she said, and left the rest hanging. Living by myself, I had developed that sort of independence of clock and calendar that irritated more rational minds. Estelle knew better than to fight it.

After she left, I settled back with my paperwork. My mood improved, as I took grim satisfaction in knowing that Sonny Trujillo would be stone sober for some time if Judge Hobart's colors ran true to form at the preliminary hearing.

And Tammy Woodruff would wake up jail-cell sober in a few hours. I had no doubt that her father would put her on the straight and narrow. At least he would try to. But Tammy was no child anymore. I had no intentions of getting myself involved in that family fight. An hour later, I left the office.

Shortly after 2 A.M. that Saturday, I pulled off Guadalupe Terrace into the driveway of my adobe house, buried under gigantic

18

cottonwoods in an old quarter of Posadas south of the interstate. The place was rambling, dark, and quiet. No sounds filtered through the two foot thick walls.

In the kitchen I made myself a cup of coffee, drank a third of it, and then went to bed. The musty old bedroom pooled all the aromas that were a comfort to me into a potpourri that should have put me to sleep. And they did, for one blissful hour.

At 3:46 A.M., the telephone jangled me awake. For a moment I lay quietly, eyes open wide like one of those jungle lemurs. I answered on the fourth ring.

"Gastner."

"Sir, this is Gayle Sedillos." Our dispatcher waited a moment for that to sink in.

"What's up, Gayle?"

"Sir, you really need to come in. We've got a real problem with Sonny Trujillo."

I snapped fully awake and sat up in bed with a grunt.

"What do you mean?"

There was a slight pause, about four heartbeats' worth. "He apparently choked to death in his cell, sir."

THE cot was pushed against one wall of the jail cell with the brown wool blanket crumpled at the foot. The sheets and pillowcase told me all I needed to know. The final seconds of Sonny Trujillo's life had not been a pretty way to go.

"Were you here?" I asked Deputy Tony Abeyta.

He shook his head. "No, sir. Not at first. Gayle called me on the radio for assistance. She was the only one in the building."

I grimaced. That wasn't unusual for a tiny department like ours, but it wasn't going to make Gayle feel any better.

"We both attempted CPR until the ambulance arrived. It was just a few minutes."

"Is everyone else at the hospital now?"

"Yes, sir. Sheriff Holman went directly there from home. And Gayle called Estelle just after talking to you. She went over to the hospital as well."

I turned away from the cell and started down the short hallway that led to the front offices and dispatch. "You've written up a statement of what happened?"

"Yes, sir. It's in the folder on your desk."

"All right. Why don't you call Bob Torrez back in for a little while to sit the radio. Stay here by the phone until Bob gets here. And then patrol central. We may need . . ." I waved a hand. "Who the hell knows what we'll need." I heard voices out front.

Frank Dayan stuck his head around the corner, saw me, and said, "Ah, here he is."

"Hello, Frank."

The publisher backed away to give me room to maneuver in the narrow doorway.

"Some night, huh?" he said.

"Yes, it is."

"Do you have a couple of minutes?"

"No, I don't."

"I was just down at the hospital, and Sheriff Holman said I should come and talk with you."

That's because he doesn't want to be bothered talking to you, I almost said. "Frank, we're not going to have anything for you for several hours yet. It's that simple."

He followed me past the row of bulletin boards and the snack machines by the drinking fountain. "Linda was going to stick around for a little while, if that's all right with you."

"Have at it."

"You'll have a statement, then?"

I stopped, turned, and looked at Frank Dayan with a combination of weariness, exasperation, and curiosity. If the Omaha, Nebraska, where he was from was not the center of the hot news universe, then where did that put Posadas, New Mexico? Long before first light of a Saturday, Dayan was worrying about his six- page Monday edition.

"Frank . . . yes. Now give us a break." He nodded and backpedaled a step. I caught Gayle Sedillos's eye and beckoned her into my office.

I closed the door and put my arm around her shoulders as we walked across toward my desk. I saw that she was carrying the brown hardcover ring binder that included the jail activity logs. "You all right?"

"Yes, sir." She took a deep breath. "I think so."

"Did you check on Tammy? In the last few minutes?"

"Yes sir. She's sleeping." The three upstairs cells were reserved for juveniles and, on the rare occasions when we had them, women. The cells were small, neat, clean, and remote.

I motioned toward the swivel chair by the window. "Do you want anything?"

"To go home and go to bed," she said. She managed the beginning of a grin.

"Wasn't Tom Mears supposed to be working desk midnight to eight?"

"He called in sick. Ernie stayed until I came in at two."

"Half the world is sick," I said. I leaned back in my chair and tried to twist a kink out of my neck. "So tell me what happened."

Gayle Sedillos was the best dispatcher and office manager we'd had in years. She had begun working for the Sheriff's Department the summer of her high school senior year, and for the next six years had been steady, bright, and efficient.

I had tried, along with others, to get her married off on several occasions. We'd had no success. The standard department joke was that Bob Torrez, six-foot-four, movie-star handsome, and eligible, would eventually fall for Gayle Sedillos, petite and pretty, like a Mexican porcelain doll—if only we would schedule them on the same shift often enough.

She opened the log. "I checked the cells at two-oh-five downstairs and two-twelve upstairs. Trujillo was awake and restless. Woodruff was asleep." Her finger traced the entries down the page. "I checked every fifteen minutes until about three. At that time I heard coughing sounds from upstairs."

"Upstairs? Miss Woodruff?"

"Yes, sir. When I checked, I found that she had vomited. I asked her if she was going to be all right. She said she was, and that she was sorry about making such a mess."

"That was at three or shortly after?"

"Yes, sir. I changed her pillowcase and cleaned up the floor by her cot. She kept apologizing for not being able to make it to the sink."

22

"Did you call anyone?"

"No, sir."

I made my tone as gentle as I could. "You should have, you know."

"Yes, sir."

"Even if it's just calling the road deputy in for a few minutes. When you have to be in a cell with a prisoner, call someone. You're not a jailer."

"Yes, sir."

"If no one else is available, call me. But call someone."

"Yes, sir."

"Then what happened?"

She consulted the log again. "I checked every five minutes or less, and by three-twenty she seemed to be resting comfortably. Trujillo was sound asleep. I was more worried about the Woodruff girl. When I checked at three-twenty-five, Trujillo was restless again. He wouldn't say anything and I was going to call Deputy Abeyta in, but before I got to the radio, I heard violent gagging and choking sounds from his cell."

"That's at three-twenty-six or so."

"Yes, sir. I went back to check and Trujillo was convulsing."

"He was choking?"

"Yes, sir. I could see that he was turning blue. I tried everything I knew how to do. He lost consciousness and I tried to put a ventilator in place." Gayle wiped one of her eyes. "It sure wasn't like the CPR classes, sir."

"You went into the cell with him, by yourself?"

"Yes, sir."

I shook my head. "And at what time did you call for assistance?"

"Right after that," she said. "I ran down here and called Tony."

"And you asked that he call the ambulance?"

"Yes, sir. I didn't want to spend the time at the radio. He called as he was driving back here."

"And you continued your efforts at resuscitation until the ambulance crew arrived?"

23

"Yes, sir."

Deputy Abeyta opened the door long enough to tell me that Bob Torrez had arrived to sit the radio and that he would be on the road.

"Is the young lady riding with you?"

"Sir?" Abeyta asked.

"Miss Real. The reporter."

"Oh." The young deputy looked over his shoulder. "I guess so, sir. She's standing by the front door."

"Have fun," I said. "And when she asks for details about either Tammy Woodruff or Sonny Trujillo, just tell her I'll have a statement sometime today."

"Yes, sir."

The door closed and I played with a pencil for a few minutes while I framed my thoughts. "When the ambulance arrived, was Trujillo showing a pulse? Were there any signs that he was responding?"

"No, sir. I continued CPR until Deputy Abeyta arrived. He relieved me and worked until the EMTs arrived a few minutes later. Neither of us could find a pulse, and from the time I started CPR, Trujillo never took a breath on his own, sir. I knew he was gone."

"And after the ambulance arrived, you called Sheriff Holman, me, and Estelle."

"Yes, sir. I called you first, then Estelle. And then the sheriff."

"Sonny wasn't living at home. Did Holman call the Trujillos?"

"He said he would try to locate them, sir."

"And did someone call from the hospital to let you know that Trujillo had, in fact, been pronounced dead?"

"Yes, sir," Gayle said softly. "Estelle called." She scanned down the page. "At four-twenty."

"Just before I walked through the door."

"Yes, sir."

"Gayle, I hope you know that you did everything you could." She looked down at the floor. "These things happen," I said. "We can't have an ambulance on standby for everyone on the planet at every minute." I glanced at the wall clock. "You can be sure that Sheriff

Holman will be stopping back here when they're finished at the hospital."

For the next fifteen minutes, Gayle and I talked about inconsequential things until I was sure she was all right. Then I left her alone in my office so that she could write out a detailed statement without interruption of what she had just told me.

Out of habit, I walked upstairs and checked on Tammy Woodruff myself. She was curled in a tight fetal position, sleeping the deep sleep of the truly drunk, still hours away from the dawn of a new day and the new life she'd made for herself. She'd missed all the excitement, and that was just as well.

Try as hard as I might, I couldn't bring myself to feel too sorry for Sonny Trujillo. As I trudged back downstairs, I did wonder how Frank Dayan was planning to bolt this entire mess together for his newspaper. It would be easy to misunderstand the incident at school with Trujillo, and just as easy to make a cesspool out of his death . . . even though he'd been given medical assistance for his bruised nose before he was jailed.

The back door opened and Sheriff Martin Holman walked in. Usually, he was as dapper as they come, impeccably dressed and with a catalog of just the right things to say poised at his lips. Like the talented used car salesman he had once been, he could convince almost anyone of almost anything at almost any time.

This wasn't one of those times.

He saw me and said, "Jesus, Gastner," as if that just about covered it.

5

Sheriff Holman sputtered, ranted, and barked for about five minutes, and I listened without comment. Finally he stopped, took a deep breath, and looked sideways at me.

"Are you listening to me?"

"Sure."

He walked over and toed the door of his office closed. "So what do you think we ought to do?"

"First of all, Martin, it doesn't really matter what the newspaper does or says in all of this. We have no control over them."

"I know that."

"Then don't worry about it." He looked heavenward and I added, "From what Gayle tells me, from the way she describes the incident, it sounds more like Trujillo had a heart attack than anything else. An autopsy will show for sure. And second, if Sonny Trujillo's parents decide to sue us, and they probably will, that's what the county attorney is for. They don't have a case, but they can do what they want."

Holman shook his head. "I'm not worried about that."

"Fine. Let's take one thing at a time. Now, if it wasn't a heart attack, Trujillo's death was probably avoidable." Holman looked pained, but I ticked the points off on my fingers. "Yes, we could have had a deputy with him the entire night, baby-sitting. And yes, we could have checked him into a hospital for observation, even though a physician said that it wasn't necessary and gave us a signed release. And yes, we could have done a lot of things that we didn't do. But we didn't. We assumed that he was intoxicated, which he was, and that he'd sleep it off." I shrugged. "Just like millions of other drunks before him."

Martin Holman picked at a perfectly manicured fingernail until he realized what he was doing. He thrust his hand in his pocket. "You know what worries me?"

"No."

If Holman hadn't looked so pained, I would have smiled. He'd been back less than a week from another one of those ten-day seminars that tries to teach administrators some aspect of the convoluted criminal code. As he was discovering, it wasn't really the letter of the law that mattered.

Holman walked around his desk and sat down in the overstuffed leather chair with a thump. He motioned to the swivel chair. "Sit, sit, sit," he said. "You just stand there like some calm Buddha. It makes me nervous."

I let pass his comment about my considerable girth. "I don't dance well," I said.

The sheriff smiled ruefully. "I wish to hell I had your nervous system."

"No, you don't."

"I mean, I don't give two craps if I win the election in November or not." He held up both hands and hastily retreated from that ridiculous remark. "Well, that's not true. I do care. But I want to do what's right in this mess. And you're going to have to give me a hand. I mean, you've got a zillion years of experience in these things."

"Right," I said. "That's why the newspaper has a picture of me breaking a fat kid's finger and punching him in the nose."

"He was twenty-one, wasn't he?"

27

"Twenty-two."

"Should he have been in the hospital? I mean, really? I don't care what the doctors said. What do you think?"

"Don't be ridiculous, Martin. He didn't die because of any injuries from the brawl. He choked to death on his own vomit. Either that or his heart got insulted once too often. Sure, his nose was probably a little bit plugged. But hospitals don't admit patients for broken noses and cracked fingers. It's as simple as that. And if Dayan wants to make a story out of nothing, I guess that's his department."

"That's what worries me," Holman said with finality. "Having a prisoner die in the county lockup isn't exactly 'nothing,' as you put it. But maybe Dayan will have the good sense not to run it on page one. The classified section maybe. But see, everyone knew Trujillo and his record, and quite a few of them probably will think he got just what he deserved. But the others . . ." He picked up a pencil and tapped a dozen dots on his desk blotter. "Did Trujillo have the booze with him at the game?"

"I have no idea. I'm sure no one else does either."

Holman took a long, deep breath. He looked at me for a minute, assessing. "You normally don't cover games, do you?"

"No. The deputy who took the job has the flu. Or did have."

"What prompted you to unload your gun before going in the gym?"

I shrugged. "The odds of running into armed felons inside a school during a basketball game are pretty remote, Marty. If I needed a loaded weapon, it would take only seconds to put the shells back in the gun. The most likely thing to happen during a game is just what did happen . . . a scuffle. The last thing I want is to have some high school kid jump on my back and grab a weapon out of its holster."

"And that's just what did happen," Holman said.

"More or less."

"Do the other deputies do the same thing? I mean, do they unload their weapons when they're at a game?"

"Yes. At least they've been told to do so." I grinned. "They all think I'm foolish for ordering such a thing, too."

"Imagine if it had gone off," Holman said, and I grimaced.

"I'd rather not, thanks."

Holman glanced at his watch. "Karl Woodruff will probably be down before long to spring his little girl. He called me back, about an hour after we arrested her. We talked for about twenty minutes. I'm pretty sure he's going to swear out a complaint against Victor Sánchez."

"He can do that." I shrugged.

"Woodruff contends that the bartender shouldn't have continued to serve his daughter after she was already so obviously intoxicated." I chuckled and Holman looked surprised. "It is against the law, Bill. To serve an intoxicated party."

"Yep. It's always somebody else's fault, sheriff."

"Well, wouldn't we be within our rights to ticket Sánchez for violation? Shouldn't Sergeant Torrez have done that?"

"I suppose. By the letter of the law. I can't think of when we ever went after a saloon keeper because one of his adult patrons strayed across the double yellow. If we go after one, we have to go after them all. All of them. We won't have time to do anything else. Although the way the mood of the country is right now, I wouldn't be surprised to see it come to that."

"Will you at least go out and have a talk with Victor Sánchez?"

"Sure, if you think there's any point."

"He's a hothead," the sheriff said. "I want him to know from the beginning that we're not singling him out, or his saloon, or anything like that. If Woodruff presses the issue, that is. Maybe he won't. I just don't want Victor Sánchez jumping on one of our deputies because he thinks we've singled him out."

"It would be more to the point to talk with Karl Woodruff," I said. "But I'll swing around there this afternoon."

By two that afternoon, I finally broke away from the blizzard of paperwork and a half dozen other irritations—not the least of which was attending Tammy Woodruff's arraignment before Judge Les

29

Hobart. She was cleaned up and pretty, just like the photograph the *Register* had run on the front page three years before when she'd been the Posadas County Fair Queen.

Her father was conspicuous by his absence. Maybe he was sticking to his guns, forcing his daughter to face the court by herself.

And Tammy was contrite . . . or a damn fine actress. Judge Hobart fell for it and whacked her with a hundred-dollar fine and DWI school on the one charge and restitution for the broken camera to satisfy the assault charge.

She paid with a personal check and left Judge Hobart's mobile home-office with a smirk on her face. Sergeant Torrez looked at me and shrugged as if to ask why he'd bothered to get out of bed for this show.

I'd promised Sheriff Holman that I would talk with Victor Sánchez. The sheriff was right. In an election year, good community relations were top priority.

After the arraignment I drove out State Highway 56 to the southwest. In four miles I passed the first of the Sánchez family enterprises, Wayne Feed and Ranch Supply. Victor Sánchez's brother Toby owned that business. He'd bought it from Dick Wayne's widow ten years before and never bothered to change the name over the door. I couldn't see that there were enough ranchers left in Posadas County to support the place, but maybe he sold a fortune in windmill parts.

The highway swept around the bulge of Arturo Mesa and then crossed the bridge over the Rio Salinas . . . a dry wash with pretensions during summer thunderstorms. On the west side of the bridge was a sign that announced the quiet little village of Moore. It had every reason to be quiet. The one house and the mercantile building that still stood under the brittle limbs of half a dozen dead cottonwoods were vacant and vandalized.

Three miles farther on the land flattened out, dotted here and there with marginal ranches that grazed a handful of bony, tough, range cattle. The Rio Guijarro snaked under the highway at mile marker seven. This stream managed to pass a little water most of the time.

Seeing an opportunity, Victor Sánchez had opened his Broken Spur Saloon and Trading Post on the banks of the Guijarro in 1956. And when he saw that those cottonwoods weren't about to die but were in fact thriving, he went a step further and opened Guijarro RV Park and Camp Sites in 1987. He reckoned that there was enough snowbird and tourist traffic headed down State 56 to Regal and the Mexican border crossing that he might do some good business.

I turned 310 off the highway and rolled into the Broken Spur's parking lot. Down the road I could see the blades of Howard Packard's windmill turning in the light breeze. Sergeant Torrez was right—it was a good place from which to watch the bar's parking lot.

A beer delivery truck was angled so that its side roll-up doors faced the building. Nosed into the shade on the other side of the building was a faded blue and white 1976 Ford half-ton pickup. I shut off the county car and got out, immediately wishing I'd worn a warmer coat. The wind was from the west, picking up a little as the sun dipped low.

The driver of the beer truck saw me first as he wheeled the dolly back for another load.

"How you doin'? Is Victor in there?"

He shook his head. "Junior is, though. He's in the kitchen."

I made my way inside, stepping around piles of boxes, a collection of brooms and mops, and scores of aerosol cleaning products—and all the other junk that keeps a place habitable and the health inspectors happy. Junior Sánchez was bending over the sink, snipping fat off chicken carcasses. He straightened up with a hunk of chicken in one hand and large kitchen shears in the other and blinked as I shuffled in.

"Dad's not here," he said without preamble or greeting.

I leaned against the counter and surveyed the mess he was mak-

31

ing. Not the brightest lad on earth, Junior Sánchez was lucky that he had a steady job with Dad. His older brothers had struck out on their own, Juan heading for California last I'd heard and Carlos working at Chavez Chevrolet-Oldsmobile.

"What are you fixing?" I asked.

Junior turned and looked at the pile of chicken. "Saturday's always a big fajita night," he said, and poked at a thigh with the scissors. "Got to get all these ready."

"Are you still showing the games on the big screen in there?" I asked, nodding toward the double doors that swung into the barroom proper.

"Oh, sure," Junior said.

"I might have to come over for that," I said as smoothly as if I meant it. "When's your dad going to be back?"

Junior went back to snipping. "I don't know. He had to get something fixed for the bathroom. One of the toilets wouldn't flush."

That would be more grim for a busy barroom than running out of fajitas, for sure, I thought. "Well, it's nothing that can't wait," I said. "I was just out this way, and thought I'd see him for a bit. But it's no big deal. If you happen to think about it, tell him I was here, would you?"

The kid nodded and I left him to his chicken.

I didn't hang around to see Victor Sánchez. Karl Woodruff wasn't going to file a complaint against anybody. He might grumble some, but that would be the extent of it. Tammy was out of jail and no doubt reciting her tale to anyone who would listen, and Sergeant Torrez was off duty until Monday swing shift. Victor wouldn't see him parked down at Packard's windmill for a couple of days.

What was left of the weekend passed uneventfully until late Sunday afternoon when, with the setting sun square in her eyes, Donni Weatherford overcooked it coming off the ramp from the interstate. She was driving a big custom van pulling an even larger travel trailer, and like the rest of her family was tired and cranky.

The unit apparently began to weave, and Donni's husband Chad leaned over to provide assistance at just the wrong time.

The van and trailer crashed off the pavement and reduced themselves to junk through a spectacular tap dance across the tops of the guardrail posts. Chunks of van and travel trailer littered the entire ramp and most of the intersection and underpass below by the time the entire affair came to a shrieking, smoking stop.

The younger Weatherford generation, including a hysterical teenager named Becky and a sober set of ten-year-old twins tagged Donnell and Donette, were well belted in and unhurt.

Deputy Paul Enciños arrived at the wreck minutes before I did.

33

When I scrambled through all the junk, I saw that he was trying to talk some sense into Becky. The girl was hanging by her seat belt with a head-on view of a section of bent guardrail. The jagged steel was inches from her face. The side of the van where she'd been sitting was gaping as if hit by a huge can opener.

Had the vehicle chewed another foot down the railing, Becky would have been decapitated. She was smart enough to figure that out for herself.

Paul and I popped her seat belt and helped her out. She grabbed my arm so hard with her sharp little fingers that I thought I was the one who would end up bleeding.

The twins and Mrs. Weatherford were trying to divide their attention between Becky and the man who'd caused the whole thing. Their dither was understandable. Chad Weatherford had been pitched clear of the mess, hitting a section of the steel guardrail and fracturing his right thighbone in about eighteen places.

With Becky and the twins safe, Donni Weatherford concentrated her efforts on hubby, giving her something to worry about other than the junk pile she'd made of their vehicle and their vacation plans. Through tears, she told me the family had been heading for San Diego, a long haul from home in Davenport, Iowa.

I didn't ask her how she managed to check her kids out of school in the middle of February.

The ambulance arrived. Chad's leg was field dressed and he was strapped onto a gurney for the four-minute trip to Posadas General Hospital. One of the EMTs and I assisted Donni, making sure she didn't break anything or become tangled in any of the equipment when she climbed into the ambulance.

Deputy Tom Mears played taxi and took the youngsters to the hospital in his patrol car. Mrs. Weatherford thanked me profusely, as if she had first thought that we might leave her kids by the shoulder of the highway, battered, stranded waifs.

By the time I returned to the office and made a few phone calls, it was pushing seven. My stomach was growling, having been ignored all afternoon. I needed to stop by the hospital and if I then took time to go home to clean up and change as well, I'd risk being so late for dinner that I'd miss several courses. Estelle and her family would have to take me as I was—something they were used to.

Donni Weatherford was considerably more composed when I found her in the hospital's tiny snack bar. I gave her the telephone number of the local insurance agent and recommended a motel that would put a courtesy car at her disposal.

I'm sure the kids thought being marooned in Posadas, New Mexico, was high adventure. That would wear thin in a day or two.

At 7:09, I walked through the front door of the Guzman's modest adobe on South Twelfth Street. The aroma of Mexican food as only Estelle could cook it made me slobber.

"We just finished," Francis said as he held open the door.

I stopped short, rested my palm on the butt of my revolver, and frowned at the young surgeon. "You're finished, all right."

He grinned and waved me in. "We're glad you could make it," he said. "Aunt Sofie was looking forward to seeing you again." He paused for just a heartbeat and added, "We weren't, of course."

I hesitated. I'd forgotten the Guzmans had company—proper company no less. I held up my hands, sure that I still smelled of spilled gasoline. "You'll have to take me as I am. I didn't have time to go home and get all prettied up." I shed hat and coat and then gun belt. "Where's the kid?"

"In the dining room, making a mess," Francis said. "Come on in."

Francis Guzman Jr. was belted in his high chair; he was old enough to pound out percussion with a spoon but not so old that all the food found its way with regularity to his mouth.

Estelle and Francis's aunt emerged from the kitchen and Estelle greeted me with a hug.

"You'll have to excuse the aroma," I said. "We had a mess on the interstate and I smell like gasoline and highway flares."

"Serious?" Francis asked.

I shrugged, dismissing the incident.

"You remember Sofia from the wedding," Estelle said, taking me

35

by the elbow and guiding me around the kid, who was making a multicolored mess of his food.

"Of course," I said. Sofia Tournál smiled warmly and extended her hand.

"It is so nice to see you again, sheriff," she said. Her voice was husky and thickly accented. She must have been lost in the crowds of Guzman relatives during the wedding, for I would certainly have remembered her otherwise. Five years or so younger than my own sixty-three, the Guzman family resemblance was strong. When she smiled, which was often, the angular planes of her face softened. I had a feeling those features could just as easily form impressive storm clouds as well.

"I'm glad you could visit," I said.

She nodded. "I was so sorry to have missed the *bautizo*—the christening—for the child," she said, and smiled. Her teeth were perfectly even. If tooth genes from each side of the family joined forces, the kid would never see an orthodontist. "It was very kind of you to host it, *padrino*."

"It was a lot of fun. My pleasure."

"I'm sure it was. Had my husband not been ill . . ." She let a turning of the hand suffice for the rest.

"I thought we'd let the kid eat first, and then turn him loose so we can eat in peace," Estelle said quickly.

"The kid," Sofia said softly. The tiny wrinkles at the corners of her eyes deepened as she bent down to make a face at the youngster. He responded with an explosive laugh that sprayed applesauce on his aunt. She didn't flinch. Compared to the splattered, smeared youngster, I was clean as the driven snow.

Dinner was one of those wonderful affairs that lasted all evening. After an hour, the kid decided we were too dull for his world. He sat in the middle of a sea of randomly shaped wooden blocks in the living room, building only he knew what. Each time the block tower toppled, he would shriek with delight. In twenty minutes, he toppled, too, curled in a tight ball on the sofa.

36

I had no desire to talk shop or recite an endless, tedious compendium of law enforcement war stories, but Sofia Tournál's curiosity was that of a true lawyer. She probed, she prodded, she delved . . . and always she listened with her dark, thick eyebrows furrowed slightly in concentration.

Finally, with a hand delicately over her cup to halt the fifth refill of Estelle's potent coffee, she looked across at me. "So, tell me . . ." and she rested her other hand against her cheek as if preparing for a long answer. "What do you think of Estelle's decision, then?" She raised one eyebrow.

"Decision?" I asked. "To go back to school, you mean?"

Sofia turned as Estelle came back from the kitchen. "Maybe you have not discussed . . ." she started and then let the comment linger. I could see that Estelle was on the same mysterious wavelength. She knew exactly what Sofia Tournál was talking about, and I didn't have a clue.

"I haven't talked about it with him yet, *tía*. Just with you and Francis."

I sat back and folded my hands on my belly.

"Well," Sofia said. "This is a man who is used to being in the very center of things." She beckoned to Estelle to sit back down. "You should discuss your decision with him, certainly."

"Certainly," I said, amused.

Estelle concentrated on the tablecloth for a full minute, tracing the lace design with the handle of a spoon. Neither Francis nor Sofia said a word. We waited. Finally Estelle chuckled. "This is harder than I thought, sir."

"Oh? What's harder? Fill me in. What's the big mystery?"

She looked up at me, her clear, olive skin framed by raven black hair. But it was the eyes that as always drew my attention to Estelle—black, bottomless, calm, and assessing.

"I've decided to run for sheriff, sir."

The room became so still I could hear the kid's muttery little breaths in the next room.

It was Sofia who broke the silence. "This must be quite an adventure, don't you think?

Adventure wasn't the first word I would have chosen, but I desperately wanted to say the right thing when I opened my mouth.

"Instead of law school, or in addition to?" I asked.

"Before, maybe," Estelle said. She frowned. "If I do, that is."

I sat forward. "What do you mean, if you do? You just said you'd decided."

She grinned sheepishly. "That still changes from minute to minute, I guess. There are still some very important things I haven't worked out in my mind."

"For instance?"

The telephone in the living room jangled and Francis got up swiftly to answer it. I wasn't sure that Estelle had heard it.

"I don't want to put you in an uncomfortable position," she said.

I laughed. "You mean during the election or afterward, when I have to work for you?"

She started to say something and then stopped, looking up at Francis. I twisted around. "It's Gayle Sedillos, sir. She needs to talk with you," he said.

I felt like ten tons when I pushed myself upright and away from the table. "Hold that thought," I said to Estelle. "This will only take a minute. They can live without me for one evening."

The kid stirred fitfully as I walked past him, so I kept my voice down when I picked up the receiver. "Gastner."

Gayle's voice was artificially starched. "Sir, a civilian just called in to report a shooting involving one of our deputies. Tom Mears and Howard Bishop are on their way out now."

"Who was involved?"

"Deputy Enciños, sir."

"You don't know what happened?"

"Not yet, sir."

"Where?"

"State 56, one mile east of County Road 14."

38

"We're on our way." I started to hang up the telephone, but Gayle's urgent voice stopped me.

"Sir . . ."

"What is it?"

"I think Linda Real was with him as well, sir."

7

AN ambulance's red lights winked in my rearview mirror as we passed under the interstate exchange on South Grande Boulevard and started to slow for the sweeping right-hand turn onto State 56. As I accelerated 310 out onto the highway, Estelle turned up the radio slightly, hunching forward as if to prompt the electronic signals.

"Three oh seven, PCS. Ten-twenty."

Gayle Sedillos's voice on the radio was crisp, almost mechanical. Estelle reached for the microphone and held it in her lap, waiting.

I could envision Howard Bishop reaching over to grope for the microphone without taking his eyes from the highway as it hurtled past.

"Uh, PCS, three oh seven is about a minute out. I just passed the Broken Spur." Deputy Bishop's voice was soft, almost hushed. He was eight miles ahead of us with Deputy Mears close on his bumper.

"No traffic," Estelle said. Our headlights drilled a tunnel into the black prairie.

I didn't respond. I concentrated on the highway. The drowsiness following a heavy meal had vanished with Gayle's voice on the telephone. The black macadam of the state highway stretched out in front of the county car, a ribbon that grew narrower as we accelerated into the night.

For several seconds, the only sound was the bellow of our car's engine. And then the dam broke.

"PCS, three oh seven is ten-ninety-seven." I tensed and gripped the wheel until my knuckles were white. Maybe whoever had called had sucked up one too many drinks at the Broken Spur Saloon and had gotten the story all wrong. Maybe it was a false alarm, a practice run where we all got to drive like crazy people with red lights and sirens and then got to laugh about it afterward.

We wound up through the esses that curled around the base of Arturo Mesa and then flung down the other side, to cross the Rio Salinas and flash past the tiny ghost town of Moore. I caught a wink of red far off in the distance to the southwest.

"Three ten, three oh seven."

Estelle responded in less than a heartbeat. "Three ten is just coming up on the Broken Spur."

"Three ten, is the ambulance right behind you?"

"Affirmative."

In another minute, as we shot past the saloon, I saw a group of half a dozen people standing in the parking lot, clustered around a cattle trailer and a fleet of pickup trucks. They were on their way to provide an audience, no doubt.

Two minutes later we crested a slight rise, turned a corner to the right, and came face to face with a parking lot in the middle of the state highway. I swore and braked hard. A civilian was standing in the oncoming lane waving a flashlight frantically, thinking perhaps that I was blind.

I stopped 310 diagonally across the double yellows so it blocked both lanes. Up ahead I could see Mears's and Bishop's patrol cars, one slightly ahead and one behind a third county car that was parked almost off the pavement. Half a dozen other vehicles were parked on both sides of the highway, and a circle of people nearly hid Deputy Enciños's patrol car from view.

I recognized rancher Howard Packard as I stepped out of the car.

41

"Stay back here and make sure no one else comes through except emergency vehicles, Howard," I said, and pointed back toward town. "Stay back behind my car."

Estelle was two paces ahead of me, walking down the center of the road, her hands thrust in her coat pockets. Ahead in the glare of a spotlight I saw that both doors of Enciños's patrol car were open.

I pushed my way past several curious, taut faces and knelt beside Howard Bishop. His huge frame was folded awkwardly as he tried to pump and breathe some life back into Paul Enciños.

"Any pulse?"

"No," Bishop said between grunts.

"The ambulance will be here in less than a minute." I didn't need to tell Bishop that his efforts weren't going to do Paul Enciños any good. Whoever had assaulted the deputy had used a shotgun and used it more than once.

"Sir . . ." Mears called across the car. I rose and made my way around to the other side. "I don't know what to do, sir," Mears said when he looked up and saw me.

The deputy had cause to panic. Linda Real's face, neck, and left shoulder were punctured by so many holes that Mears needed six hands to stop the gush of blood. Estelle Reyes-Guzman slipped into the backseat of the patrol car and leaned over the front seat back, cradling Linda's head while Mears and I tried to compress the multiple wounds on her left shoulder, neck, and face. After what seemed an eternity the first ambulance did arrive and I heard Bishop shout, "Over here."

A moment later a head peered into the car. "That one alive?" the EMT barked.

"Yes, just."

"Ah, here we come," he said as the second ambulance slid in behind the first. Mears, Estelle, and I stepped back as the EMTs took over.

"What a goddamned mess," I said. I looked at Deputy Mears's

42

pale face. "Take your car on up the road about a quarter mile and block the oncoming lane. No one comes through. No one." He nodded but didn't move. I took him by the arm. "Tom . . . do it now. And find out from Gayle what the deputy's last radio call was and get back to me."

"Yes, sir," he said with a start. To Estelle I said, "Let's get an inventory and then get 'em out of here."

She nodded. There were nine civilians present, and by the time we took IDs, statements, and inventories and marked where each vehicle had been parked, Sergeant Robert Torrez and Sheriff Martin Holman had arrived.

We needed the manpower to control that circus, and every time I caught a glimpse of Estelle's taut face I knew just what she was thinking. Whoever had pulled the trigger on Enciños and Real had picked a perfect spot. There had been no passersby to witness the shooting, no neighbors to hear the shots.

And the nearest telephone, when a motorist finally did stumble onto the carnage, was at a crowded saloon seven miles from town. That assured that the spectators would arrive well before any law, trampling any evidence there might have been into the fine New Mexico sand.

In less than two minutes, the handheld radio on my belt squawked. The news from Deputy Tom Mears wasn't what I wanted to hear. If Paul Enciños had stopped a vehicle, he hadn't radioed in. The last transmission Gayle Sedillos had recorded in the log back in Posadas was at 10:53 P.M., when the deputy had radioed that he was stopping at Chavez Chevrolet-Oldsmobile to talk with a motorist. He had given no name or license then, either.

That coincided with the information on the deputy's own patrol log. The clipboard rested on Enciños's briefcase in the middle of the front seat. The blood-spattered top page offered only a cryptic account of the deputy's last hours. He hadn't documented either the stop at Chavez or any event thereafter.

I felt a hand on my elbow. "Bill . . ." Sheriff Holman pulled gently, ushering me to one side. "Listen. Cassie isn't sure they are going to be able to . . . resuscitate him." Cassie Gates, the best EMT in Posadas County, wasn't usually wrong.

I nodded. "I know, sheriff."

"Maybe if they can get him back to the hospital in time . . ." His voice trailed off as he watched the first ambulance's door slam shut. After a deep sigh he shrugged his shoulders a little straighter and looked at me. "What do you want me to do?"

"Control things at the hospital, Martin." I ticked off a list while he jotted notes in the little blue spiral. "Make sure both sets of parents are notified. Paul's father lives in Scottsdale, I think. I'm not sure where his mother is now."

"She's up in Albuquerque," Holman muttered.

"And get a hold of Paul's ex-wife."

"Tiffany," Holman said.

"She lives over in the Mesaview Apartments. And Linda. I'm not sure. I think she told me once that her mother was living in Las Lunas."

"I'll take care of it." He snapped the little book shut, confident now that he had somewhere to go, something to do. "Anything else? Do we know who he stopped?"

I shook my head. "No, we don't. But right now the most important thing is what's going on at the hospital." As Sheriff Holman turned to go, I added, "And Martin . . ."

"Yes?"

"Keep the lid on over there. Frank Dayan will want to talk with Linda."

Holman frowned and walked back to me, standing so that our faces were less than a foot apart.

"If she lives, then she's the only witness to what happened here," he said, grasping the obvious more quickly than usual. The back door of the second ambulance slammed shut and then that vehicle too pulled away.

"If she regains consciousness, we have to talk with her. And that means before anyone else," I said.

Holman nodded. "I'll be at the hospital."

"I'll have one of the deputies there as soon as I can. In the meantime, if anything breaks, call me. Take my recorder in case Linda is able to speak with you. If she says anything at all, tape it. The recorder is in my briefcase on the front seat of my car."

He walked briskly back toward his car, caught in the winking of a dozen red lights. I saw the huge, dark figure of Sergeant Bob Torrez herding spectators east along the highway, well away from the scene. The routine of the drill would keep our minds occupied, at least.

The spectators would be individually interviewed and then escorted, one by one, down the macadam to where their vehicles were parked. They would be allowed to pull directly back onto the highway, their tire tracks in the sandy shoulder marked with a red surveyor's flag.

Eventually the entire fleet would be gone, leaving only the bullet-pocked patrol car parked on the north shoulder of the road. Then we would put a half mile of state highway under a microscope if we had to.

Maybe one of the rubberneckers had seen something. Maybe one of them had overheard someone say something at the Broken Spur Saloon. Maybe.

I left Bob Torrez and Bing Burkett, one of the first state troopers to arrive, to work the witnesses. Estelle was setting up her camera gear on the pavement beside Enciños's patrol car.

"Do you need any help?"

"You could hold the flashlight for me, sir."

I swung the beam over the patrol car and counted seven holes in the driver's door, doorpost, and roof.

"I'll take close-ups of those in the morning when it's light," Estelle said. "I want the side of the car and the macadam beside it right away."

By the time we finished two hours later, the list of evidence was painfully short. Paul Enciños had been driving county patrol car 308. The tire tracks showed that he had pulled his patrol car off the

45

pavement in a normal fashion. Another set of tracks was printed clearly in the sand several feet in front of 308. The origin of the tracks was obscured by both the patrol car and dozens of bootprints. Whether the tracks belonged to the killer's car was anyone's guess.

The driver's door of 308 was open, and that's the way Francisco Peña had found it when he'd happened by sometime after eleven that night. Pena worked for rancher Herb Torrance. He traveled from his line shack the nine miles down County Road 14 to the state highway and the Broken Spur Saloon often.

It had been Peña who'd raced to the Broken Spur and called Posadas. Peña said that when he'd driven by the scene, the car door was open. The engine was idling, the four-way flashers were blinking, and Deputy Enciños was on the ground by the back tire. Another person was inside the car.

The first pool of Paul Enciños's blood began four inches in front of the back tire and extended east for seventeen inches, part of the pool smeared by the deputy's upper left arm.

Another larger pool of blood actually touched the tread of the back tire where the tire rested on the macadam, extending around and under the car in a crescent. What appeared to be a blood smear on the bodywork of the patrol car began just to the rear of the wheel-well opening, extending down to the chrome strip above the rock guard.

The deputy had managed to exit the patrol car, but Linda Real never moved from her seat. "The killer fired at Linda through the driver's side window," Estelle said.

"I don't understand why Paul didn't call in, Estelle. I mean we harp and harp on that." I'm sure Estelle heard the helplessness in my voice, but there were no easy answers.

"I don't know, sir."

"Somebody does," I said.

46

8

SUNDAY slipped into Monday morning. Roadblocks on State 56 just north of the border at Regal produced nothing. Throughout most of the morning, deputies and troopers stopped just about everything with wheels in an area whose radius grew with the day. Our best efforts produced nothing. We had no idea what we were looking for.

At ten that morning, I sat morosely at my desk, staring across my small office at the chalkboard in the corner. I'd just left the hospital, where any extra people were just a nuisance. In an effort to clear my weary brain, I'd holed up in my office for a few minutes, trying to think of anything we'd missed.

On the chalkboard I had drawn a representation of the shooting scene. It was simple enough . . . a child could have drawn it. One section of empty two-lane highway and a patrol car—and two victims. That was all.

We didn't have a single set of tracks that we could conclusively link to the crime, although Bob Torrez had made a plaster of paris cast of the tracks in the sand in front of the county car. We had another set from across the highway, imprints no more than three feet long before they'd been obliterated by one or more of the sightseers. Torrez had cast those, too.

The killer had left behind no shell casings. From hurried con-

47

versations at Posadas General Hospital, we knew that the weapon that had killed Paul Enciños and desperately wounded Linda Real was a shotgun. The odds-on favorite would be a 12 gauge, statistically the most common by a wide margin. The killer's weapon had sprayed them with number 4 buck, lead pellets roughly .24 caliber in size and 21 to the ounce. A 12-gauge three-inch magnum would blast out 40 of the things at each jerk of the trigger.

We did not know where Paul Enciños had been standing, or even if he was, when the first shot was fired. Our guess was that Linda Real never moved from her seat during the incident . . . and certainly didn't move once the killer started pumping shots into the patrol car.

Gayle Sedillos appeared in the doorway. "Sir, Lionel Martinez is on the phone." I waved a hand in dismissal and Gayle smiled faintly. She was tired, too, but I needed her expertise for a few hours more. "He wants to know when you're going to open the highway."

I sighed and reached for the phone. "What's up, Lionel?"

Martinez was a man of infinite patience. He ran his State Highway Department District with good humor and tact, even when overloaded semis beat his new, expensive pavement to rubble and tourists constantly complained that there were no shaded, plumbed, padded rest areas out in the middle of desolation.

We'd put a cork in one of his highways and left it there.

"Sheriff, I need to know when your department is going to open Fifty-six."

I took a deep breath, trying to think of something tactful to say. "I don't know, Lionel."

"You can't give me some idea?"

"Not yet."

"We've got a flock of angry snowbirds who aren't takin' kindly to using Herb Torrance's road to go around you folks." I could imagine the gigantic, waddling RVs trying to negotiate the narrow, dusty, rutted county road that would take motorists around our roadblock.

"They're going to have to stay angry, Lionel. Tell you what.

48

Don't take any shit from anybody. If they want to bark at someone, send 'em to see me."

Lionel chuckled and then his voice grew serious. "Is there anything else we can do for you?"

"I wish there were."

"No progress yet?"

"No."

"Is the young lady going to make it?"

"I don't know. She was in surgery all night. Last word I had is that she's still out."

"I never would have thought something like this would happen here, sheriff."

"Yeah . . . well," I started to say, then stopped. I let it slide.

"You know, Paul Enciños was family."

"I didn't know that."

"Sure. He was second cousin to my wife. You know Rosie Salazar?"

"Yes."

"Rosie's sister Celsa was Paul's mother. She died here not so long ago."

I wasn't in the mood to pursue the complicated lineage. Paul Enciños had lived in Posadas County most of his life and I wouldn't have been surprised to learn he was related in one way or another to half the county. It would make for a hell of a lynch mob when we caught the son of a bitch who killed him.

"I had forgotten that," I said, and glanced up as Gayle Sedillos appeared in the doorway again and tapped her ear.

"I'll keep in touch, Lionel," I said, and as soon as I started to hang up Gayle said, "Estelle needs you out on Fifty-six. And she asked if you'd bring the county's cherry picker."

"The cherry picker?" I looked at Gayle stupidly.

She held out her right hand, palm up, and raised her arm. "You know, the cherry picker they use to fix electric lines and things like that."

"I know what it is, Gayle. I was just trying to imagine what Es-

49

telle would want with it. There's not much higher than cholla cactus out where she is."

Gayle shrugged. "That's what she said."

"Then that's what she'll get."

Twenty minutes later I was driving west on 56 with the county's utility truck rumbling along behind me. One of our reserve officers met us at the roadblock, and five hundred yards after that I stopped, the county truck edging up behind me so that its massive front bumper was only inches from the back of 310. The driver, Nelson Petro, sat patiently with both hands locked on the steering wheel while I got out to confer with Estelle.

"I need to show you what we've found, sir," she said. I caught the eagerness in her tone. I looked toward Enciños's patrol car and saw the webbing of heavy nylon fishing line attached to the car in several places. The nylon lines stretched from the car across the highway, converging to a single spot five feet above the ground, tied to the top of a wooden pole driven into the hard soil of the highway shoulder. A camera tripod rested on the north side of the highway's center line, and several more nylon lines ran from points inside the car to it.

Ignoring the spiderweb of lines, Estelle walked quickly to where her briefcase perched on the hood of Bob Torrez's patrol car. Torrez leaned against the car, his arms folded. "First, we got lucky," she said, and handed me a plastic bag. I looked at the attached evidence tag and then turned the bag so I could see the shell casing inside clearly.

"Twelve gauge," Sergeant Torrez said quietly. "Winchester-Western, number four buck." He straightened a little, towering over me by a head. "Recently fired."

"Has to be it, then," I said. "Where was it?"

Bob indicated the south side of the highway where the dense rabbitbrush and kochia choked the shoulder. "Twenty-eight inches from the pavement." I saw the small red flag off to one side of the wooden web-stake.

"Sharp eyes," I said.

"Luck, sir," Estelle said. "I almost stepped on it when I was adjusting the camera tripod."

"Sharp eyes," Bob Torrez added. He was right, of course. Estelle rarely did anything by accident.

"Any others?"

"No, sir. Just the one," Estelle said.

"But at least three shots were fired, maybe more."

"That's right, sir. But this tells us something we didn't know. Number one, the killer probably picked up the spent shell casings that he could find. The other two may have landed on the macadam. They would be easy."

"In the dark, it would have been a tough search to find this one," I said, and dropped the plastic bag back in Estelle's briefcase.

"He . . . or she, maybe . . . took the time to pick up spent shells, but missed this one, because it was kicked out to the side."

"And that eliminates any shotgun that ejects its shells straight down, sir," Torrez said.

"In all likelihood," Estelle added quickly. "Let me show you." I followed her across the macadam to the far shoulder. The red surveyor's flag was nestled in the midst of a thick, healthy rabbitbrush. The wind was cooperating and the spiderweb of fishing lines stretched silently, reflecting the sunlight.

"If the killer had been standing here," and she pointed at the wooden pole, "off the shoulder of the highway, a shotgun that ejects downward wouldn't have flung the casing more than seven feet to the right, into the bush," she said. "And if the killer inadvertently kicked it, it wouldn't have flown around here, to land nearly at the back side of the bush."

"Unlikely that it would. So, you've got a casing. Maybe we'll be lucky and be able to lift a readable print. And if you've got a side-eject shotgun, that eliminates only about one percent of the shotguns on the market." I looked at Estelle thoughtfully. "It's a good start."

I turned and gazed at the strings. I imagined the muzzle of the shotgun pointed across the road, and my eye followed the shimmering strands of fishing line as they angled across the highway.

"Let me show you what I want to do," Estelle said, and I followed her back across the road. She stepped close to Enciños's car and pointed at the roof. "One of the pellets glanced off the roof, right here, just above the center pillar between the front and back doors."

I saw a four-inch scar—at first only a faint lead mark on the paint and then becoming deeper until it actually showed a trace of bare metal. The end of a piece of nylon line had been carefully taped to the roof of the car so that it lay in the missile track.

"That's not going to be exact," Estelle said, "but it gives us a starting point." She indicated another hole, this one in the top window frame of the back door. "This one is a relatively clean puncture of the first two layers of metal. Enough to establish a probable angle." She turned and pointed back across the highway, along the stretched lines.

"How many contact points did you establish?" I asked, and then counted the lines for myself. Seven strands ran from the car across the highway.

"The rest either struck Paul or passed behind him, over the back window and trunk of the car," Bob Torrez said.

"All right. It makes sense. That's the first shot." I backed away a step. "You've got two others."

"The killer walked across the highway after firing the first time," Torrez said. "He got to about here," and he rested a hand lightly on the camera tripod, "and fired again. One round was fired downward . . ." He hesitated and glanced at me. "Estelle thinks Paul was on the ground, by the back tire, trying to get up."

"That accounts for the smeared blood on the fender," I said.

"Yes. The second shot was fired from close range." Torrez indicated the pattern path from the tripod and then knelt down, his knee near the second bloodstain that trailed under the car. One of the nylon strands ran from the tripod to a spot actually under the

52

rear rock guard of the patrol car, some fourteen inches behind the tire.

"This is the only pellet mark we found, sir," Estelle said as Torrez touched the tack that had been pushed into the macadam to hold the fishing line. "From the second pattern."

"If there are others, they'd be lost in the loose gravel there," I said. "And the third round went into the car?"

"Yes, sir." I walked around the other side of the car, following Estelle. "One of the pellets cut across the top of the seat." She indicated one of the lines that attached just above where the passenger's left shoulder would have been. "We found a total of nine pellet holes or tracks that show the shot was fired from a point two or three paces from the driver's side door, through the window."

"About ten to fifteen feet," I said. "The pattern wouldn't have been very big."

"No, sir. The majority of the blast went behind Linda's head, shattering the right rear window and tearing the window post. We think she was also hit by some of the pellets that deflected off the driver's side upper window frame."

I bent down and squinted. "So the killer was shooting a little high and to the right. Otherwise Linda Real would have taken the full charge right in the face."

"Yes, sir."

I straightened up with a grunt. "So the son of a bitch fired once from across the road as Paul stepped from the car. Then he walked across the road and fired once more at Paul, point-blank, while the deputy was on the ground."

"Yes, sir."

"And in the dark, with all the confusion of the headlights, maybe even the spotlight, he might not have noticed that Paul had a passenger until he crossed the highway. Then he saw Linda and fired a third time."

Estelle nodded. "I think that's the way it went, sir."

"What did you want the picker for?"

53

"I'd like photographs from above, sir. The sun is just right to glint off the lines. If he parks the truck over behind the pole, then we can adjust the angle from there."

Nelson Petro idled the truck forward under Bob Torrez's directions. He parked in the soft sand along the side of the highway, far enough from the pole that no part of the truck would be in the photographs. He extended the truck's hydraulic outriggers, then swung the boom out and lowered the bucket. For the first time Estelle hesitated.

"There doesn't look like there's room in there for both of us," she said.

"Yeah, we'll fit," Nelson said. "You just tell me what you want."

They squeezed into the red bucket and then with a whine were lofted into the air. Bob Torrez and I backed away, squinting into the sun and watching the performance. Nelson maneuvered the bucket to a point directly behind the string-post and then, with Estelle bracing the camera, lifted the bucket straight up, gradually increasing the angle of sight along the strings. Finally, hovering fifteen feet up and as many feet behind the post, Estelle found what she was looking for. A few minor adjustments and the bucket hung quietly while she burned film.

She shot photos from several other positions before nodding that she was satisfied.

"Anything else, just holler," Nelson said a few minutes later, and then the county truck rumbled back toward town.

"You want to meet in my office in a few minutes?" I asked. "Or down at the hospital?"

Estelle looked down at the macadam thoughtfully. "Francis is going to let me know the instant there's any change in Linda's condition, sir. I'm going to head over that way. I have a couple of questions to ask the medical examiner, and then I want to follow up with Mr. Peña."

"He's pretty upset," Torrez said. "I tried to talk with him, but he wasn't much help."

"I'll give it a try," Estelle said. She would pry out any information the old ranch hand knew, in one language or another. "And I want to use one of the hospital's stereoscopes. See what the shotgun casing has to offer."

Slim evidence, but maybe the killer had been confident that we'd never find the shell casing in the first place. I found myself hoping he'd stay confident and give us something more.

9

SHERIFF Martin Holman sat in my chair, leaning forward with his elbows on the desk and his hands clasped at his forehead as if he were deep in prayer. A newspaper was spread out under his elbows. He looked up from the *Posadas Register* as I entered and dropped one hand to the paper so he could mark his place with an index finger.

"Ron Schroeder wants to see you."

I hung my Stetson on the hat tree behind the door, taking my time so Holman wouldn't feel rushed about getting out of my chair. He didn't move.

"Schroeder knows where I work," I said.

"No, no, Bill. This is a summons into The Great One's presence." That wasn't entirely fair, since District Attorney Ron Schroeder was as hardworking as they come—bright, diligent, ambitious—all those traits that somehow never quite seemed to make up for the giant streak of condescension running down his back.

Holman turned the newspaper so that I could see it and then pushed it across the desk.

I sighed and fished what was left of my glasses out of my pocket. "Somebody else worked all night, too," I said, and before my eyes could focus I was already wondering how Dayan had managed to

56

sneak a crime scene photograph when we hadn't allowed so much as a centipede through the roadblocks.

But I had forgotten about Sonny Trujillo and the Friday night follies.

"Not very flattering, Bill," Holman said. There I was, in perfect focus, spread across three columns at the top of the page. The photographer had popped the flash at the instant that Trujillo's fat fist made contact with my cheek and glasses. In the picture, my glasses were askew, Trujillo's mouth was open and bellowing, and there in the bottom left corner, perfectly in focus, was my service revolver. My left hand was clamped around the barrel and cylinder, obviously twisting hard.

"Nice picture," I said. I squinted at the caption. *"Despite being physically attacked, Undersheriff William K. Gastner managed to wrestle a handgun away from Salvador Trujillo (left) during an altercation at Friday night's basketball game."* I grunted. "That's nice. They had to label him 'left' so people could tell us apart?"

"At least the caption doesn't mention that it's your own gun, Bill."

"There's always that." The three column headline below the photograph read *Veteran Cop's Quick Thinking Prevents Tragedy.*

"You may need that headline," Holman said, and I looked up sharply. "Schroeder said that he needs to see you in connection with Trujillo's death."

I started to fold the newspaper. "I don't have time for that shit, Martin. You talk with him. We've got a murder investigation, for God's sake. You'd think Schroeder of all people would have his priorities straight on this one. And you'd think that Linda's own goddamned newspaper might feature something about her, rather than this nonsense."

Sheriff Holman held up both hands to slow me down. "Whoa, whoa. The DA said he needs to talk with you when you have time. Not this instant." He made little rotating motions with his hands, as if I were supposed to turn the newspaper over.

"That'll be in about seven years, the way things are going."

I turned the folded paper over and a box with a heavy black border at the bottom right corner of page one drew my eye. The shooting late Sunday night had caught the *Register* right at deadline. The article showed that Frank Dayan was as frustrated as we were. I read it quickly.

Deputy Killed, Reporter Wounded

Police are investigating the apparent murder of a Posadas County Sheriff's Deputy and the wounding of *Posadas Register* reporter Linda Real last night.

According to Posadas County Sheriff Martin Holman, the double shooting occurred sometime after 10 P.M. last night on State Highway 56, nine miles west of Posadas. Holman reported that Deputy Sheriff Paul Enciños, 26, was dead on arrival at Posadas General Hospital.

Ms. Real, 25, is listed in critical condition in Intensive Care with shotgun wounds to the head and neck, Holman said. Ms. Real had been riding with Deputy Enciños as a civilian passenger, Holman said.

No other details were available, although Sheriff Holman said that several leads were being pursued.

I dropped the newspaper on my desk and shook my head. "Christ, I wish I had some answers, Martin."

"Something will turn up. I really believe that. I have confidence something will break."

I shoved my right hand in my trouser pocket and groped with my left for a cigarette in my shirt pocket. Of course there were none there, but old habits died hard. "We've got nothing on this one,

58

Martin. Nothing. No gut feelings that tell us where to go or where to look. Nothing. Some stranger could have burned 'em both and been to hell and gone over the border long before Francisco Peña ever happened by."

"Estelle can give us full time on this one?"

I grunted a monosyllabic reply to what I thought was an abysmally stupid question.

"And you'll make a note to see Schroeder today or tomorrow? Try to fit in a few minutes."

"I'll see."

"There has to be a hearing on Trujillo no matter what."

"I know it, sheriff." I took a deep breath. "It's hard to put some useless drunk choking to death on his own vomit in the same ball-park as one of our deputies being murdered, and the kid who was riding with him shot to pieces as well."

Holman shrugged and raised both hands, palms up. "Schroeder tells me that apparently Juanita Smith has decided this is her chance to get back at all of us."

"Who the hell is Juanita Smith?"

"Sonny's mother."

"I didn't know he had a mother." Holman grinned and I added, "I mean alive and living in town."

"She married Woody Smith a year or so before he drank himself to death. Before that she was living with Sal Trujillo Sr. Remember? Sal and his cousin were the ones . . ." I held up a hand.

"Please, Marty. I'm not ready for this. What you're saying is that this woman, whoever she is, has crawled out of the woodwork and is yelping that her one and only, her brilliant and talented son, was murdered by the gestapo. Is that about it?"

Holman leaned back in my chair and hooked his hands behind his head. "Basically, yes." As a sudden dawning spread through his brain, Holman's eyes grew large and bright and he lunged out of my chair. "Do you suppose . . ."

"No, Martin."

He waved a hand wildly. "No, no. Hear me out. Do you think that somehow . . ."

"One of Sonny Trujillo's friends decided to avenge his death and saw the opportunity out on State Fifty-six somehow? No."

"You don't think there's a chance of that?"

"No."

Holman deflated slowly as he scanned my face for signs that I might give in.

"Why not? It's as good as anything else you've got."

"I'll grant you that, Martin." I shook my head. "First of all, Sonny didn't run around with the kind of friends who'd have enough brains to pull something like this. Whoever did it was a cold son of a bitch, Martin. The killer took the time to pick up his damn shell casings, for God's sake. He shot Paul once from across the highway, then walked up and pumped another into him while Paul was lying on the ground. And then he shot Linda Real, shot her right through the driver's window. If the glass hadn't deflected some of the pellets, he'd have blown her head off."

"Christ, Bill."

I picked up the newspaper, idly folding it. "And then he picked up his casings, Martin. All except one that he couldn't find."

"And you did?"

"Estelle found it, yes."

"Then that's something, isn't it?"

I shrugged. "Damn little."

Holman made his way around my desk and headed toward the door. "You've been over to the hospital?"

"No. Estelle said her husband would let us know if there was any change."

"Is someone assigned to the hospital?"

"Peggy Mears is over there. And I asked for some assistance from the state police. Ray Galiston will be there until four." I glanced at my watch. "And they'll send someone else then if they can spring somebody."

"If Linda regains consciousness, she might be able to tell us what we need to know."

"Maybe."

"She's the only witness, Bill."

"So far, yes."

Holman stopped at the door with his hand on the knob. "Will there be someone there to question her at any time? I mean, if she should surface for even a minute, whatever she knows might be really valuable."

"Right now, that's not our highest priority, sheriff."

Holman looked confused. "I don't follow."

"Paul Enciños is dead. Nothing we do is going to bring him back. Much as I'd like to catch the son of a bitch who killed him, I don't want to do anything that might jeopardize Linda Real's life. I don't want two dead. So we're going to let the doctors alone to do their best. Later, if she can . . ."

"She's got to know, Bill. She's the key witness."

"Only if she's alive, sheriff."

Holman nodded and turned to go. I had a stack of patrol logs and radio logs I wanted to sift through in peace and quiet, but Holman wasn't finished.

"Will you give the eulogy?" I stopped short, and Holman added, "At the service. It's Thursday morning at ten."

"I'm not very good at that sort of thing, sheriff."

"You don't have to be good at it, Bill. And I hope that you never get enough practice that you become good at it. But it will mean more coming from you than from me. I mean, I'll say a little something, but the official department sentiments should come from you. You've been in this business for a long time."

I nodded.

"Thanks. Let me know if there's anything else you want me to do."

"There is," I said, and Holman looked expectant. "Sergeant Torrez has a plaster cast of some tire prints. He's got about eighty-five million other things to do. It'd be a hell of a deal if you'd take them and find out what kind of tire we're dealing with."

For a second or two, Holman looked as if he wanted to say, *"How do I do that?"* But he thought better of it. "Where are they?"

"The deputy has them with him. He's over at the county maintenance yard, in the old shop building."

He nodded. "I'll pick them up. I'll be in my office until five, and then I'll be at the hospital."

After Sheriff Martin Holman left, I retrieved a stack of patrol logs along with the radio and telephone logs for the previous week. I spread the paperwork out on my desk, closed my office door, and got to work. I had no illusions that I would find anything of importance in that mass of documentation.

The logs would show, in terse, repetitive jargon, exactly what I told every new deputy who ever joined our tiny department—and what I told the others on a regular basis. The threat of rural law enforcement lay not in the constant dangers of hoodlum patrol. Leave that to the big cities. We might go weeks, months, even years with nothing but yawns, and then be smashed in the face with fifteen seconds of panic.

After living in the doldrums, it was easy to be caught off guard.

Paul Enciños had been caught off guard and it had killed him. His handgun had been found still snapped in its holster. The electric lock on the dashboard of his patrol car that held the shotgun had not been tripped. The deputy never had time to recognize his moment of panic.

10

SERGEANT Robert Torrez was bent over the fender of 308, his brows knit tightly together in concentration as he peeled the backing off a one-inch bright-blue circular sticker.

"Estelle's better at this than I am," he muttered.

I surveyed his handiwork, impressed. Centered over each mark of pellet damage was a colored sticker. He had used yellow dots for the first shot pattern, blue for the second, and red for the third. In place of the atomized driver's side window, he had stretched a piece of clear plastic and then, by carefully extrapolating where the pellets had struck other surfaces of the car's interior, he had dotted the probable locations of the pellets' entry through the window.

I turned and looked at the dozen yard-square pieces of brown butcher paper that were laid on the garage floor. Each one had been blasted once with a shotgun. Each was carefully labeled.

The top six targets had been shot using one of the department's 12 gauge riot guns, a pump action weapon with a twenty-inch barrel. The shots had been fired at distances beginning at five feet and then extending out in five-foot increments to thirty feet. The diameter of the pattern was clearly labeled.

The second set of targets had been riddled using the same type three-inch magnum number four buck ammunition, but this time fired from a shotgun with a standard length barrel.

63

"You can see a pretty significant difference in spread between the two guns," I mused, kneeling down with a grunt and a loud cracking of the knees. "What was the choke on the field gun?"

"Modified," Torrez said. "There's a bunch of other combinations I could have tried, but this gives us a pretty clear picture."

He picked up the last target in the riot gun series, the one fired at thirty feet, and walked to the car. "If you compare the size of the yellow pattern, the one we think was fired from the opposite shoulder of the highway, you'll see that it'd be pretty easy to imagine a close match."

"You sound overwhelmed with confidence," I said. "None of the other series are that large."

"Right," Torrez nodded. "In order to get a spread like this with a regular field gun, you'd have to be backed off fifty or sixty feet."

"You don't really have very many definite pellet marks on the car to establish that pattern size, though."

"Eight, sir. That's why I said you could imagine a match. I'd hate to have to defend this in court."

"Eight pellets out of a possible . . ."

"Forty-one. I know that isn't a very good percentage, but it gives us a starting point. For the round fired through the window, I had only six definites to work with and another half a dozen probables." He laid down the target and picked up another. "The round fired through the window was really tight when it hit the glass. Just under a foot in diameter."

"And with a field gun, you'd still have to be backed away twenty or thirty feet for a pattern that big."

"Right."

I took a deep breath. "So we're looking for a sawed-off twelve-gauge three-inch magnum shotgun that ejects its empties to the side."

"Or a bottom dumper that the killer held on its side, like the Hollywood hotshots do." Torrez mimed the stance, right elbow cocked high. I grimaced.

"In short, we don't really know very much, do we?"

"No, sir."

I straightened up and surveyed the perforated patrol car and paper targets. "We're going to be able to figure out pretty much what happened from the time the trigger was pulled for the first time," I said. "And that just about shoots our wad. We don't know who, we don't know why, we don't know how many people were involved." I looked at Torrez, hoping that he had some other answers that he'd been saving for last. He didn't.

"Howard Bishop and Bing Burkett are coordinating highway searches, airport checks, that sort of thing," I shrugged. "Good cooperation all around. I imagine that there's something like a hundred deputies, troopers—even some of the critter cops working every corner of the state. No one's turned up anything." I thrust my hands in my pockets. "Did Sheriff Holman swing by and pick up the tire casts from you?"

"Yes, sir." Torrez sounded a little skeptical. I grinned at the big deputy.

"The sheriff is not as stupid as we all son   es think he is, Roberto." Torrez had the tact to remain silent. "Did you tell the county yard foreman that we'd need this garage bay for several days?"

Torrez nodded. "He said whatever we needed. He said he's got the only other key, so people won't be wandering in and out until we give the word."

The deputy carefully walked around his targets and frowned at me. "Sir, I've been wondering about the car, too. You know, we have a couple of coincidences here that are kinda interesting. One, Paul takes three oh eight here, instead of the car he usually drives. Two, he was out in the vicinity of the Broken Spur Saloon, which is where I had my last go-around with Victor Sánchez. And three, this all happened during the swing shift, which is when I work."

"You're thinking that maybe someone out there had it in for you and shot at Paul by mistake?"

"It's possible, sir."

I shook my head. "Not likely. For one thing, you don't look a damn thing like Paul Enciños, even from a distance. You're a head taller and fifty pounds heavier. However, I suppose that maybe at night, with the adrenaline pumping, a cop looks like a cop."

Torrez turned and surveyed the riddled patrol car. "And what about it being my car?"

I snorted. "First of all, it isn't your car, Roberto. True enough, you drove it most of the time during your shift. But on days, Tony Abeyta was using it. And half the time Howard Bishop drives it midnight to eight. So . . ." I strode quickly over to the car. "And finally," I said, holding thumb and index finger to gauge the height of the black number decals behind the rear window post, "these little numbers are only three inches high. We notice 'em because it's part of what we do. But to the average civilian, one patrol car looks like any other. Who's going to notice a number and assume that the deputy inside is Robert Torrez?"

I stepped away from the car. "Victor Sánchez is a hothead, Robert, and that's what makes a case of mistaken identity even *more* unlikely. If he's got a complaint, he'll climb right into your face. An ambush from across a dark highway isn't his style."

"Should I go out and talk with him?"

"No. Let me do that."

"You want me to come along?"

I smiled and shook my head. "I want you to keep doing what you're doing. Finish with the car and make sure you have a set of perfect photos. Then, when the sheriff tracks down the make and model of tires from those casts, hunt the right species down and get some photographs of those, too. Estelle is putting the shell casing under the microscope and we should have fingerprints a little later, if our boy got careless. By then, we can start pushing the Office of the Medical Examiner for whatever the autopsy showed."

I shrugged with resignation. "None of the roadblocks turned up a thing. I canceled them just before I came over here. If the killer was someone just passing through, he's long gone anyway. If it was someone local, then maybe pulling down the barriers will encourage him to stick his head out. I don't know. In the meantime, it's important to pay attention to all the little details." I nodded at his targets and stickers. "Good work."

"You sure you don't want company going out to see Sánchez?"

"I'm sure."

The late afternoon sun was dipping toward the San Cristobal Mountain peaks to the southwest as I drove out State Highway 56. The air was brilliantly clear with no breeze. For the first four miles, I didn't pass a single car, coming or going. A handful of cattle didn't bother to lift their heads as I motored past. Goddamned pastoral, is what it was.

I wondered what Linda Real and Paul Enciños had been talking about as they drove this very macadam twenty hours before. Just kids, I thought. Both of them less than half my age. Kids idling down the highway during a pleasant evening, assuming that come Easter they'd be part of a family gathering, or that they'd be ready for a week's vacation in June, or that they'd get to see the fireworks put on in the Posadas Village Park on the Fourth of July. I thumped the steering wheel with my fist in frustration.

I looked out across the sweep of prairie, my eyes following the gradual curve of the highway around the base of Arturo Mesa. Two sodium-vapor lights burned brightly and marked the yard and pens of Wayne Feed and Supply, a business that sprawled over a dozen acres.

If you needed a cutter bar for a 1924 Eustice hay-flailer, you could probably find one there. You'd have to tramp out through the creosote bush, cactus, and rattlesnakes to find it yourself on one of the legion of rusting hulks. Toby Sánchez hadn't bought the business so that he'd have to work.

In another two minutes, I would drive past the empty buildings of Moore, just as Deputy Enciños and Linda Real would have done. I glanced down at the papers beside me.

Deputy Enciños's patrol log for the evening hadn't offered much. A photocopy of the last page of that log lay on top of my briefcase.

```
16:06    308 starting 98390.8
16:38    10-8
16:54    W/W KGY-399 neg.
16:56    10-87 Cal Hewlett 10-15 Efren Padilla PCDC
17:25    10-8
17:32    MVA I-10/NM 56
18:18    PGH, confer Dr. Perrone, op. Weatherford
         ng/ba, inf. t/o/t Mears
18:30    10-7 NSI
18:48    10-8
18:50    10-19 L. Real
19:00    10-8
20:11    10-62 Rosalita Ibarra, 579 Serna Place. Ani-
         mal nuisance t/o/t PPD
20:35    10-8
21:05    10-62 R. Ibarra, animal nuisance, neighbor
         threats. Talked with neighbor Saucilito Ortiz,
         agreed to corral dog. PPD nr
21:40    10-8
22:53    E. Bustos Ave. ref. afterhours activity. Neg.
         contact, t/o/t PPD
22:59    10-8
```

In his last hours of duty, Deputy Enciños had entered the starting mileage of his patrol car—completely routine. A few minutes later, he'd asked for a wants/warrant check on a license number. There was no hint in his log about whether he had actually stopped the vehicle. The dispatcher's log had confirmed that he had not.

Cal Hewlett, one of the U.S. Forest Service law enforcement officers, had requested assistance in transporting a prisoner, one Efren Padilla, to the county lockup. I knew Padilla. The old man had probably been cutting green piñon again, on the feds' turf.

At five-thirty-two, Enciños had responded to the Weatherfords' traffic accident. That had kept him occupied until six-thirty, when

68

he'd eaten dinner at the North Star Inn, the big chain motel near the interstate ramp where the Weatherfords had trashed their van and trailer.

At six-fifty, the deputy had returned to the Posadas County Sheriff's Office and picked up *Posadas Register* reporter Linda Real. If she was expecting an exciting night, the first calls didn't offer a preview. Rosalita Ibarra had been complaining about Sauci Ortíz's dog for years. She would have complained even if the old man didn't have a dog. Rosalita and Sauci had been neighbors for sixty years. They'd argued and shouted at each other for sixty years. They loved it. The only thing that made it better was a good audience.

Deputy Paul Enciños had provided the audience. Twice. He'd tried to turn the complaint over to the village cops, but they weren't buying it . . . if one or the other of them had been on duty. It must have been the deputy's first time trying to handle the Ibarra/Ortíz show. Otherwise he would have known better.

The last entry was equally routine. At fifty-three minutes after ten, Deputy Enciños had been directed to East Bustos Avenue. The dispatch log, and Gayle Sedillos's memory, said the call had come from the manager of Mark's Burger Heaven, one of the teen hangouts.

The manager had said that kids were driving around behind the fence of the business across the street. She didn't know what they were up to. She didn't have much imagination if she couldn't figure out what two kids in a car wanted with darkness, away from streetlights and prying eyes.

Deputy Enciños had checked and then, at one minute before eleven o'clock, he had called in 10-8, meaning that he was in service and free for assignment. That was his last call.

He and his passenger had then driven to the other side of the county and gotten themselves shot.

I drove through Moore, looking hard at the huge dark blob that once had been Beason's Mercantile and Dry Goods. Until the vein ran out, folks in Moore had assumed their town was going to grow and prosper, maybe even make mention in the 1920 census. Beason thought so, enough to build the two-story edifice that now stood empty and crumbling.

State 56 was so straight between the back side of Arturo Mesa and the banks of the Rio Guijarro that for two and a half miles a laser beam wouldn't have strayed from the dotted center line.

After crossing the bridge, the highway fishtailed a little, dipping through the grove of cottonwoods that surrounded the Broken Spur Saloon.

Monday at suppertime would be slow, and a good time to capture Victor Sánchez's full attention, but I didn't pull off the highway. I scanned the parking lot as I drove by. There were two pickup trucks, one with a long livestock trailer attached. The trailer was empty. Half of the ranchers drove around with the humongous things permanently attached to their trucks, clanging and banging over every bump in the road. I figured it was a kind of status symbol.

Three miles down the highway was the turnoff to the north— County Road 14, a dusty ribbon that wound up through the prairie and the old lava beds, past windmills and stock tanks, and up over the top of San Patricio Mesa. It had been down that jouncing two-track that Francisco Peña's old GMC pickup had trundled the night before.

I drove southwest, toward that intersection with the county road. My hands involuntarily gripped the steering wheel tighter as the white lines clicked by. Peña would have pulled up at the stop sign, at which point he would have been able to see the headlights of the parked patrol car a quarter-mile east, to his left.

A dark smudge and some white chalk on the pavement, along with a few trampled weeds on the shoulder, were all that marked the spot. I slowed 310 to an idle. An oncoming car dashed by, no doubt curious why anyone would stop in the middle of nowhere.

Paul Enciños and Linda Real would have had no reason to do so unless another vehicle was stopped along the shoulder of the road.

In another quarter of a mile, I turned right onto County Road 14,

70

and as 310's front tires crunched onto gravel, the late afternoon sun winked off metal to my left, further up the highway. Someone was parked in a small grove of elms that struggled for life near one of the highway department's stash of crushed stone.

I continued up the county road for half a mile and then turned around, nearly planting the front wheels of my patrol car in a small arroyo. As I drove back, I opened my window and took a deep breath. Francisco Peña said he didn't see anything until he actually drove by the scene of the shooting. And true enough, most of County Road 14 ambled up and down through dips and cuts and arroyos, around runty stands of juniper and cholla. The state highway intersection wasn't visible until I approached within a hundred yards of the stop sign.

At any time during that hundred yards, though, I could see east along the state road. Had there been more than one vehicle parked along the shoulder of the highway, Francisco Peña would have been able to see it.

I hesitated at the stop sign and then turned right. The car I had seen was parked behind a mound of crusher fines, impossible to see eastbound, and not much more than a glint for westbound traffic. I circled the pile, drove around a parked asphalt roller, and pulled up beside the other vehicle.

I saw the passenger side window buzz down and I switched off the engine of the patrol car.

In the distance I could hear oncoming traffic, so I waited until it shot past—a single late-model sedan with New Mexico plates. The tire noise faded and that wonderful, heavy silence of the open prairie settled once more.

Estelle Reyes-Guzman looked across at me. From the lack of radio traffic, she knew as well as I did that our roadblocks sealing Posadas County had produced nothing but expense and inconvenience.

I wasn't particularly surprised to find her parked in the middle of nowhere, with nothing but the sound of night winds, coyotes,

71

and rare traffic for company. As a little kid growing up in northern Mexico, Estelle Reyes had probably been the sort to seek out a dark corner for private moments.

I conjured up a mental image of her as she might have been twenty years before and saw a tiny, thin six-year-old waif sitting with her back against a cool, dark adobe wall, arms folded around her knees, skinny elbows jutting out. Under the mop of black hair were those two incredible eyes looking out at the world, contemplating, evaluating.

"What have you decided?" I said, and even though a vehicle's width and more separated us, my quiet question sounded like a shout.

Estelle Reyes-Guzman didn't answer for a long moment, but finally she shifted a little in her seat and said, "I think you and I need to go over and talk with Victor Sánchez, sir."

11

DURING the twenty-four hours since the shooting, a dozen cops of one stripe or another had talked with Victor Sánchez. The owner of the Broken Spur Saloon and Trading Post was no charmer in the first place. Quick-tempered, beady-eyed, his saloon was his own private hot rock under which he lurked.

And as Sergeant Bob Torrez had discovered in days past, Sánchez evidently felt he was the target of cops who had nothing better to do than harass an honest business man. I was certain that Sánchez had sold his share of liquor to intoxicated customers over the years. And I was sure that he didn't check IDs as closely as he could have. But I went into his saloon that evening just as sure as I could be that he had nothing to do with the murder of Paul Enciños and the wounding of Linda Real.

I didn't know what Estelle had in mind. She probably could have earned a good living as a high-stakes poker player with her inscrutable face. She'd tell me what she was thinking in her own good time—I'd learned that over the years.

Neither Estelle nor I had had the chance to talk with Victor Sánchez since the incident. Other officers had interviewed the man, and according to their reports, the saloon owner knew no more than the rest of us.

But Estelle was chewing on something, and a few minutes of

peace and quiet in a dark, cozy saloon wouldn't hurt. Whatever the owner's rattlesnake personality, the Broken Spur provided infinitely more creature comforts than parking behind a gravel pile along the highway.

We drove into the saloon's parking lot and I parked 310 beside a blue Dodge three-quarter-ton pickup whose bottom half was armored with inch-thick, sun-dried caliche. A blue Queensland healer pup stood guard in the back over a rubble of ranch tools, oil cans, and half a dozen partial spools of barbed wire.

As I got out of the patrol car, the dog stood on two of the full wire rolls like a king of the mountain, looking down at me.

"I would think that would hurt," I said, and the dog lowered his head and beat the air into a frenzy with his tail. Either his paw pads were tough or he was too stupid to mind the barbs.

Estelle parked her unmarked car beside 310. She got out and stood for a minute, listening, looking, surveying the parking lot. The pickup that belonged to Victor Jr. was parked beside the building in the shade of several elm saplings. On the other side of the Dodge and the healer pup were three other vehicles, two local and one with California plates. Beyond that, parked diagonally for easy exit, was another ranch truck hitched to a twenty-foot-long livestock trailer.

The Broken Spur Saloon and Trading Post was cave dark, and our eyes, tired from a day of squinting into the New Mexico winter sun, were slow to adjust.

I stepped in the door and stopped next to the cigarette machine. Across a faded, scuffed Mexican imitation of a Navajo rug was a glass counter full of belt buckles, packets labeled as rattlesnake eggs, porcelain figurines, and other detritus that must have attracted tourists now and then. Maybe if I had to live in some place like Cleveland I'd get a kick out of showing my friends the New Mexico scorpion encased in plastic that I'd bought "right down there near the border."

My gaze drifted up to the zoo of antelope trophies gathering dust on the dingy white plastered wall. Two big buck pronghorns kept

74

musty vigil over a piece of plywood framed with braided rope. The plywood displayed a collection of *"Barbbed Wire of Posadas County."* There must have been fifty varieties of rusted wire tacked to the mount, with some dating back to the late 1870s when they were first patented. By the 1940s, most of the county ranchers had decided it wasn't so much barbed wire that they needed for successful cow-calf operations as it was rainfall.

"Two for dinner, sir?"

I hadn't heard the girl approach, and I turned with a start. The hostess smiled pleasantly, her plump, acne-scarred face framed by long, curly black hair. She was the kind of kid who probably didn't turn many sober heads now, but when she reached fifty she would have grown into her features. Her gaze shifted from me to Estelle and back again.

"Is Victor here?" I asked.

"Mr. Sánchez? Let me go see."

The bar was through a doorway to the left. To the right was a small dining room. Straight down the hall was the kitchen, and the hostess headed that way. Estelle browsed the foyer and then stepped briefly into the bar. I didn't follow. The tobacco smoke would be thick and I didn't need the temptation. The cigarette machine behind me was bad enough.

I saw the hostess stop in the kitchen doorway, leaning against the doorjamb as if she weren't allowed to trespass. After a minute's earnest conversation, she recoiled a step and Victor Sánchez appeared, a large carving knife in one hand and a bunch of celery in the other. He looked out at us and then waved the celery in dismissal. He disappeared and the hostess turned and smiled at us hopefully, maybe thinking that we'd see the obvious and leave.

I remained rooted under the *Barbbed* wire, so she padded back down the hall, her head down in that "please don't kill the messenger" posture she'd probably learned early in this job.

"Mr. Sánchez said he can't talk with you now."

"Ah, busy night, huh," I said. The girl nodded, her face brightening with the hope that I wasn't going to be as cranky as I looked.

75

I stepped past her and walked down the hall toward the kitchen. The hostess didn't object or offer to present me to his highness. She murmured something to Estelle and then vanished into the bar to deal with customers she understood.

The kitchen smelled of Saturday night's fajitas, grilling hamburger, and cleaning compounds. Victor Sánchez was working at the cutting board, chattering the celery into slivers with the knife. He looked up and saw Estelle and me standing in the doorway. He stopped cutting.

"I said I was busy."

"I see that," I said.

Sánchez was a squat man, beefy through the shoulders with short, muscular arms, thick wrists, and powerful, stubby-fingered hands. He tipped the board of celery into a bowl and turned toward the stove.

"You want something to eat?"

"No, thanks. I guess not." I did, but Sánchez was fixing something that looked and smelled like chicken soup, and as far as I was concerned, that was health food.

"*Y tú?*" he asked Estelle. I knew about ten words of Spanish, just enough to be surprised at the familiar greeting.

She shook her head. "*Queremos unos pocos minutos de tú tiempo, señor,*" she said.

Sánchez banged the bowl down on the table and turned to glare at us. I knew the look—I'd used it myself many times in the marines when conversing with idiot recruits.

"You know how many people I talk to today, *querida?*" Estelle's face remained impassive. He took a step closer and shook a stubby finger in her face. "All day long, in and out, in and out. Like flies. They ask, what's this, what's this, what's this?"

"What do you expect?" I said quietly when he paused to take a breath. "One of our officers was killed just down the road. Do you think we're going to wait until there's a lull in your bar traffic to talk to you?"

Sánchez dropped the knife on the cutting board and wiped his hands on his clean, starched apron. "What does this place have to do with what happened?" he demanded. He turned back to Estelle and hunched his shoulders like an old bulldog. His words came machine-gun fast, and I guess maybe he thought Estelle would flinch. She listened impassively. *"Nada pasaba aquí. Nada. Ni siquiera una persona vio nada. Ahora, quita de medio."* He chopped the air with the edge of his palm.

"He said nothing happened here, that no one saw anything . . . and to get out of his way," Estelle said to me. Victor grunted.

He waved a hand in my direction. "He knows damn well what I said, *chinita*. All these cops, you drive away my customers. You cost me money."

He turned back to his celery and dumped it into a stainless steel cooking pot on the stove. The tidbits disappeared into the bubbling soup and my stomach twinged a little with anticipation.

"Victor," I said using my most conciliatory tone, "one of your customers might remember something. In a case like this, we don't have much to go on. Any little detail that someone might remember. It could help us. Anything that happened that was even a little unusual."

Several pieces of chicken were spread out on the cutting board as Sánchez went to work with the big knife, deftly separating skin and excess fat. He studiously ignored the two of us. As far as he was concerned, the conversation was over.

Estelle stepped close to the table and leaned over so that she was talking within two inches of Victor Sánchez's ear. I saw one of his eyebrows rise a little.

"He oido decir que alguien cerca de aquí sabe mas," she said, her voice husky. *"Con tú ayuda . . ."*

Victor Sánchez straightened up slowly, the knife motionless on the cutting board. He looked at me and grinned, at the same time nodding his head toward Estelle as if to tell me he knew he'd almost stepped in it.

"You tell your compadres, señor, that if I think of something I'll let you know." He pointed directly at Estelle. *"Tú, chinita, sola-*

mente." He pointed then at the door behind us. "Now leave me alone to my work. You want something else, you bring a warrant."

Estelle ignored Sánchez's dismissal and instead pulled out a small notebook from her purse. She leaned against the prep table and leafed through the pages.

"Señor, you told one of the deputies earlier that Francisco Peña came in at twelve minutes after eleven and shouted that there had been a shooting."

Sánchez grunted something I didn't hear. "How did you happen to know it was twelve after eleven?" Estelle asked.

"Because I was standing at the bar and happened to be facing the door."

Estelle flipped forward a page in her notes. "And there is a clock right by the door, sir."

Sánchez looked up sharply at her. *"Basta,* you think I didn't tell the truth . . ."

Estelle shook her head. "I need to make sure that the deputy who told me was correct, señor. You told him that Francisco busted in like maybe he had an accident or something. And then?"

"You know the story as good as me," Sánchez muttered as he hacked at the chicken.

Estelle dutifully continued. "After Francisco settled down enough to tell you what was wrong, you called the state police. The nine-one-one relay connected you with the Sheriff's Department. Most of your customers went outside, and at least four of them drove down the road to the scene."

"Six of them went outside. I told 'em *no toquen alguna cosa . . .* nothing," Sánchez said. He wagged a finger. "Don't touch nothing."

"All right. So . . ." I turned to Estelle quizzically.

"Mr. Sánchez said that last night he had no patrons other than those known to him. I have a list here, if you want to see them."

I shook my head. "So, no strangers in the place all evening?"

"That's right," Sánchez muttered.

"And there were no disturbances of any kind that amounted to anything, *no luchas?"* Estelle prompted.

Victor Sánchez dumped a pile of hacked chicken into the soup pot and walked over to a refrigerator to collect a package of baby carrots. He took a deep breath as if becoming resigned to our presence.

He spilled the carrots out on the board, slicing each one lengthwise and then across, building a mound of perfect little carrot quarters. After processing about ten, Sánchez shrugged. "Pat Torrance, he drank too much. It looked like he was going to puke, so I asked him to go out back before he made a mess of my bar."

"And that's all? One drunk cowboy?"

"Es todo."

"It appears that it was a pretty quiet night up until then, sir," Estelle said to me. "No strangers, nothing unusual." She closed her notebook and slipped it back in her purse. "Mr. Sánchez, when was the last time you spoke with Sergeant Torrez?"

For a moment, Victor Sánchez's face was blank. Estelle folded her arms and leaned against the table. "The deputy who arrested Tammy Woodruff, sir."

Sánchez's eyes narrowed. *"Conózcolo, señorita."* Estelle ignored the emphasis Sánchez placed on the jibe at her age and appearance. True enough, Estelle Reyes-Guzman was far from matronly.

She smiled faintly. *"Bueno. Cuando estaba el tiempo último cuando hablaba con él?"* Sánchez shot a sideways glance at me. I raised an eyebrow as if I understood Estelle perfectly and was waiting for an answer.

"I spoke with him Friday night only."

"Not since then?"

"No."

Estelle looked down at the growing pile of carrots. "Did someone mention to you last night . . . after Francisco and the others left and the police came . . . did someone mention to you which patrol car was involved in the shooting? Did someone mention who the deputy was?"

It was Sánchez's turn to look puzzled, and if he was faking it, he was a great actor.

"Nobody said nothing about which one, señora. I found out that it was Paul Enciños only after Pat Torrance came back and told me that is who it was."

"Torrance was recovered by then?"

Sánchez shrugged and almost smiled. *"Podria andar.* But he did not go down to the place. He said he heard from someone else out in the parking lot that it was Enciños. I know him, you know. I know his family."

"Enciños, you mean?"

"Yes."

"But no one said anything about which patrol car was involved?"

Sánchez cocked his head and frowned at Estelle. "No. What difference does it make?"

She didn't answer but pushed away from the table as Sánchez collected the last of the carrots for the soup.

"Sir, thank you. If there's anything else, I'll be in touch."

Sánchez shook his head and started toward the refrigerator again. *"No más, chiquita, no más."*

We stepped outside. Beyond the circle of the sodium-vapor light in the parking lot, the prairie stretched away into the chilled darkness of that February evening.

"He's got all kinds of pet names for you, doesn't he?" I asked. "What's *chinita* mean?"

Estelle smiled wearily. "Around here, you'd translate it about like, 'little half-breed darling.' "

"Cute. He's a sweetheart, isn't he?"

"He's known my family for generations, sir. He knew my Great-uncle Reuben. In fact, Reuben built one of the fireplaces in the barroom for him. Years ago."

"I should have known. You asked about the patrol car. You don't seriously believe that the killer thought that Paul Enciños was someone else? Bob Torrez told me earlier that he was thinking the same thing."

80

Estelle shook her head. "No, sir. I don't think anyone would notice the number on a patrol car. I just wanted to see the look on Victor Sánchez's face. That's all."

"No connection?"

"No connection, sir."

I sighed. "You want to go down to the hospital with me for a bit?"

"If you'll stop on the way for something to eat, sir."

I laughed. "I didn't think you ever stopped to eat, drink, sleep . . ."

Estelle grinned. "No, sir. *You* need something to eat. I saw you watching that soup. And I want to show you something."

My spirits lifted. Earlier, while parked behind the highway department's gravel pile, Estelle hadn't just been ruminating about Victor Sánchez. There was something else brewing in her mind.

12

❖❖❖

I was too tired and depressed to care much about eating, and that alone said something about my condition that evening. Because she wanted to talk on the telephone privately with her husband, Estelle suggested we meet at her house.

Francis Guzman's aunt met us at the door. She frowned hard at Estelle and muttered something in Spanish that I didn't catch. I recognized the word that had something to do with sleep, and true enough, we both had ten-gallon bags under our eyes. But that wasn't unusual. The entire department would be operating on fumes if something didn't break quickly.

Señora Tournál wore a tailored blue suit of casual cut, the white blouse fluffed and lacy at the throat. Her black shoes were mirror-perfect. She was not the image of the perfect nanny. Rather, she looked like she was waiting for a tardy junior partner to arrive so that she could begin a board meeting.

Sofia Tournál had no children of her own. I wondered if, behind that handsome face that registered only concern for her niece, Mrs. Tournál really enjoyed being corralled as a baby-sitter.

As if she could read my mind, Sofia Tournál glanced at me and offered a half smile. "The *kid* is asleep, Estellita."

Estelle nodded. "We're going to be in and out. I'm sorry."

"No tengas lástima," Sofia said, and ushered us toward the dining room table—Estelle's office.

"No tú invitamos para ser nana para el niño, Sofia," Estelle said, and hugged the older woman.

She waved a hand in dismissal. *"Por un día o dos."* Sofia Tournál may not have minded baby-sitting the kid for a day or two, but spending those days near a hot stove wasn't in her plans.

Her favorite solution to immediate food problems was American fast food—and her particular passion was fried chicken, the higher the cholesterol the better. She didn't even cast a second glance at my girth as she vanished out the door, Estelle's car keys in hand, headed off to fetch a barrel of the crunchy stuff. She knew where my heart was.

I settled in one of the chairs near an uncluttered spot on the table and heaved a sigh.

"Are you all right?" Estelle called from the kitchen.

"Yeah, I guess," I said, not convinced.

She reappeared and set a tall glass of orange juice in front of me. I grimaced. "You got anything to put in this?"

She grinned and ignored my request. Instead she opened her briefcase and drew out a large, clear plastic evidence bag containing what looked like a streamlined socket wrench with no handle. "I found this off the shoulder of the highway," Estelle said, and handed it to me. While I looked at the wrench, she fished a piece of graph paper from her briefcase. "Right here."

She had drawn the deputy's patrol car and then labeled everything else with distance flags. The wrench had been lying sixty-five inches from the edge of the pavement, thirty-five feet in front of patrol car 308.

"You want to tell me how anyone missed this?" I asked. Estelle shrugged and I added, "We all walked through that area a hundred times. This thing is what, about a foot long?"

"Nestled in a clump of rice grass," Estelle said. "The way it was lying, it was obvious that it was dropped recently."

"How so?"

"Nothing on top of it. Not even dust."

I held the bag by the zipper lock and turned it this way and that. "It's brand-new."

"Just a few scratches. Do you know what it is?"

"Sure. It's a lug wrench . . . or part of one. The ratchet part. And you're right. No dust, nothing. You could have one of these stowed in your vehicle for years, and never use it. But it would collect dust and dirt with the passage of time. This one is clean as a whistle."

"Brand spanking new," Estelle said.

"So, you found a lug wrench," I said. "Or half of one. This part fits over the lug nuts . . . or the jackscrew." I made little twisting motions with my hands and the tiny crow's-feet at the corners of Estelle's eyes deepened ever so slightly. "There's another part, the actual ratchet handle, that slips over this end."

"General Motors has been using those since about 1988," Estelle added. She pointed with the tip of her pencil. "There are a few marks on the black paint where the handle was attached, sir."

I frowned. "So . . . we've got half of a lug wrench. It may have been dropped recently. It's from one of the major manufacturers, which means that we've narrowed the vehicle down to one in a couple billion."

Estelle nodded. "Since we're starting with nothing, this," she said tapping the bag, "is more than we had."

"I won't argue that," I replied. "You're going to run it for prints?"

"Tonight." She leaned forward. "Sir, this might be connected."

"It might be."

"If someone had a flat tire and stopped to change it, it's easy to imagine that in the dark, one piece or another of that wrench could be dropped, or kicked, or misplaced somehow. If the person was unfamiliar with the equipment, it's even more possible. If that person was in a hurry, or nervous, it might be even more likely."

I leaned back in my chair and Estelle watched me, as if what I would have to say might make a difference. I reached out and toyed with the glass of orange juice. "The shots came from across the highway, Estelle."

"I think there were two vehicles involved."

"Two?"

"Yes. I think that Deputy Enciños parked behind what he thought was a disabled vehicle." She nodded at the wrench. "It was disabled. It's too desolate out there for it to be coincidence, sir."

"All right. You've got a vehicle stopped." I gestured at the wrench. "Flat tire. The deputy comes along. Yes, he would stop. It's automatic."

"*Automáticc* " Estelle mused.

"That, too," · said. "And the second vehicle?"

"Either across the road . . ."

"Facing east, back toward town?"

"I have no way of knowing that, sir. It could have been. Or it could have been parked with the disabled vehicle, and the killer could have ducked across the highway when he saw headlights coming."

I frowned. "Or just passing by at the wrong moment. I don't buy lying in wait. That seems a little far-fetched. As Paul's car approached, the killer would have no way of knowing it was a cop, in the first place. And to dart across the road and hide, deliberately waiting, would mean that he had reason to believe that a cop was in fact coming and would have reason to be suspicious. And we know that he didn't know Paul was coming, because Paul never said anything on the radio after he left Bustos Avenue. Other than that, someone with a scanner wouldn't have known much about the deputy's location."

Estelle gazed at me from across the table, her chin resting in her hand. She slowly shook her head from side to side, as confused as I was.

A car pulled in the driveway and the few rapidly evaporating gastric juices I had sprang into action. "She's back," I said, and grunted to my feet. I opened the door and saw not Sofia Tournál with fried chicken but Sheriff Martin Holman, a grin splitting his face from ear to ear.

"I got it," he yelped, and bounded up the steps.

"Come on in," I said as he charged past into the house. I tried to keep the disappointment out of my voice.

"Gayle said you'd be here, so I figured that I'd . . ."

"Good, good," I interrupted him. "Come on in." I directed him to the dining room. "Now, what have you got?"

"The tires," Martin Holman said. He straightened his shoulders, pleased with himself. "The cast taken in front of the patrol car? Easy as can be." He dug a paper out of his pocket. "LT235/85R by 16E all seasons."

"Brand?"

"A good match to General, Bill."

I sat down with a thump. "Well, that's too bad," I said, and was amused at Sheriff Holman's immediately crestfallen expression.

"No, I mean it's great that you've got a positive ID. I was hoping that maybe it'd be a brand that someone here in town sells. Maybe some neat little local thread like that." I shrugged. "No such luck."

Holman shook his head. "Generals are one of the tires that come as standard equipment on dozens of vehicles."

Estelle leaned across the table and Holman handed her the paper. "A big tire," she said. "From a truck of some kind. Like the lug wrench, sir."

Holman grasped the back of one of the dining room chairs until his knuckles turned white. He rocked the chair this way and that and I looked up at him, curious. He was enjoying himself, and after a minute said, "But there was something else."

"Oh?"

"The tires were brand-new. I mean brand-new."

Both Estelle and I regarded Holman with interest. "You're sure?"

"Positive. The little mold dinguses that stick out weren't even worn off." Holman didn't bother reminding us that he'd spent fif-

86

teen years selling cars and should have learned enough to be able to tell a new tire from an old one.

"Wouldn't they wear off just in a mile or two?" I asked.

Holman shook his head. "Not the ones that stick out sideways into the tread channel. Thousand miles or so, probably. I think you're looking for a new vehicle."

"Then it fits," Estelle said.

"What fits?" the sheriff asked.

Estelle handed him the bag with the wrench inside. "We found this out there, sir."

"A lug wrench?"

"Yes."

"And it's brand-new."

"Yes."

"Then that's it. We are dealing with someone who was driving a brand-new truck of some kind. Pretty unusual to have a flat tire right off the bat."

"But it happens. Maybe they hit something in the road."

Holman stood up, excited. "It'd have to be something big enough to really slice the sidewall. Just running over a bottle, or board, or something like that wouldn't do much to a brand-new steel-belted tire. It'd have to be a pretty good road hazard of some kind." He headed toward the door.

"Martin . . . where are you going?"

He stopped short. "I was going to take a drive out that way, scan along the shoulder of the road."

I beckoned him back. "If you're going to do something like that, you need to call dispatch and see if Gayle can spring a deputy free to go with you, Martin." His face went that wonderful blank that told me the proper synapses in his brain had failed to fire. "Until we nail this thing down, no one is roaming out in the boonies by themselves at night."

"Oh," he said. By the tone of Holman's voice, a bystander would have guessed that the sheriff was a freshly hired rookie, not the top dog.

87

"But there's something you need to do first. Howard Bishop was making a blanket check through NCIC for stolen vehicles or any other wants. You might shag Nick Chavez back down to his office and start him helping you on a trace of dealers in the Southwest who might have had inventory stolen off the lot."

"That should be covered by NCIC, shouldn't it?" Holman asked.

"It should be, sir," Estelle said. "But it's possible that something was missed."

Holman looked pained. "You think that the vehicle involved was taken from some dealer's lot?"

"It's just as likely as being stolen from an individual's driveway," I said. "We'll cover all the bases."

Holman shook his head. "I'd think those new ones, with all the antitheft devices and all, would be tough to steal."

I glanced at Estelle and smiled with sympathy. "They got yours, right? Right out of the airport parking lot. No broken glass, nothing." I shrugged and leaned back in my chair. "There's a ready market for trucks, sheriff—especially the carryall class like Suburbans, Explorers, RamChargers . . . anything with lots of room and four-wheel drive."

"In Mexico, you mean," Holman said.

"That's right. And as fast as engineers think up antitheft devices, the thieves come up with a slick solution."

Estelle frowned. "And we might not be dealing with auto theft at all, sir. That's just one trail we're following. It could have been a dozen other things."

"Like what?" Holman asked.

Estelle took a deep breath. "The deputy might have run into a felon who got nervous. Maybe on the run from somewhere else . . . anywhere else." She held up her hands in frustration. "We've got the entire continent to choose from. Or maybe Paul stepped into the middle of something else, like a drug deal going down."

"Out there?"

"Why not? Sir, remember that guy last year who landed his twin-engined plane on the only straight stretch of County Road

88

Fourteen? That was two hundred kilos right there."

"But you caught him," Holman said, as if that settled that.

"We didn't catch him, sir, the Forest Service did. And only then because the pilot snagged a wingtip fuel tank in a juniper thicket when he was trying to turn around. If he hadn't been delayed with that mess, all the Forest Service would have found was a cloud of dust."

I heard another vehicle in the driveway and recognized the wheezy exhaust note of Estelle's little sedan. "Have you had dinner yet?" I asked Holman. He shook his head. "Then sit a minute and have a piece of chicken. It'll help you think. It's going to be a long night, Martin."

Holman didn't look happy. He had been raring to go, to gallop out into the night. He didn't like hearing that we were operating like a frustrated posse, hunting for pony tracks after a buffalo herd had already thundered by.

13

◆◆◆

NOT so many hours before, Linda Real had smiled at me from across the Sheriff's Department parking lot as she walked toward the patrol car, lugging her camera bag, notebook, and God knows what else reporters carry. And then the last time I'd seen her, on that Sunday night when she should have been on her way home from a date with a nice, friendly kid who knew how to behave himself, she was a torn, bloody rag doll.

Now, lying at the mercy of all the hissing, clicking intensive care gadgetry, she seemed tiny, frail, childlike. Her head was bandaged with the exception of her right eye and cheek. Drip tubes stabbed into the back of her right hand. Her left hand was curled at the wrist, as if she were trying to hold on to something.

Holman, Estelle, and I had arrived at the hospital shortly before nine that Monday evening. We entered through the back service entrance, and outside the double doors of the intensive care unit I was relieved to find only the village cop who was working security.

Standing beside the hospital bed, I watched what I could see of Linda's face and wondered where she was.

I could remember distinctly a long, complex dream that I'd had sometime during the swim to the surface after open heart surgery three years before. After hiking for hours along an abandoned narrow-gauge railroad bed, I'd found a red glass crystal bell from a

Shay locomotive. Then I'd spent days trying to find an antique dealer who would give me an honest appraisal for the imaginary artifact.

Maybe Linda's mind was off somewhere, engaging itself in adventures of its own while her assaulted body recuperated.

Estelle reached over and took Linda's left hand in hers. There was no response.

I glanced over at Dr. Francis Guzman. Estelle's husband looked as weary as the rest of us. A full head taller than I was, he leaned against the wall, hands thrust in the pockets of his white coat.

"Any changes?" Martin Holman asked. He stood at the foot of the bed looking like a priest in his dark suit. If Linda awoke suddenly and saw him, she'd know she was in trouble.

Francis pushed himself upright and nodded toward the door. We went out in the hall; Patrolman Tom Pasquale looked up hopefully.

"Why don't you go get yourself a cup of coffee," I said, and Pasquale was off like a shot. He wanted to be out chasing bad guys, and there weren't going to be many in the hospital hallway. Dr. Guzman crossed his arms.

"She's stable. That's about all the good news there is."

"Stable?" Holman asked.

He nodded. "We've got the bleeding under control. That was our biggest worry." He put his hand on the left side of his neck. "Two pellets did significant damage to the vessels in her neck. That was worrisome. One of them caused . . ." he hesitated, searching for the right word. "Well, a traumatic aneurysm is the best description. Fortunately for her the pellets were low velocity, comparatively. One of them nicked the wall of her left carotid. We had a balloon forming there."

"She was lucky," I said.

The physician nodded. "Another millimeter and the artery would have ruptured. That would have been that."

"When do you think she'll be able to talk?" Holman asked.

Francis managed a tired smile. "I can't read a crystal ball, sheriff. She's had nine hours of surgery so far. You assault the body

91

that much, and it retreats. With the pain she's going to be in when she regains consciousness, she'll be under heavy sedation anyway."

"Nine hours for a neck injury?" Holman said, puzzled.

"Not just the neck. She's lost her left eye and the outer orbit is fractured. One of the pellets broke off two front teeth and did all kinds of damage before rattling around in her left sphenoidal sinus." Holman winced, but Guzman didn't stop. "And another pellet hit her jaw just under her cheekbone, an inch or so under the eye. Nasty, splintery fracture. There's going to be lots of cosmetic surgery required down the road."

"A long struggle ahead," I said.

"You bet." Francis took a deep breath. "A long, painful road. There's a pretty long list of minor injuries that we haven't even begun to think about yet. If she pulls out of this, there'll be more surgery, more physical therapy. And with the loss of vision and the disfigurement, you can count on some psychological trauma as well. And by the way, Frank Dayan was here just a few minutes ago. He told me that his company is going to offer a ten-thousand-dollar reward. Did he talk to you about that?"

"I haven't seen him since last night," I said. "But anything will help."

"Any leads?"

"None to speak of," I said. "All we can guess is that the deputy stopped along the shoulder of the road for some reason, maybe to assist what he thought was a stranded motorist." I held up my hands. "Shots were fired from across the highway, and then from right beside the patrol car. Three shots. That's it."

"No radio calls?"

I shook my head.

"Then Miss Real may be the only witness, is that right?"

"That's it."

"So there may be some risk for her."

"I don't think so," I said. "My gut feeling is that the killer is long gone. Some scumball just passing through."

92

"But you've arranged for an officer to be posted here for the time being . . ."

I nodded. "Just a precaution. And to be here in case Linda regains consciousness and can answer a few simple questions. Someone needs to be here."

Guzman looked absently down the hall in the direction the patrolman had gone. "My guess is that tonight is going to be the critical time. You might want an officer here who's a little more . . . ah . . . concerned? Pasquale has the bedside manners of a pickup truck."

I smiled. "Gayle Sedillos is coming in at ten, doctor. And the rest of us will be in and out."

The young physician reached out and took Estelle by the elbow, shaking it affectionately. "How's Sofia?"

Estelle grimaced. "Eating fried chicken and feeling left out of things."

"I bet. I'm going to run home for a few minutes while Dr. Perrone is on the floor. I'll ask Lucy Padilla to come over to the house and give a hand. I didn't mean for Sofia to get stuck as nana." He looked over at me. "My aunt likes children at a distance."

"I noticed that," I said.

"Maybe Sofia can come up with some interesting ideas," Francis added, and I shrugged. I was open to anything.

Estelle Reyes-Guzman retreated to her tiny cubicle at the sheriff's office to dust the lug wrench for prints. Holman and I were within fifty yards of Nick Chavez's house on Fourth Street, behind the high school, when the radio crackled.

"PCS, this is three ten," I replied, and shot Holman a glance. "Now what," I muttered.

"Three ten, ten-nineteen." I recognized Estelle's voice then, and immediately pulled into a handy driveway to turn around.

"Why doesn't she just say what she wants on the radio instead of asking us to drive all the way back to the office?" Holman asked.

93

"Because she doesn't want half the county to hear the conversation," I said. "And it's only a few blocks."

It wasn't Estelle who wanted us. The sheriff and I walked into the dispatch room to be greeted by Howard Bishop, who looked almost awake.

"I thought you'd want to know," Estelle said, and nodded at Bishop.

"Sir," the deputy said, "NCIC has a hit on a stolen 1996 Chevrolet Suburban, white over blue." He stopped and I impatiently beckoned him to continue. "Taken from Todd Svenson Motors in Albuquerque sometime between eight P.M. Saturday and nine A.M. Sunday morning. The only reported auto theft of a new vehicle since the previous Monday."

"This one was taken right off the lot?"

Bishop nodded. "The manager's name is Kenny Wilcox. I called him a few minutes ago. APD took the report shortly after nine Sunday morning, when Wilcox drove by the car lot on his way to church and noticed the Suburban was missing."

"Keen eye."

"Well, he said he had it parked on one of those inclined ramps for show."

"How was it taken?" Holman asked.

Bishop frowned. "No broken glass. If they jimmied the door or window, they didn't leave any traces behind. Wilcox said he had one of those steering wheel bar-locks on it, and that the axle was chained to the ramp."

"The chain was cut somehow?"

"Yes," Bishop said, puzzled by the obvious question.

"How was it cut, Howard?" Estelle prompted quietly.

"Wilcox didn't know. They didn't leave the chain behind."

I looked at Holman. "Now there's neat and tidy, Martin."

Holman's eyes narrowed. He was happy to be on familiar turf. "Did they have a lockbox on the truck?"

Bishop shook his head. "Wilcox said they don't use window lockboxes anymore. Too easy just to crush. Even kids were swip-

94

ing the keys. Wilcox said they take all the keys in at night."

I sat down on the edge of the nearest desk. "Did you happen to ask the man what kind of tires the truck had on it?"

"Yes. He wouldn't swear to the brand. That wasn't on the invoice. Two other vehicles that came in the same shipment from the factory had Generals. But the size was listed on the invoice, and we got a match with the cast the sheriff worked on. Sixteen-inch LT235/85Rs. Standard size for that type of vehicle."

"Bingo," Estelle said softly, then added, "it's something, sir. The first real lead we've had to follow. It may be just coincidence that the wrench we found is the same kind that comes as standard equipment on those vehicles, but it's worth pursuing."

Holman let out a high-pitched chirp of delight when the full import sank in. I smiled at Bishop. "Good job, Howard. Get on the horn to the Federales in Chihuahua and tell 'em what we're looking for. If the killer was headed over the border, he's had all the time in the world. He could be halfway to Mexico City by now. But they may turn something up."

"I'll have prints off the wrench in another few minutes," Estelle said. "You might call Wilcox back and have APD dust down that ramp, if they haven't already. We might get a match."

Bishop nodded and I slapped Holman on the arm. "Let's go talk with Nick Chavez."

Holman glanced at his watch, ever the politician. I chuckled. "It doesn't matter about the hour, Martin. This is the best time of day to work. You don't have to worry about crowds."

14

At ten o'clock that Monday night, the streets of Posadas were deserted. Sheriff Holman and I drove west on Bustos Avenue past the park, and then turned south on Fourth Street.

Nick Chavez's home was one of those cinder block things that were built in droves during the fifties when the mines showed signs of life. Contractors had bulldozed the field behind the high school and dumped enough concrete to make fifty or sixty slabs, then slapped the houses together. The three bedroom "homes," as realtors were fond of calling them even when they were empty, came with all the options—metal windows that let in fine dust during every windstorm, flat roofs that only leaked when it rained, and stucco that began peeling even before the second summer of blistering New Mexico sun was over.

Nick could have afforded something more fancy, but his Fourth Street home had served him well, with additions sprouting and spreading as the years and the kids went by. A hundred yards from the front door was Pershing Street and Posadas High School's football field. Eleven Chavez kids had graduated from PHS, the last just two years after my own youngest son.

For sixteen years I had been driving a Blazer that I'd purchased new from Nick Chavez . . . and for the past fifteen years he had never let slip an opportunity to try to sell me a replacement.

Somewhere deep in the house a television blared, but eventually the doorbell broke through the din. In a few minutes Nick Chavez opened the door, blinking against the harshness of the porch light. Any father with eleven children—even if they are all grown and flown—is going to jump to the worst conclusions at ten o'clock at night with two cops at the door. Nick put on a hospitable face.

"Hey, Bill," he said. "Kind of past your curfew, isn't it?" He grinned at Holman, who looked uncomfortable. "Sheriff, how you doin'?"

"Nick," I said, "we're in a bind. Can you spare us a little of your time?"

"Sure." He held open the storm door and beckoned. "Come on in. Marty, are you tired of playin' cops and robbers yet? You want a real job?" Martin Holman may have sold used cars at one time in his varied career, but he'd never voiced the slightest inclination to return to the lot. I knew his purchase order for election year campaign posters and cards had already gone to the printer. And when he stepped through the door, Holman squared his shoulders a bit and looked like a proper sheriff—trim build with broad shoulders, a little gray just beginning to creep into his neatly clipped sideburns. I always felt like an old worn-out basset hound standing next to him.

Nick Chavez closed the door and frowned. "I heard what happened yesterday. It's hard to imagine who would do such an awful thing. How's the young lady?"

Thanks to the efficient media, the entire world had heard one version or another of the shooting. I didn't answer Nick's question, but instead gestured toward the formal living room, untouched by humans except for regular dusting. "Can we talk in here, Nick?"

"Sure. Sure. Let me get you something to drink. Coffee?"

"No, thanks." I shook my head.

"How about you, sheriff?"

Holman nodded. "That would be just right. Black."

I sat on the edge of a flowered sofa while Holman prowled the room, examining Mrs. Chavez's collection of porcelain figurines. She tended toward gnomes, elves, and other small, ugly caricatures.

Holman picked up a casting of a leprechaun examining a rabbit's injured paw and turned the figurine this way and that. He set it down carefully and picked up a business card that someone had placed on the mantel.

"Florie Gallegos for Assessor," he read. "She's been in office a hundred years." After carefully replacing the card, he added, "You know that Estelle is going to run against me." He said it as a statement, with just a hint of self-pity mixed with accusation creeping into his voice.

"She told me yesterday. We didn't have a chance to discuss it."

"Do you think it's a good idea?" He thrust his hands in his trouser pockets and leaned against the fireplace mantel.

I took a long time to answer and finally settled for, "No."

Holman's eyebrows shot up and he started to say something. But Nick Chavez returned, carrying two mugs of steaming, fresh coffee. He set one down carefully on the small end table near my elbow.

"You say you don't want any, but you really do," he said. He handed Holman's mug to the sheriff. "Spill any of that on the carpet and my wife will cut your heart out," he grinned, then turned serious. "Now, what can I help you gentlemen with?"

I looked at Nick Chavez's open, expectant face, round and friendly like one of the porcelain figurines. He settled his short, chubby body onto a chair that looked like something out of *Wuthering Heights* and clasped his hands between his knees.

"We're chasing shadows, Nick," I said.

"I don't follow."

I hesitated, then said, "This is just between us."

He nodded vigorously. "Sure, sure."

"We have reason to suspect that the deputy was shot after he stopped to assist a motorist. Maybe shot by that motorist, maybe by a third party."

"Ay," Nick said softly.

"We also have reason to think that one of the vehicles involved was both brand-new and disabled somehow." I saw Nick's eyes narrow a little. "Svenson Motors in Albuquerque reported a Chevy Suburban stolen sometime Saturday night. There is some circumstantial evidence that points to that as the vehicle involved. Maybe."

"Maybe?"

I shrugged. "As I said, it's circumstantial. Pretty thin. But it's our only lead. That's it. Period."

Nick pursed his lips, then said, "A stolen Suburban is going to be hard to find, Bill. If he's got some hours head start, he's in Mexico by now, that's for sure. Are you working with the Federales?"

"Yes. But they won't turn up anything."

Nick shrugged his sympathy for our frustrations with Mexican law enforcement. "What can I do for you, then?"

I sipped the coffee. He was right. The coffee was just what I needed. "How do you steal a locked vehicle without breaking anything?" Nick Chavez grinned and settled back in the chair. "You've got to protect your own inventory, Nick. You're as much of an expert as anyone around."

"The easiest way is to steal the key." He made a little twisting motion with his right hand. "But other than that? We take the keys in at night. On some of the high-profile vehicles . . . like the Blazers and Suburbans . . . we use a steering wheel bar-lock. But I tell you . . ." He leaned forward. "Nothing works too good if someone really wants the vehicle. See, first of all, we all used to use window lockboxes. Everybody did. But the damn kids would break them and take the keys. So now, they pop a window and they're inside."

"What about the steering wheel bar-lock?" Holman asked.

Chavez shrugged. "I heard that sometimes they spray the lock mechanism with Freon and then tap it hard with a hammer. Just shatters. I'm not sure about that. But the easiest way is just to cut a little chunk out of the steering wheel rim."

"It's that easy to do?" I asked.

"Sure. They have to make the steering wheel kind of soft, you know. The metal, I mean. So it bends and deforms in a wreck and doesn't cut the driver into little pieces. Thieves know that, and with a good pair of wide-jawed bolt cutters . . . snip, snip."

"But if they break into the truck by shattering a window, that would leave some glass on the ground."

Nick shook his head. "Not necessarily. Hold a towel over it and rap it inward. Maybe one of the smaller back windows. You can do it pretty clean." He grinned slightly. "Or you can slip the door lock other ways, I guess. You know, as fast as they come up with antitheft systems, there's some smart thief out there who spends all day long figuring ways to beat the system. Count on it."

"And you can hot-wire these new ignitions? What about all the interlocks, and cutoffs, and what not?"

"Like I said, as fast as the engineers design something, there's a solution. And it's a big market down south, let me tell you."

"Maybe with NAFTA, it'll dry up," Holman said.

"Sure," Nick said, and grinned.

"When's the last time you had a truck stolen from your lot?"

Nick puffed out his cheeks in thought. "Eight years ago. We keep the inventory down, though."

"Nothing since then?"

"No. You remember that time. When the Alvaro kid took the Z-28 and went joyriding all night before he blew up the engine?"

"What have you been hearing from other dealers?"

He shrugged. "Nothing out of the ordinary. There's a lot of theft, especially in the bigger cities. But not from dealers. It's too risky. The lots are well lit now and some of them even have security all night."

I looked down at the dark coffee and swirled the cup gently, watching the patterns. Nick Chavez sat and waited. "Nick," I said, "the deputy's last call to dispatch was from the general area of your dealership." I set the cup down and retrieved a small notebook from my breast pocket. After thumbing a few pages I found the entry I wanted. "He radioed dispatch at fifty-three minutes after ten from your dealership."

"What was going on?" Nick asked. "No one called me."

"Someone apparently called the police and complained that kids were driving around behind the dealership. Maybe parking in some dark corner, doing who knows what. Deputy Enciños noted in his patrol log that he responded and made no contact. Six minutes later he noted in that same log that he was ten-eight . . . that he was in service and available."

"And then . . ."

"And then he drove about ten or eleven miles west on State Highway Fifty-six and was killed."

Chavez looked at the floor, his hands clasped tightly with the index fingers steepled together. "Do you have much trouble down at the lot, Nick?" Holman asked, and Nick looked up at Holman as if he had just seen the sheriff for the first time.

"No," he said. "None. I guess we've been lucky. The other place," he said, referring to D'Anzo Auto Plaza, "they had more trouble . . . but they're closed now, so we're the only game in town. We've been lucky, I guess."

"Isn't the shop area fenced off in back?" I asked. "There's nowhere anyone can go, other than just skirting the building, right?"

Chavez nodded. "The main service building is fenced, yes." He stood up quickly. "You fellas got time?"

"To . . ."

"Let's take a run down there. Right now."

"Nick," I said, "don't misunderstand me. I'm not suggesting that there is any connection between the stop the deputy made at your place and what happened afterward. We're just trying to re-construct what happened that night."

The dealer nodded vigorously, and held up one index finger close to his face, like a schoolteacher savoring a moment of ex-planation. "You never know," he said. "Now you got me curious."

"About what?" Holman asked.

Chavez walked to the foyer and lifted a *Posadas Jaguars* wind-breaker off the hook. He shrugged it on. "You said that the deputy responded to the call from your dispatcher at ten-fifty-three, right?"

101

"That's right." I knew Nick's next question before he asked it, a nagging little gap in events that had been eating away at me all afternoon. "And six minutes later, he's clear."

Nick Chavez nodded. "So what is he doing for six minutes, Bill?"

15

IF kids wanted a dismal place to party, the narrow space behind the Chavez Chevrolet-Oldsmobile back fence was certainly it. Between the chain-link and the ragged edges of Arroyo Cerdo were fifty feet of sand, goat-heads, creosote bush and bunchgrass . . . mixed with debris and junk that the wind had brought in, or that Chavez's mechanics had tossed over the fence from time to time.

Inside the eight-foot, barbed wire topped fence a row of vehicles waited for repairs that would probably never be made, or waited to surrender vital parts so some other junker could waddle a few more miles. As we walked along the fence, I noticed that several of the stripped vehicles were newer models than my own Blazer.

"Now this inner gate is locked all the time," Nick said. He fumbled with a large set of keys.

I surveyed the eight-foot-high chain-link fence. "The person who called in the complaint from across the street wouldn't be able to see back here. The building is in the way. She just said that there was vehicle traffic."

"Kids," Chavez said, as if that covered all the sins of the world. "They can pull in off the street, sneak around here, and be out of sight." He pointed at the tire tracks outside the fence.

He opened the gate and motioned for the sheriff and I to follow.

103

"The service manager opens this each morning," he said. "That way the four back service bay doors can be opened and we can drive vehicles straight through, out and around." He made a circular motion with his hands.

I grunted and turned slowly, surveying the yard. "Nothing," I said to myself.

"Pardon?"

"I said, 'nothing.' There's nothing here that tells me a damn thing."

"I wish we knew who the deputy talked with," Holman said. "That would answer a lot of questions."

"It might," I replied dubiously. "We have no connections, Martin. None. We can assume either way—that what Deputy Enciños did here had something to do with the later shooting, or that there is no relationship." I shrugged. "You take your choice. Nothing either way."

"Who called in the complaint?" Nick asked.

"Across the street. The Burger Heaven's night manager. She called to say that she saw kids driving around behind this building."

"Then all they could do is park outside the service yard fence," Nick said. "They're not going to climb over the barbed wire."

"Who talked to the manager?" Holman asked.

"Tom Mears. He said that she couldn't identify what kind of vehicle was involved. She was busy, the light was bad, it's a hundred yards distant . . ."

"But she took time out to make the call to police," Holman said. I looked at him with mild surprise. Given another four-year term, he might turn out to be as cynical as the rest of us. There was hope yet.

We dropped Nick Chavez back at his house after extracting the standard promise that if anything cropped up he'd give us a call. I wasn't optimistic. Unable to let go, I drove back to the car dealership and pulled into the lot.

"Now," I said, looking at my watch. "It's ten-fifty-three. I've just checked out the lot, found nothing, and called the PD to inform them."

"All right," Holman said. "What do we do for six minutes?"

"Suppose we just sit here. Suppose the deputy and Linda Real were just talking. About what, we don't know. But they're sitting in the dealer's lot, watching what little traffic there is, and chatting. They finish their conversation, and Enciños calls ten-eight."

"So they drive twelve miles west on State Fifty-six."

"Why would they do that?" I asked.

"Why not?"

I glanced at my watch. "The deputy's shift ends at midnight. It's already eleven. So to give himself time to finish up paperwork and so forth, he's only got a few minutes. It's been an interesting shift. He assisted at the Weatherford crash on the interstate, and he may want to talk with Mears about that report. He's had two domestic dispute calls, and the odds are good that a third one might come in before the night's over. So it makes sense, both from timing and need, that he'd tend to stay central—that he'd stick close to town for the last few minutes of his shift."

"But instead, he headed west."

"Right," I said, and pulled 312 into gear. "He heads west. It's just about eleven, dead up. Driving at moderate speed will bring him twelve miles out on State Fifty-six in fifteen to twenty minutes."

"Maybe he wanted to stop at the Broken Spur for something." Holman's face brightened. "Or maybe Linda did. Remember, she'd been there just the night or two before. With Torrez."

"Then why did they drive beyond the saloon, Martin?"

"I don't know." He slumped in the passenger seat and watched the night slide by. "Maybe a patron left there drunk, and the deputy decided to follow him."

"Follow a drunk? Not for three miles before he pulls him over. Maybe a thousand yards."

105

"Maybe he was just trying to make sure he got home all right."

"Martin, if one of your deputies does that and I find out about it, he can go earn a living flipping burgers. The only place they'd better be escorting drunk drivers is into the backseat of the patrol car."

Holman shot a quick glance at me. "It was just a thought."

"Watch the highway and the right-of-way for junk," I said. "Remember? If the theory is that something ruined a tire, then that's what you should be looking for."

"Testy, testy," Holman grinned. He straightened up a little and watched the roadway. After a minute, he said, "Why is it I always feel like I work for you?"

I looked over at him in surprise. "Sorry, Martin. I'm tired, that's all. And old habits die hard."

Holman shrugged. "Well, in a way, I suppose I do work for you. I'm elected, you're not." He lowered his window an inch and inhaled deeply, holding the air in like someone smoking a joint. He finally let out the air with a monumental sigh. For a moment, I thought that he was going to start rattling on again about the election, but instead he said, "It's not going to tell us much, even if we do find something."

"Anything at all is a piece of the puzzle," I assured him. "Have you ever tried one of those two-thousand-piece jigsaws, where all the pieces are shaped almost alike? The box top shows a big picture of some Swiss castle or some such? One piece at a time. And if you're missing one piece, it's all just that much harder."

Holman snorted with disgust. "My daughter talked me into helping her with one of those. It was a picture of a field of horses." He looked across at me. "About two-hundred damn pieces of blank blue sky, Bill. It took forever, and even then she figured it out just by trial and error."

"Then that's what we'll do here."

"It's not the same thing."

"Oh yes. It is the same thing, Martin."

We reached the Broken Spur Saloon. The parking lot was full, the patrons no doubt taking advantage of having a good story to kick about. I slowed 310 and pulled off the highway. I switched on the spotlight, swiveled it, and played the light across license plates as we idled along the shoulder of the highway. A westbound truck laid on the air horn and passed us so fast the car rocked in its wake.

"Jesus," Holman murmured.

And just beyond the parking lot, as I was pulling back out onto the highway, the sheriff found his missing puzzle piece.

"Stop," he barked, and I did so, the patrol car half on and half off the pavement. "Turn the light around this way." The fender of the patrol car blocked the beam and I backed up. "What's all that stuff?"

I craned my neck, pulling myself up against the steering wheel. "The remains of an old sign base, maybe."

Holman was out of the car before I finished the sentence. My guess was correct. Hidden in the bunchgrass just far enough off the highway's shoulder that the mowers wouldn't hit it in summer was a concrete slab two feet square and a foot thick or more. The sign base rested skewed, sunken into the ground where ants undermined it and occasional careless drivers coming out of the saloon's parking lot clipped it. One corner of the concrete had spalled and crumbled to pebbles.

Martin Holman knelt down in the grass and played his flashlight back toward the saloon. The harsh artificial daylight from the parking lot's single sodium-vapor light washed out the flashlight's beam, but I could see what excited Holman.

"Look there," he said. "You can see impressions in the grass where people have pulled out of the parking lot, driving right over this thing. If you cut the corner more than just a little, bang." He played the light around the base. "He must have had an old sign up on this at one time."

"Uh-huh," I said, and grunted down on my knees. "Enough here to rip up a tire, that's for sure." A three-inch spike of naked rebar angled up from the back corner of the pad.

"Are there traces of rubber on that?" Holman asked, the excitement raising the pitch of his voice so much he sounded like a teenager on his first date.

"I'm not a human microscope, Martin," I replied. I sat back on my haunches. "And even if there were, what would it mean? This thing's been hit a hundred times over the years."

"Maybe there's some kind of match-up we could make with the rubber?"

I grimaced and stood up. "Martin, think on this, now." I held up a hand and ticked my fingers. "First, we have the assumption that the disabled vehicle had a flat tire."

"Didn't it?"

"Maybe."

"What about the lug wrench?"

"We don't know for sure that the wrench belongs to the vehicle in question, Martin. Second, if we assume that the wrench belongs to the vehicle in question, we can further assume that maybe, just maybe, that vehicle was one that was stolen up in Albuquerque— we assume that on the thin basis that the wrench was new and fit the type. Now, we assume even further that if the vehicle had a flat tire, it must have been because of a road hazard." I shrugged. "Maybe. And then we have to assume that this thing," and I nudged the concrete slab with my toe, "is the hazard."

Holman rose to his feet and stood head down. Maybe he was thinking, maybe he was crying. Maybe he was just plain flummoxed.

"And then we have to *assume*," and I leaned on the word, "that if all the other puzzle pieces are what we think they are, that this thing managed to gouge a brand-new, steel-belted radial in just such a fashion that it held air for roughly two miles." I pointed off into the dark. "Two miles that way, until the driver was forced to stop and deal with it."

"But can't we match rubber fragments?" Holman persisted.

I grinned in the darkness. Martin was game, I had to give him that. "No, sheriff, we can't. In the first place, the rubber compound that makes up a given line of tires—a given batch regardless of size—is all the same. A match wouldn't tell us anything. In the second, far more important place, we don't have a damn thing to match to. We don't have the suspect's vehicle."

Holman squared his shoulders and turned toward the patrol car. "Yet," he said with finality.

16

◆◆◆

THE first five rings of the telephone merely enhanced a ridiculous dream. The first jangle came as my son Kendall was waiting patiently while his wing commander argued with me about the weight of an airplane. It wasn't an airplane that either he or Kendall was preparing to fly, but it was parked in the way. Why the weight was important was anyone's guess. Why I was on my son's aircraft carrier was also a mystery.

The wing commander heard the second ring and said something about the operations' Klaxon and that we'd better settle this problem before we had four incoming jets land in our laps.

I argued, somewhere between the third and fourth ring, that there was no point in doing anything until we knew the weight of the aircraft. Kendall stood off to one side, occasionally gazing out across the blue, calm Caribbean, not interested. That irked me, since it was an airplane that belonged to his squadron. And then I awoke with a start.

The phone rang again. The two-inch, glowing digital numbers on the nightstand clock announced 3:16 A.M. I rested on my elbows for a moment and let the phone ring three more times. I'd fallen into bed at one-thirty after dropping Martin Holman at his home. Dispatch knew where I was, so I groaned and reached for the receiver.

"What?" I said, not the least bit cordial.

"Sir," Estelle Reyes-Guzman said, and her husky voice sounded loud in the dark, predawn silence of my ancient adobe house. "I'm sorry if I woke you."

"Uh," I said, and lay back down, the phone buried in the pillow. "I guess I dozed off for a little bit. What's up?"

"Sir, I'm down at the hospital. It looks like Linda Real might be gaining some strength."

I frowned in the dark, trying to remember all the pieces. "She's awake, you mean?"

"Not yet, sir. But a few minutes ago, one of the nurses said something to her, and she responded. She murmured a few sounds in response."

"Did you get a chance to talk with her?"

"She can't talk, sir, and she drifted off again. Francis said that's normal. But she's close to the surface now, sir."

I pushed myself upright and swung my feet over the bed. "Did you have a chance to process the wrench handle?"

"Yes, sir."

"And?"

"Several clear prints, sir. I'm going to have Tony Abeyta run it up to the state lab later today. Maybe they'll find something I missed. It's going to be time-consuming to separate the prints, though."

"Separate?"

"If it's a new vehicle, sir, then there'll be prints of the factory worker who put the wrench in the kit, in addition to the person who used it."

"It won't be hard to trace the Detroit end, or wherever that thing was made."

"No, sir."

"Did you make any comparisons?"

"Just one, sir. I checked Victor Sánchez's prints more out of curiosity than anything else. We've got them on file. No match."

"That's not surprising," I said. "If Victor Sánchez ever kills

111

someone, there'll probably be a hell of an audience. By the way, Holman thinks he found the road hazard that ruined the tire."

"Oh?"

"A chunk of concrete near the Broken Spur. It's got a piece of rebar sticking out of the side."

Estelle caught the tone of my voice and said, "And you don't think so?"

"Well, I think he's jumping at the first thing he sees. Yes, here's an object that could wreck a tire. To make the jump to proving it's *the* object is just that . . . a jump."

"Especially since we don't know for sure that that's what happened," Estelle said.

"That's about the size of it." I stood up beside the bed. "Give me about ten minutes to pull myself together and I'll be down."

"That's probably not necessary, sir. Anything else can wait."

"Hell, I can't sleep the night away, Estelle. Hang in there for a few minutes and I'll relieve you."

I arrived at Posadas General and padded down the silent hall past the snack bar and gift shop that the auxiliary operated, past the small waiting area for radiology, stopping finally at the nurses' station. A young lady looked up through the Plexiglas partition and saw the apparition of an old fat man in a red-checked flannel shirt and gray trousers. Except for the absence of a white beard, I probably looked like an off-duty Santa Claus.

"Hi," she greeted me. Her name tag said she was Peggy Hadley, LPN.

"Everything quiet?"

"Very, sir." She smiled a snaggletoothed grin that was as charming as it was crooked. "At this time of night, everything is always quiet."

She leaned forward so she could look down the hall toward the double doors leading into intensive care. "Miss Reyes-Guzman is down there with Linda, sir."

"Thanks."

112

Someone had carried a heavy Naugahyde chair in from the separate ICU waiting room across the hall and found a corner for it among the tubes, machines, adjustable tables, and IV stands. Estelle was curled up in the chair like a little kid, sound asleep. I had three seconds to stand in the doorway before she opened one eye and looked at me.

"Hey there," I whispered. But it wasn't Estelle's unfolding from the chair that drew my attention. Under the white sheet of the bed, Linda Real's right foot moved.

I heard soft footfalls behind me and turned as Helen Murchison entered the room. She shot a tight, begrudging smile my way and then concentrated on her patient. Helen was dean of the old school of nurses, flinty, efficient, and brooking no nonsense from physicians, patients, or visitors.

She'd been one of my own nurses after surgery three years before. I'd received the best of diligent care, but I didn't remember much sympathy. Maybe that was because once I had told Helen that beneath her crusty exterior beat a heart of stainless steel.

I heard a faint, distant sound, a single syllable that sounded like an owl's first tentative hoot half a mile away through the woods.

"Is she awake?"

Helen had absorbed all the information the machinery had to offer in a single, cursory glance. Now she bent close to Linda, one hand light as down on the girl's right cheek. I noticed with surprise that Helen's knuckles were twisted and swollen with arthritis. It seemed unfair somehow that someone like her would get old the same as the rest of us.

Linda's right eye was open, but unfocused. As Helen continued to touch her cheek and whisper encouraging nothings, Linda closed her eye again and after a moment reopened it, this time looking directly at the nurse.

"How's she doing?" I whispered.

"She's a brave girl, this one is," Helen said, her back still to me. She held Linda's right hand in her own and turned to face me. "She's not going to be able to talk to anyone, you know. For some

113

time. You should all go home and get some rest." She sniffed her disapproval. "The gathering of the living dead," she said. "You're all so tired you can hardly think straight."

"Can she hear you?" I asked, stepping close to the bed. Linda's right eye looked at me from the depths of a dark hollow, haloed by bandages and oxygen tubing. As if in answer, she blinked once. Her eyelid reopened so slowly I was afraid it would stall at half-mast. "Linda, can you understand me?" Again the blink. "Let me hold her hand," I said to Helen, and she surrendered what felt like a tiny, fragile, child's hand, all its energy and vitality gone.

I bent close and my back twanged in protest. I stood hunched, my knees braced against the side of the bed. Linda's good eye scanned my face. She was probably trying to figure out just what kind of nightmare she was having.

"Linda," I whispered, "can you squeeze my hand?" The response was the slightest flexing of the fingers, a tentative experimentation. And then a second, definite squeeze. "That's the girl. Linda, I need to ask you a couple questions. Just a couple. Can you do that? Squeeze my hand once for yes. Don't squeeze at all for no. All right?"

For an agonizingly long minute, there was no response. But then a single squeeze came, as if she had to concentrate every undamaged fiber of her body for that one action.

I sensed Estelle's presence on the other side of the bed, heard a faint *snick*, and knew that Estelle had turned on her tape recorder.

"Linda, do you know who I am?" The squeeze came immediately, and this time her grip didn't relax, but held my hand. Her index finger flexed and traced a line on my palm.

"Do you know where you are, Linda?" Her index finger flexed.

"Linda, do you know what happened to you?" Even old, crusty Helen held her breath. The index finger flexed, and this time her fingernail pressed into my hand. She closed her eye and I could see the fine muscles of her cheek twitch. She held her finger pressed into my palm for a full minute, and even in that tiny motion, the anger was translated clearly. She opened her eye again and a tear

114

had welled up and now bathed the lower lash.

"Linda, you're telling me that you do know what happened. Do you know who shot you?"

The question hung there in the room, punctuated by the soft hum of one of the monitors on the wall behind us. Her index finger didn't move.

"Linda, did you understand what I asked you?" The stab of her finger came instantly. "You do understand, but you don't know who shot you?" She blinked and her fingertip remained still.

"Linda, did Deputy Enciños stop a vehicle out on the state highway?"

No.

"It was already stopped? Perhaps disabled?"

Yes.

"Did you recognize the disabled vehicle?"

Yes.

I looked up at Estelle, but she didn't return the glance. Her dark eyes were locked on Linda Real's face.

"Linda, you said you recognized the vehicle. Was it from Posadas?"

Hesitation, then *yes.*

"It was local, you're saying. Was the person who shot you in that vehicle?"

No.

"The person was not in that vehicle? Not in the disabled vehicle?"

No.

"Linda, was there a second vehicle?"

Yes.

"Was the second vehicle parked across the highway?"

Yes.

"Was it there when the deputy first stopped?"

No.

I paused and straightened, grunting audibly. Linda's finger touched my palm, and I smiled at her. Her eyelid was at half-mast

115

and I knew she was about to slip off into her drug-washed slumberland.

"Linda, do you know who was in the first vehicle?"

I didn't think I was going to get an answer, but finally it came, a faint, light finger touch.

"You do know who was in the car?"

. . . Yes.

"Was it someone we know?" Linda's hand lay limply in my old paw, unresponsive.

"She's drifted off," Helen said, and her crusty voice was softened to a whisper. I stood there for a minute holding the kid's hand, thinking. The small click of Estelle's recorder startled me, and I looked across the bed at her.

"How do you figure," I said, and placed Linda's hand on the sheet with a final pat. But Estelle was already collecting her purse and heading for the door.

"Thanks, Helen," I said, and I caught Estelle by the elbow just outside the swinging doors of the ICU.

"What are you thinking," I asked her.

"Would you stay with her, sir? She may come around again in a couple hours. She needs to see you, sir. She needs to see a familiar face."

I nodded. "Sure, I'll stay."

"And if you find a writing pad, sir. A legal pad, maybe. If she can hold a pencil, maybe she can write a name for us."

"And you?"

"Sir, if Linda knows the person involved, then the fingerprints on the lug wrench will match something we have in the file."

"If that person has a record for anything, yes. And that's a long shot."

"Maybe, sir, except for one thing."

"What's that?"

"The person who Linda recognized is involved, sir. Somehow. Otherwise, we would have found a third body out there, too."

116

"There are any number of ways someone could have slipped away, Estelle."

"But if they were just an innocent bystander to a homicide, then they would have contacted us. Or someone. No one watches two people get shot and then just drives away."

I looked at Estelle, trying to assess if she still had enough of an energy reserve to avoid making a whopper of a mistake. "What can I do for you, then?"

"It's important to stay here, sir." And as if reading my mind, she added, "I'm going to go home for a few hours and try to clear my head." She half smiled. "Francis keeps threatening to slip me a sedative. Later this morning I'll go down to the office and see if there's a match for prints." She reached out a hand and touched my arm. "Will you call me if Linda can give us anything?"

"Of course."

I pushed open the ICU doors. Helen Murchison was fiddling with one of the monitors, and when it behaved as she thought it should, she straightened up and frowned at me.

"What now? You're going to stay?"

I nodded and pointed at the chair in the corner. "It's my shift."

"Oh, that's choice," Helen snorted, and headed for the door. She stopped with one hand on the push plate. "Can I get you anything, sheriff?"

"No, thanks, love." And then as an afterthought, I added, "Yes, there is something. I really need a legal pad. Something to write on."

"That shouldn't be difficult," she said, "although a pillow would do you far more good." She smiled that wonderful half smile again, just enough to show the gold of one of her front bridges.

I awoke being scrutinized. Dr. Alan Perrone and Dr. Francis Guzman stood at the foot of the bed, Perrone holding a chart, Guzman with his hands thrust in the pockets of his white coat.

Perrone had led the charge when this same hospital had cut me open for an overhaul three years before.

I blinked and looked at Linda Real. She appeared to be peacefully sleeping.

"The young lady is doing a first-class job, sheriff," Perrone said. "If she keeps it up, we'll move her out of ICU in two or three days." He leaned forward, tipped his head up slightly, and peered at me through his bifocals. "Then we can move you in."

I waved a hand and pushed myself up out of the chair. "No, no. I'm just an innocent bystander, doctor." My watch said I'd slept almost three hours, just enough to feel wretched—stiff, groggy, discombobulated. There were no windows in the ICU, but the sun would be up, even in February cheerful as always, peeling paint off cars and incubating melanomas.

I rubbed a hand over my face and shook my head. "Effective guard," I muttered.

Perrone laughed. "Don't worry about the nap, sheriff. There's a most alert sentry outside the door." I looked out one of the windows in the swinging doors and saw Deputy Howard Bishop sauntering back and forth, a cup of coffee in his hand.

"Marty Holman was by earlier," Francis said.

"He should have said something."

He shrugged. "He figured you needed the sleep. I'm not sure that the DA agreed with him, but Schroeder's always impatient. There wasn't anything going on here, and they stayed just a few minutes—just until the deputy got here."

"Schroeder was with him?"

Francis Guzman nodded. "I don't know what he wanted, other than just to be in on things."

"I can guess," I said, and moved to the bed and touched the back of Linda's right hand. Her skin was dry and cool.

"She's heavily sedated right now," Francis said. "For the next day or so, all the surgery she's had around her eye and jaw is going to be hurting like hell. She's not alert enough to have a self-starter for the pain." He pumped an imaginary button with his thumb. "Maybe later. Estelle tells me that you managed a conversation of sorts with Linda earlier."

I grunted. "Hardly a conversation. But she's a champ, I'll tell you that." I looked up at Guzman. He'd taken to wearing a neatly trimmed beard. If a Hollywood casting agent walked by, he'd sign the young physician up to play Ivanhoe in an instant. "We need a name, Francis. That's the information she has that we need. A name. She said that she knows the person that the deputy stopped out on Fifty-six."

"That's what Estelle said."

"Linda can't talk, so I was holding her hand and she was responding to yes and no questions with a touch of her finger. If she gains enough strength to hold a pencil, she can scribble the name on a pad for us."

"That's a long shot," Perrone said. "Maybe by the end of the week."

Francis rested a hand lightly on my shoulder. "Estelle wants you to stop by the office this morning when you're finished here."

I chuckled. "When we both wake up, you mean."

119

"That, too. But I think she's got the name for you."

I turned and stared at Francis. "I beg your pardon?"

"She matched a print."

The young physician must have seen the annoyance as well as astonishment cross my face and he interpreted it correctly. He held up both hands. "Hey, have you ever tried making that young lady do something she doesn't want to do? Right now, rest isn't on her agenda."

I planted my hat firmly on my head and hitched up my trousers. "I'll check with you gents later," I said, and headed for the door. As I walked out to the car, I realized it wasn't Estelle's nonstop pursuit that annoyed me. Hell, that's one of the traits that made her such a formidable cop. What unsettled me was that she was burning up the trail while I slept in a chair. Old, fat, retired grandfathers dozed their lives away, not cops in the middle of a murder investigation.

Martin Holman's office was the first door on the left on the way to dispatch. His door was open when I passed and I saw him and Ron Schroeder deep in conversation. Holman looked up and saw me walk by.

"Bill!"

I stopped and backed up to stand in his office doorway.

"Can we see you for a minute?"

I didn't step into the room. "I've got about ten seconds," I said. The district attorney was lounging with one elbow propped on Holman's desk. He didn't get up, but tapped his pencil on the legal pad he'd been filling with notes.

"Bill, where are we at with this thing?" He waved a hand in summons, but I stayed put.

"This thing?"

"The shooting." He enunciated the word carefully, as if there might be a chance I'd misunderstand him.

"I can tell you better in a few minutes. After I talk with Estelle."

"But so far you've got nothing. Other than a possible tire print and the report of a stolen vehicle from Albuquerque."

I didn't say anything. He hadn't said it as a question and I was too tired to play word games.

"How's Ms. Real?"

"She's gaining," I said. I didn't add that Linda and I had played talking fingers.

Schroeder nodded and tapped his pencil again. After a few seconds he pushed himself upright and sat back in the chair. He folded his hands across his stomach and regarded me evenly, his eye blinks reminding me of when Camille, my eldest daughter, was taking piano lessons and had the metronome set on largo for some funereal piece she was studying.

"I've asked Captain Eschevera if he'll handle the investigation into Sonny Trujillo's death, Bill."

"Him personally?" I asked, and Schroeder nodded. I'd known Adolfo Eschevera for years. He was as much of a dinosaur as I was, and ruled his dominion within the New Mexico State Police in true *patron* fashion. Martin Holman stood up quickly and motioned toward a chair.

"Sit down, Bill. Sit down." I did and he looked relieved. I don't know what he had expected. I tossed my Stetson on the edge of the sheriff's desk.

"So," I said.

"We wanted to move fast on this," Schroeder said.

I glanced at the wall clock. "At five after seven on a Tuesday morning? I guess so. It must be an election year." Holman grimaced.

"That's not the case, Bill," Schroeder said. He leaned forward. "We have to have a formal inquest into Trujillo's death anyway, you know that. You know for a fact that his relatives are going to sue the county . . . and you . . . for all we're worth. I mean, this is their opportunity to set themselves up for life, Bill."

"We've heard that Sonny Trujillo's mother, Juanita Smith, has hired someone from Bacon, Ortiz and McNally in Las Cruces to represent her," Holman said.

121

"So we're all supposed to face Mecca and bow three times?" Schroeder chuckled. "They don't have a case, but Bob Weems and I want to make sure. No mistakes. If someone from the Sheriff's Department investigates, they're going to make an issue of it."

"Of course. I would, too, if I was them," I said. "A dentist doesn't drill on his own teeth. And Addy Eschevera is the best there is." But I didn't share that view of Bob Weems, the county's attorney. He represented Posadas County part-time, attending meetings of the County Commission. I couldn't remember the last time he'd been able to give the commissioners a direct, positive answer to a question. The thought of Weems representing the county—and me—in a wrongful death lawsuit was enough to take away my appetite.

Schroeder picked up a manila envelope from Holman's desk. "And Frank Dayan at the *Register* provided us with these." He pulled the eight-by-ten photos from the envelope and handed them to me. "I didn't even have to try a subpoena." Dayan had managed to take a series of five photos during the brawl at the school, and they told the story pretty well. I adjusted my glasses and examined them with interest.

The first photo on the negative strip included the general melee, with only a small portion of me edged into the right side of the picture. The second shot clearly showed me holding Sonny Trujillo's right hand, my fingers clamped over the cylinder of the revolver. The barrel of the gun was close to my face.

"That's the most interesting part," I said, and held the photo so Schroeder could see it. "Trujillo's finger is in the trigger guard, clear as a bell."

"And the trigger is pulled all the way back," the district attorney said with satisfaction. "He pulled it and held it."

The third photo caught the two of us just as Trujillo's fist made contact with the side of my face, sending my glasses askew. The fourth image was slightly blurred from camera motion. Trujillo was down on the floor, I had regained possession of the handgun, and my right hand was groping around behind my belt for handcuffs.

The last blowup showed a cowed Sonny Trujillo, blood running down his face, being escorted away, village officer Tom Pasquale on one side, me on the other.

"Great stuff for your scrapbook when this is all over, Bill," Schroeder grinned.

"I don't keep a scrapbook," I said. I stood up and handed the envelope back. "What do you need?"

"I just wanted to tell you that someone from Eschevera's office will be here sometime this week to talk with you. We have your sworn deposition already, but I'm sure they'll want to speak with you as well. Just to cover all possibilities."

"There aren't any possibilities," I said shortly. "We all know exactly what happened."

Schroeder pursed his lips. "Bacon, Ortiz and McNally have a pretty good reputation, Bill. This isn't something to take lightly. I can tell you right now what course they're going to take."

"What's that?"

"That you shouldn't have punched the kid in the nose. It's that simple."

I gestured toward the envelope of photos, but Schroeder shook his head. "They'll say that the officer should have been able to restrain an intoxicated young man without breaking his nose." Schroeder saw my eyes narrow and he added, "That's what they'll argue. I didn't say they were right."

I looked across at Holman.

"The whole affair is ridiculous," he said. "I agreed with Ron that we should have Eschevera come in, Bill. That frees us up. I don't want to just prove that you—that the department—did the right thing, Bill. I want to pound this kind of harassment right into the ground. I want to show that you defused a dangerous situation quickly and efficiently and that, if anything, Gayle Sedillos endangered herself when she entered that cell out of concern for the prisoners."

I raised an eyebrow, impressed at Holman's dramatic speech.

I stood up and retrieved my hat. "Well, all this shit is perfectly timed, I'll tell you that." My fingers groped for a cigarette and settled for patting my breast pocket.

"Why don't you join us for breakfast?" Holman asked. I shook my head.

"Maybe later." I left the two young *políticos* to their designs and hustled my way to Estelle Reyes-Guzman's dark corner down the hall. The door was closed and locked. Irritated, I stalked to my own office and opened the door.

Estelle was seated in one of the chairs in front of my desk, notepad on her lap. Seated in the other chair, looking pale and scared, was Karl Woodruff.

18

"MORNING," I said shortly. I didn't tack on a "good," since Karl's face told me it was anything but that. I read equal parts embarrassment, apprehension, and resentment in his expression. Estelle rose quickly from her chair and beckoned me back toward the door.

"Will you excuse us for just a moment?" she said to Woodruff. Estelle and I stepped out into the hall and she closed my office door behind us. At first she spoke so softly I couldn't hear her.

"I can't read lips, Estelle," I said. "And how come you didn't wake me up?"

"Sir, it was pure chance. I decided to run the fingerprints on the wrench for a match, so I just started with the most recent prints we had on file. From this weekend."

"Well, that makes sense." I looked suddenly at my office door as if I could see right through the old dingy mahogany. I could see Karl Woodruff sitting in that room, alone, his pulse hammering away in his ears. "Not him," I said.

"One of the prints on the wrench belongs to Tammy Woodruff."

"To Tammy?"

Estelle nodded. "A perfect match, sir. No mistake. I sent the wrench to Santa Fe early this morning for backup analysis, but I'm right. There's no mistaking that print."

125

Estelle held up her right index finger. With her left index, she drew a corkscrew line from the corner of the nail down across the pad, ending at the joint line. "Tammy has a scar across the pad of her finger. Friday night when we booked her, she told me she sliced her finger last year, when the top of a wine bottle that she was trying to open broke."

"Tammy Woodruff," I mused. "What the hell was she doing out there."

"Changing a tire?" Estelle offered.

"Why did you call Karl in? Tammy's the one we should be talking to, Estelle. She's no minor."

"I thought maybe her father might know where she is."

"You checked?"

Estelle nodded. "She's not at her apartment, sir."

"Shit," I muttered, and added, "Let's go see what he has to say."

Karl Woodruff watched us reenter the office; his eyes tracked my face as I closed the door. Estelle sat down and once more picked up her notebook, this time sliding her pencil into the spiral binding as if to announce that we were off the record. She then folded her hands on her lap.

The casualness of that little motion was not lost on Karl Woodruff, and he took a deep breath and tried to relax back in the hard chair.

"Sir, I asked Mr. Woodruff to join us for a few minutes this morning," Estelle said to me. I glanced at my watch. Woodruff's RxRite pharmacy would open in six minutes. "Is this a bad time, Karl? Do you have someone covering for you, or . . ."

He shook his head quickly. He leaned forward, taking most of his weight on his elbows, pushing against the arms of the chair. His hands were balled into his gut as if he were about to toss his breakfast burritos. "No, it's fine," he managed. He was a spare man anyway, one of those folks whose nervous system hangs on the outside. He'd make a lousy poker player.

"You want a cup of coffee or something?"

"No, thanks."

I sat down behind the desk, behaving for all the world as if I knew what the hell was going on, as if I had orchestrated this reduction of a confident, successful merchant and chairman of the Republican party into a nervous wreck. Estelle pulled the pencil out of the notebook binding again.

"Sir, I asked Mr. Woodruff to come down because of the information we've received that places his daughter Tammy at or near the scene of the homicide Sunday night."

Woodruff blanched. *Homicide* was one of those grim words that was a real attention grabber. I leaned forward and propped my chin on one hand. Woodruff was terrified, which was to our benefit, since if he knew anything at all he'd tell us—in a great rush of words that would try to wash away the grime of that single pronouncement.

Tammy Woodruff was twenty-three years old. She didn't need daddy's permission for anything, as she'd proven the previous Friday night at the Broken Spur Saloon with Sergeant Torrez. And we sure as hell didn't need daddy's permission to arrest her attractive young butt if she'd gotten tangled in something far dirtier than public drunkenness.

But for all her majority, nothing could erase her from her father's mind as a little kid—a little kid winning 4-H ribbons at the fair, a little kid screaming out her first cheer, a little kid . . . all those sentimental things had to be swimming in Karl Woodruff's mind just then. I felt sorry for him. I had four "little" kids of my own.

Estelle bent slightly and retrieved the lug wrench from her briefcase, which had been leaning against her chair. She held it out toward Karl Woodruff.

"Mr. Woodruff, this is part of a lug wrench from a General Motors product—a newer model truck of some sort. It's the sort of wrench that we discovered in the grass just a few feet in front of where the deputy's patrol car was found parked Sunday night. We have reason to believe that the deputy stopped that night, perhaps to assist someone." She held up the wrench and turned it. Karl Woodruff's eyes followed it.

127

"I don't . . ."

"Mr. Woodruff, your daughter's fingerprints were found on the wrench."

"On that?"

"On the lug wrench that we found near the scene of the shooting. Yes, sir."

"I don't understand."

"Nor do we, sir." Estelle said it so quietly I almost didn't hear her. And then she let the moment of silence hang.

"Her fingerprints?"

"Yes, sir."

He pushed against the arms of the chair, rising up an inch or two. "I don't understand. How does that wrench . . ." He stopped abruptly, cocked his head, and frowned. "What did Tammy tell you? I mean, she must have a simple explanation for all this. Just because she handled a wrench doesn't mean . . . I mean, she could have touched it at any time. It doesn't mean she had anything to do with that . . . with what happened out there."

"Indeed not, sir. But it's a connection we need to track down. I was hoping you could tell us where she is, sir. So we could ask her a couple of questions."

Woodruff looked relieved, as if he had the right answer. "Well, I assume she's at her apartment, detective." He tried for a grin and managed a lopsided grimace. "She's not an early riser."

"She's not at her apartment, sir."

"She's not?"

"No, sir."

"Well, a friend's then. She frequently stays with a friend." Woodruff shifted in his chair, uncomfortable having to admit that his healthy, wild-hair daughter didn't live the life of a nun. "But wait, now." Woodruff looked at me as he tried to rise to the offensive. "I don't understand any of this. Why would Tammy's fingerprints be on that . . . that wrench in the first place? She doesn't even drive a Chevrolet, or whatever you said it's from. Hell, you know what she drives." He chuckled weakly. "Doesn't drive it too well, sometimes, either."

Estelle lifted a page in her notebook. "Mr. Woodruff, is the white over gold 1993 Ford half-ton extended cab pickup that's registered to your daughter her only vehicle?"

"Sure. She'd live in that thing if she could, I think."

"In the past few days or weeks, has she had occasion to drive any other vehicle?" Woodruff looked puzzled and Estelle added softly, "To your knowledge?"

"No. Of course not. I mean, as far as I know, no. She drives that truck everywhere."

"Who is your daughter seeing right now, Karl?" I asked.

He frowned and bit the corner of his lip. "You know, for quite a while there she was hitched up pretty steady with Brett Prescott. He's a nice enough kid."

"Gus Prescott's boy?"

Woodruff nodded and said with considerable chagrin, "That was Gus's new truck that Tammy backed into Friday night at the bar. She told me that she'd had some sort of tiff with Brett. She doesn't talk much to her mother and me about who she sees. Bill, you went through the same thing with your girls, I imagine."

"Sure." I hadn't, but what the hell.

"The latest thing I heard was that she went to the fire department's Valentine's Day dance with . . ." he hesitated. "Someone came in the store and mentioned how nice a couple they made. Who the heck was it." He frowned hard and stared at the dark pine flooring. The lightbulb finally lit and he said, "Torrance. One of the Torrance boys."

"Pat Torrance, maybe?" Estelle offered.

"I think so, yes."

Herb Torrance raised beef, sheep, emus, and nine kids on his ranch west of Posadas. Patrick was somewhere in the middle of the nine in age.

"You don't know if Tammy has been seeing the Torrance boy

129

regularly, then?" I asked, and Woodruff shook his head. I folded my hands and tapped the tips of my thumbs together while I gazed across the desk at Estelle.

"I really wish I knew what was going on," Karl Woodruff said miserably. "I just can't believe that Tammy would be involved . . ."

"Karl," I said, getting up and walking around the desk, "it's probably nothing. We'll talk with Tammy and find that out, I'm sure. A hundred to one that it's just a fluke, some crazy coincidence." I patted him on the shoulder. "We don't even know what kind of vehicle was stopped, or for that matter even if there is a connection between that incident and the shooting."

Woodruff looked hopeful and pushed himself to his feet. "Bill," he said, "will you call me the minute . . . the second . . . that you know anything? I'll be at the store all day, until nine tonight. And everyday. Just call, all right? As soon as you hear from Tammy, as soon as you have the chance to talk with her?"

"You bet, Karl."

We ushered him out of the office and I closed the door. "What do you think?"

"I think . . ." Estelle started to say, then stopped. She tapped her notebook. "I think we've got several sets of questions, sir. If Tammy Woodruff is the one whom Linda Real recognized, then that's one scenario." She cupped her hands and moved them to one side, as if all those questions were floating in a puddle of water. "And one set of questions—like what vehicle was she driving, and why. And did she know the killer? And why hasn't she come forward to talk to us?" Estelle paused to take a breath and cupped her hands again.

"If Tammy is *not* the person Linda saw, and is *not* the person Linda thinks we all know, then how did Tammy's prints get on the wrench? And what was the wrench doing out there? And when was it dropped? And does that incident have anything at all to do with the shooting?"

"And who was with her," I added. "Who was the person Linda saw?"

130

"Just so, sir," Estelle said. "Who's with Linda now?"

"Howard."

She nodded. "If you're going back to the hospital, I'd like to spend some time trying to track Miss Woodruff down. You know, it's interesting . . ."

"What's that?"

"You remember our conversation with Victor Sánchez?"

"Dimly. I was depending on your note-taking skills."

Estelle smiled and flipped back through several pages in her notes. "I think it's interesting that Señor Sánchez mentioned that Pat Torrance was in the bar, drinking himself sick. It's not unusual that Pat was there, certainly, since his family's ranch is just up County Road 14 a bit. But it's interesting that, if Tammy Woodruff was out in that desolate corner of the county, near an establishment that she frequents, near a saloon where her maybe boyfriend is chugging the brew . . . it's interesting that either she never stopped at the Broken Spur, or that she did stop but Victor didn't see her."

"What's really remarkable," I said, "is that you understand what you just said, Estelle." I ran a hand through my hair and slumped against the side of the desk. "Now listen. I don't want you out in that corner of the county by yourself, you understand me?"

"I wasn't planning . . ."

"Yes you were. If you didn't find Tammy right away, you were going out to the Torrance ranch to find young Patrick. I don't want you doing that by yourself."

"That's a logical next step, sir."

"Sure, it is. And when you take that next step, make damn sure you have someone else with you."

Estelle picked up her briefcase. "I don't think there's anything to worry about, sir."

"So you say. Remember one simple thing." I saw her eyebrow lift in that characteristic expression of attention. "You say Tammy isn't at her apartment. If she was out on State Highway Fifty-six and witnessed a murder, she may very well be cactus fertilizer right now."

131

19

❖❖❖

DEPUTY Howard Bishop saw me as I rounded the corner by the nurses' station. He started down the hall toward me at a brisk walk, unusual for a man to whom exercise was a nice nap in a shady hammock.

"Her mother's here," he said.

I stopped in my tracks. "It's about time. How long has she been here?"

Bishop glanced at his watch. "About half an hour. She's calmed down some."

"I can imagine that she'd be upset."

"It was quite a show there for a while," Bishop mused.

"No show, I'm sure, Howard," I said. A twitch in his expression said there was something else, but he settled for a shrug and accompanied me back up the hall to intensive care.

Helen Murchison stopped me just as I began to push the swinging doors into the ward.

"Sheriff," she said. She kept her voice low but it was pure steel. "Now you listen to me." She drew me to one side. Over her shoulder I could see the ghost of a smile crinkle the corners of Deputy Bishop's eyes. I'm sure Helen and I made quite a pair, squared off the way we were—she a matronly block of efficiency, dark eyebrows glowering over those wonderful blue, piercing eyes, long thin lips compressed with anger. And there I was, a tired old bulldog with too many hours on the clock.

"This can't go on," she said.

"What can't?"

"The young lady's mother has arrived," she said with finality. "And she has been questioning every step we take. She insists that Ms. Real be transferred to the city. She questions every medication and every dosage." Helen stopped and inhaled deeply, the air hissing past her clenched teeth. "And not ten minutes ago she told me that if Linda loses the sight in her left eye, it will be our fault." She looked at me, her fierce blue eyes scanning my face. "I suggested that she wait in the ICU waiting room, and she practically struck me."

"Does she actually know the extent of Linda's injuries?"

"I tried to tell her, but it's impossible to get a word in edgewise. The woman is . . ."

"Distraught," I said. "Let me talk to her."

"I would appreciate that."

I nodded and pushed open the ICU doors. Linda was awake, and this time she managed to shift the position of her head slightly. She brought me into focus and blinked several times. Mrs. Real stood on the other side of the bed. She was nearly as wide as she was tall, her round face framed by jet black hair teased into a wild conflagration. I nodded at her.

"Good morning, ma'am." She raised her nose slightly as if sampling the air. Maybe it had been too many hours between showers for me.

I took Linda's right hand in mine and touched her cheek lightly with my left. "How's it going, doll."

She blinked and then, ever so softly, eased a couple of words past wired jaws. "Eh . . . eh."

I nodded. "Linda, I need to talk with your mother for a few minutes outside, all right?" She blinked and I looked up at Mrs. Real. "Just a few minutes," I said.

The mountainous woman followed me out into the hall, and I

133

motioned toward the waiting room. "Let's go have a cup of coffee," I said.

"I don't need coffee," Mrs. Real snapped.

I flashed her my most engaging smile. "I do," I said. "Come on." I held the waiting room door open for her. "Come on." She relented and bustled past me, her wake of perfume wide and strong.

"Now who are you?" she demanded.

"I'm Undersheriff William Gastner, Mrs. Real. Let's talk about Linda for a few minutes."

"I already spoke with the sheriff," she said, as if that settled that.

"I'm sure you did. Now you're going to speak with me." I gazed at her, unblinking, for a long minute. "The head nurse tells me you have some concerns about Linda's care. Now, as a physician, I'm sure you realize . . ."

"I'm not a doctor," she said quickly.

"Ah. I thought perhaps you were, to know medications and the like so well."

"I was an LPN. I retired a number of years ago."

"I see. Did they explain the exact nature of Linda's injuries to you?"

Mrs. Real looked behind her, located a chair, and sank her considerable bulk into it. She let out a long sigh. "One of the doctors—maybe he was just an aide of some kind—spoke to me earlier for less than half a minute. He was in such a hurry to be elsewhere . . ." She waved a hand.

"Linda has made great progress in a very short time, Mrs. Real. She was gravely injured. I won't kid you."

"But if there's damage to her eyes, then she should be transferred immediately to a facility where she can receive the best possible care."

"She's receiving that here, ma'am. I'm sure that if Dr. Guzman . . . is that the doctor you spoke with?"

"No. He was a foreigner of some kind."

"Dr. Perrone?"

"That may have been it."

"He's chief of surgical services, ma'am. What I wanted to say was that if the physicians think she should be moved, she will be. It's that simple. And I'll be the one to tell you, if no one else has. Linda is blind in her left eye. Permanently." I didn't see the need to tell the woman that Linda didn't even have a left eye anymore.

Mrs. Real looked at me incredulously. "He didn't say anything about . . ."

"I'm telling you now, Mrs. Real. Now listen. Linda is very lucky to be alive. Very lucky. I'll spare you the details, but basically the shotgun blast struck her in the side of the head. She has serious injuries all around the left orbit, and to the sinuses on that side of her skull. Her jaw is broken and there's damage to lots of the soft tissue inside her mouth on that side." I held up my hands. "She has a long road ahead, Mrs. Real. But she's already much stronger. The surgeries went well. I'm sure she'll need more." I smiled. "She's a tough young lady, though."

"And you've caught the ones who did this?"

"No, we haven't." I walked over to the small coffeemaker and felt the side of the pot. I poured myself a cup. "You sure you don't want any?"

She dismissed the offer with a sniff.

"But we're going to catch them, ma'am."

The woman heaved herself to her feet. "And you stand here drinking coffee when you could be—" she stopped, fuming and groping for the right words, "out there."

I sipped the coffee, wondering what the woman had been like a quarter of a century before when she watched her daughter as a tot taking her first staggering steps.

"Ma'am," I said, "we have people 'out there' working themselves sick. We have some officers who haven't had any sleep since Sunday night, when this happened."

"Well, then maybe you can tell me what Linda was doing in that police car in the first place?"

"She frequently rides with one of the officers, Mrs. Real. On occasion, she writes an article about the department for the newspaper. Other than that, I don't know why she spends so much time with us. Perhaps she's husband hunting." I regretted the comment the instant I said it, but it was too late. Mrs. Real's eyes narrowed into slits and her heavy jaw thrust forward—an expression I was sure that Mr. Real, if he still cowered somewhere on the planet, had learned to dread.

"You had no business allowing her," she snapped, and she shook her finger under my nose. "No business whatsoever."

"Mrs. Real," I said wearily, knowing already that it was a waste of breath, "Linda is an adult professional. She has the right to observe public agencies such as ours as much as she likes. We extend her the courtesy of riding with officers when she deems it necessary. She signed a waiver of responsibility with the county attorney. It's her call. We're as sorry as anyone that this happened."

"Now, you say that. But you let . . ." she began.

"You might remember, ma'am, that one of our deputies was killed in that same incident. You might bear that in mind. We're hunting a killer. Your daughter is lucky. Just plain, flat lucky."

"She shouldn't have been allowed," Mrs. Real said, and she made for the door. There were tears in her eyes and I let her go. She headed straight across the hall like a huge, waddling missile. I closed my eyes and drained the coffee.

Mrs. Real was still snuffling into a tissue when I slipped back into the ICU and walked up to the bed, yellow legal pad in hand.

"Oh, just leave us," the woman said.

I ignored her and took Linda's hand again. "Linda, I'm going to lay a pad of paper under your right hand," I said. I slid the legal pad between her hand and the sheets.

"May I interrupt?" A young voice chirped behind me, and I turned to see Patsy Montaño, face sober and brow furrowed with concern.

"Sure."

"I need to check the patient's drip," Patsy said seriously.

Right this instant? I almost replied, but nodded. "You do whatever you have to do." I watched closely, but Mrs. Real remained

136

rooted. The nurse slipped past her. I leaned over close to the bed. "Linda, if I put a pencil in your hand, can you make a few marks for me?" She blinked and said something like *umph.* "And penmanship doesn't count," I added. I slid the pencil between her fingers and she held it like an old pro, tip poised over the yellow paper. "I'm turning on the tape recorder, Linda. All right?" She blinked.

I slid the tablet under the pencil. "Linda, yesterday you indicated to me that you knew at least one of the people in the vehicle on State Highway Fifty-six on Sunday night. The vehicle that Deputy Paul Enciños stopped to assist. What was the name of that person, Linda?"

Even wandering as it did, even with hesitation now and then, Linda's freehand writing was better than mine at its best. *Tammy Woodruff.*

"Tammy Woodruff," I repeated for the recorder's benefit. "Was she with anyone else?"

No.

"She was alone. All right. Linda, yesterday you told me that the vehicle was already stopped along the shoulder of the road when the deputy stopped. Is that right?"

Yes.

"Was the vehicle disabled somehow?"

The pencil wavered for several seconds, and Linda's eye closed. I could sense the regret as she wrote, *Don't know.*

"When you say 'Don't know,' do you mean that you couldn't see anything obvious? You didn't see a jack, for instance, or a tire, or something that might indicate to you that the vehicle was disabled?"

No.

"You didn't see any of that. Was Tammy Woodruff out of the vehicle?"

Yes.

"Did she walk up to the patrol car when the deputy stopped behind her vehicle?"

No. To front.

137

"Toward the front of her vehicle?"

Yes.

I slid the pad out and turned the page. Patsy Montaño had finished checking her machinery, but we were still parked right in the center of her day, making life difficult. She stood near the head of the bed, not sure what she should do.

"Can you give me just a few more minutes?" I said.

Patsy nodded.

"Can you answer a few more questions?" I asked Linda.

Nothing else to do. She was getting used to driving that pencil without looking at it, and the words came smoothly.

I chuckled and squeezed Linda's hand. Her mother's eyes narrowed again.

"Linda, what kind of vehicle was the parked vehicle?"

The pencil tip drew a little spiral as if a memory was refusing to swim to the surface. Then she wrote, *Chevy pickup.*

"A Chevrolet pickup. Do you remember what color it was?"

White.

"All white?"

Just saw back.

"But it was just a regular pickup?"

Yes.

"You're sure?"

Yes.

Yes. She paused. *Think so.*

"Were you able to make out the license plate, Linda?"

No. Wasn't one.

"No license plate?"

No. It had . . . The pencil stopped and I looked at Linda's face. Her eye was closed.

"She doesn't have the energy for all this," Mrs. Real snapped. "You should leave now."

The pencil wavered. *Thinking.*

"Take your time," I said.

Temp tag in window.

138

"It had one of those paper permits in the back window? Like it was just purchased?"

Yes.

"Linda, I need to ask you about the second vehicle. What direction did it come from?"

West.

"From the west. It came toward you then. And it stopped on the other side of the road?"

Yes.

"Was Deputy Enciños out of the patrol car then?"

Yes. Standing by front fender. She shifted her grip on the pencil and I moved the pad a bit to give her room. *Think was going to talk to Tammy.*

"And you didn't see the driver of the second vehicle?"

No. Headlights too bright.

"Did the person fire from the vehicle?"

No. Got out. Paul backed up.

"Paul backed up? Can you tell me what you mean?"

Linda made a small groaning sound as the memories surged back. *Stepped back. I saw hand move down toward holster.*

"The first shot came from across the highway."

Yes. Right away. Then he walked across. He walked across road.

"But you couldn't see who it was?"

No. I tried to get down. Tried. So scared. The pencil's tip drifted along the line an inch or so before touching the surface again. *So scared.*

I put my hand over Linda's for a moment. The room was silent. Mrs. Real's eyes bored into mine, but I ignored her.

"Linda, can you tell me just one or two more things?"

"Uh."

"Do you know why Deputy Enciños decided to drive out Fifty-six so late in his shift?"

No.

"It was just chance?"

Maybe he wanted . . . The pencil stopped. Her forehead, what

139

little of it I could see, furrowed, but this time in pain. *Hurts so much,* she wrote. *Hard to think.*

"We'll let you rest."

No, wait. The pencil almost stabbed the paper with determination. *Paul thought Tammy maybe drinking.*

"He thought she was drunk? When?"

This time, the pencil moved slowly, painfully. Linda wrote the sentence with her eye closed. A tear formed under the long black lashes and trickled back toward her ear.

She was parked on Bustos near MacA. Paul stopped, talked to her. She didn't know how to tune radio. He helped. He laughed.

"Was this the same truck you saw later out on Fifty-six?"

Yes.

"And then the deputy headed out on Fifty-six as well."

He joked.

She stopped writing and I placed my hand on her right cheek. She opened her eye and gazed at me. Then, ever so slightly, she shook her head. The movement cost her, and she closed her eye again. The pencil wavered and scratched.

He said might as well check on Bob's drunks one more time.

"Bob's drunks." I smiled. Sergeant Robert Torrez would appreciate that. "Did he have any idea that Tammy Woodruff was headed out that way?"

Yes. We drove around some, saw her later, not too long. Saw truck go under interstate, turn onto 56. Paul checked some buildings near interstate, then we went that way, too.

She dropped the pencil and her hand curled up on the pad.

I took a deep breath and straightened up. I clicked off the little tape recorder and slid it into my pocket.

"You should leave now," Mrs. Real glowered. "You've put her through far too much already."

"Lady," I started to say, then stopped. Instead I touched Linda's right cheek once more. "Nobody will bother you for a while. You get some rest."

Her eyelid fluttered. I moved to the door and beckoned Mrs. Real

140

to follow. She did so, and when we were out in the hall, I waved Deputy Howard Bishop over.

Mrs. Real surveyed Howard with distaste and I said, "Mrs. Real, the ICU waiting room is across the hall, right there. You're welcome to wait there. I'll remind you that your daughter, besides being gravely injured, is a material witness in a homicide investigation. You're going to have to wait out here. Deputy Bishop, I want you to arrest anyone who enters that room other than medical staff until I return. Is that clear?"

"Yes, sir."

Mrs. Real's jaw dropped. "Now I'm her mother . . ."

"I don't care who you are."

"I have the right . . ."

"No, ma'am, you don't. Deputy, any questions?"

"No, sir." He moved toward the doors of the ICU.

"I'll be back shortly after noon." I nodded at Mrs. Real. "Ma'am," I said. "Make yourself comfortable."

As I walked off, I heard Mrs. Real mutter, "I don't have to put up with this." But she pushed open the door of the waiting room.

20

◆◆◆

I hustled across the hospital parking lot to 310, anxious to find out what Estelle Reyes-Guzman had tracked down and disappointed that our lead on the stolen Suburban out of Albuquerque had been shot to hell by Linda's story. I settled into the car's front seat and wrinkled my nose as a waft of air blew just right to carry the aroma of me upward.

"Christ," I muttered. "No wonder the woman was so grouchy."

I drove directly home without bothering to call the office. Hell, Gayle Sedillos was working dispatch, and she always knew exactly where I was. An instinct of some kind. Or maybe just stink. I hadn't thought of that before.

The long, hot shower was pure bliss, and I damn near fell asleep standing up. Afterward I dressed in comfortable wool flannel pants and my favorite blue-checked flannel shirt. I looked like an ad out of *Retired Lumberjack Magazine*. I sat down on the edge of the bed to draw on a fresh pair of socks and then made the mistake of lying back on the cool bedspread for just a moment.

My eyes slammed shut and that was that. I might have slept all day had Linda Real's mother not intruded. She appeared vividly in a dream where I was once again a patient. She, of course, was the floor nurse. No matter how much I protested, she still insisted there was nothing wrong with the king-size hypo she was about to jab in

142

my butt. I could see that the tip of the needle was bent, as if it had been dropped point first on a Formica countertop. The needle looked fine to her.

I awoke with a start, paralyzed. My feet were still flat on the floor, my back was flat on the mattress, and my sixty-three-year-old spine had mistaken the resulting curve as a permanent set. I cussed and dragged the arm whose wrist held a watch up close to my eyes. It was quarter to four.

I hauled myself to a sitting position and sat for a while with my head hanging, trying to clear my thoughts. "Tammy, you're the key," I said aloud. I pushed myself upright and padded in stocking feet down the long tile hall to the kitchen. I loaded grounds and while the coffeemaker did its thing I telephoned the office. Gayle answered on the second ring.

"Gayle, it's Gastner. Any messages for me?"

"Let me check, sir." An instant later she added, "Nothing while I've been here, except the sheriff asked for you a couple of times."

"Anything important?"

"He's got Captain Eschevera of the state police with him. They've been rummaging around here all afternoon. Eschevera had me in Holman's office for nearly an hour."

"Yeah, well, give 'em whatever he wants. Has Estelle checked in?"

"She was in earlier for a few minutes. Let me see." Voices mumbled in the background and then Gayle said, "Bob Torrez wants to talk with you, sir." The phone clicked and Sergeant Torrez's soft voice came on the line.

"Sir," he said, "did Estelle tell you about the Suburban?"

"No. But I found out that it's not the vehicle we're looking for."

"No, sir. It was recovered in Taos. So that's that."

"Bob, when you talked with Tammy over the weekend, did she say anything about getting a new truck?"

"No, sir."

"Sunday night, Linda Real says that Tammy was driving a white Chevy pickup. Brand-new. Temporary sticker in the window. Linda

143

says that's the vehicle that Paul stopped to assist. I want that truck, and I want to talk with Tammy Woodruff."

"Is there any chance she could be mistaken?"

"Of course," I said cryptically, and Torrez understood the tone of my voice.

"I'll get a bulletin out, sir."

"And do you know where Estelle is at the moment?"

"I saw her before lunch. She said she was going home for a little bit. And then she said something about going down to Regal. You want me to flag her on the radio?"

"No. No. I'll catch her later. What did you find out today?"

"Estelle asked me to try and run down the shotgun ammunition that was used, sir. No number 4 buck has been sold anywhere around here recently. One of the Albuquerque detectives is running a check of dealers up there, but so far nothing. And nothing in Cruces. Not too many dealers sell the stuff in the first place."

"And they don't have to keep records of sales anyway."

"No. It's just a question of maybe a chance recollection, sir."

"Well, keep after it. And by the way, while you're at the office, look at the duty roster and make sure we're covered tonight by someone who isn't dead on his feet."

"Gayle's working on that, sir. We're shorthanded. I think she's got Tony Abeyta on swing, with Mears coming in at midnight. Here, she wants to talk to you again."

"Sir," Gayle's pert voice broke in, "remember the Weatherfords?"

"Sure."

"The mother called early this morning. I forgot to tell you."

"What did she want?"

"Just to thank you and the deputies for all the help. Her husband was discharged late yesterday afternoon. She said that they plan to leave today, if things work out. As soon as they can make arrangements. She said he's still in a lot of discomfort, but apparently he can travel now."

"Well, good. I'm glad something worked out well. Gayle, if you need me, I'll be out and about. I'm going to see Karl Woodruff for a few minutes and see if he's had time to think of a few answers."

If anyone was wishing for answers, it was Karl Woodruff. He hadn't seen his daughter since bailing her out of the drunk tank Saturday morning.

We stood in the corner of the pharmacy next to the selection of foot pads. Karl's face was worried as I told him what Linda Real had said.

"She doesn't have a new truck, Bill. I'd know it if she did. You can guess who holds the paperwork on the one she's got." He jabbed his chest with a thumb. "Dear old dad here."

"Maybe she borrowed it from a friend."

Karl Woodruff shook his head in disbelief. "Anything's possible, I suppose." He reached out and grasped my arm. "But where is she? If what Miss Real says is true, then what did Tammy do? Just drive off? Where?"

"We hope that's what she did, Karl."

Woodruff bit his lip. "She could be in some sort of real danger from this, couldn't she?"

"Yes."

"My God," Woodruff said, and looked off into the distance in the general direction of the vitamin supplements. He looked back at me. "What can I do?"

"Karl, we have to find her. We have a bulletin out for her, and for that truck. If you or your wife think of anything in the meantime, get right to us. If you hear from her, we have to know. If you think of any old favorite places she might be, let me know so I can have one of the deputies check it out. If there's a relative she might have traipsed off to visit out of town, then we'll look there."

Karl Woodruff buried his hands in the pockets of his white lab coat. I could see that his fists were clenched.

"I've never been so frightened," he said finally. When he looked at me, his eyes were pleading. "For her, I mean."

I nodded and patted him on the shoulder. "We'll do what we can,

145

Karl. What's important is that you keep in touch with us. Don't let anything wait. If you think of something that might be of help at three in the morning, give the department a call."

I left the drugstore thinking about forks in the road. The myriad possibilities had narrowed to two that nagged. If Tammy Woodruff had been an innocent bystander that night, an unwilling, unlucky witness, then the odds were excellent we'd never see her alive again. And that shiny new truck she'd been driving, no matter whose it was, would be deep in Mexico, out of our reach, a nice bonus for the killer's night of work.

The other possibility was that Tammy Woodruff had been party to the shooting in some way.

Karl Woodruff had every reason to be frightened.

21

⬥⬥⬥

TUESDAY afternoon in February wasn't a time of unrelenting sales in any store in Posadas, and folks sure weren't standing in line to buy cars. Shoehorned into the showroom of Nick Chavez's auto dealership were four vehicles, their svelte plastic bumpers a hair's breadth from touching. Not a single customer salivated over the prospect of adopting one of those machines.

I let the door close behind me and had time for two deep breaths before a tall young woman I didn't know meandered her way across the showroom toward me. The cars were perfectly placed. In order to avoid a collision of thigh and plastic, she had to waltz her rump first one way and then another. I trudged forward and met her at the Olds station wagon.

Her smile was megawatt as she tried to read first impressions. Was this old man dressed up in his go-to-town clothes ready to buy himself a new sedan? Maybe one of those humongous pickup trucks with four doors and dual back wheels, powerful enough to haul any stock trailer all the way up Regal Pass without dropping out of overdrive.

"May I help you, sir?" she said. Her voice was the kind of husky that takes hours of practice at home in front of a mirror.

"Nick Chavez, please." I offered her a friendly smile.

Immediately her radiant expression wilted a touch. "I'm sorry,

147

Mr. Chavez is with . . ." That's as far as she got before Nick stuck his head out of an office door at the other end of the showroom, behind the blue Camaro.

"Bill!" he bellowed, and beckoned with both hands.

The girl nodded brightly. "I guess he's free now," she said.

I thanked her and waddled my way across the showroom, zigzagging around the polished automotive snouts and rumps with far less grace and elegance than the girl.

Nick stretched out a hand as if to save me from drowning. His handshake was one of those rock-crushers that my arthritic knuckles dreaded. "Bill, come on in. By God, I didn't think I'd ever get you back here."

Two other men were sitting in his office and Nick introduced them as if they were going to take part in the feeding frenzy. "Bill, you know Rusty Archer, my service manager." Archer stood up and stretched a hand across the desk. He looked like a thirty-years-younger version of his father, high school principal Glen Archer. Rusty had attended the same school of knuckle-dusting handshakes as his boss, and I flinched involuntarily.

". . . and Carlos Sánchez, our business manager." As we shook, this time with courtesy but no agony, I reflected that young Carlos had been spared his father's looks. While Victor Sánchez bulled around his saloon like an old grumpy rhino, Carlos was lean, almost fine boned. The slight aquiline curve of his nose set off an intelligent, aristocratic face.

"Sit down, sheriff, sit down," Nick said, gesturing toward one of the conference chairs. "We were just putting a new ad campaign together." He smoothed his glossy black hair and then remained for a moment with his hand locked to the back of his head, brow furrowed. "Bad season of the year, Bill," he said. "One good sale yesterday, and son of a gun, that's it for the past week." He grinned toward Sánchez and Archer. "These guys are going to get hungry if we don't do something to lure you hard cases in."

He beckoned toward the chair again. "Sit down. Take a load off."

148

"I don't really have the time, Nick," I said. "I wonder if I could talk with you just a bit."

Nick Chavez looked momentarily surprised, then nodded vigorously. "Sure, sure. Guys," he said, "give us a few minutes."

When we were alone, I closed the glass door.

"Nick, we're looking for a 1994, white Chevrolet pickup truck. Temporary sticker in the back window."

He sat on the edge of his desk, face serious. "Is this the one involved out there?" He waved a hand toward the west.

"We think it might be."

"Just plain white? No accent colors?"

"We don't know."

"Half-ton? Three-quarter?"

I shook my head. "We don't know that either."

"Extended cab?" He saw the look on my face and finished for me. "You don't know that either."

"Right."

"Bill, the only truck we've sold recently is the mother of all Suburbans. You know those nice folks who wrecked their van over the weekend?"

"The Weatherfords."

"Right. They bought a brand-new one, fully loaded. With that cast her husband has on his leg, I guess they want him to be able to stretch out in style. Anyway, they picked that up early this morning. Easiest sale I ever made. The kids loved it—they always make it easy."

I whistled silently. "That's a pretty penny."

Nick grinned. "It'll pay the light bill for a while longer." His grin widened. "He's a lawyer. It must be hell not having anyone to sue except his own wife. But that's it since I sold Penny Samons a little S-10 last week. We've moved a couple of cars, and a bunch of used inventory. But as far as trucks go, that's it for the past month."

"Is there any way you can check around for me? Check with other dealers?"

149

He frowned. "Sure. I guess. What kind of area are we talking about?"

"Five state."

Nick's whistle was shrill. "Jesus. Nobody got a look at the sticker to see who the dealer was, then."

I leaned forward. "No. We can do it if you don't have time, but the inquiry might be a little more discreet coming from you. Don't you folks have some kind of computer network for information like that?"

Nick shook his head. "What a dealer sells is between him and the customer, sheriff. The only way I can find out what's sold is by calling each dealer." He frowned. "And that's a lot of calling."

"Then maybe you have a dealer directory we could borrow for a day or two. I'll put one of the part-timers on it."

"That, I got." He held up a hand. "But look, I'll be glad to co-operate with you. I'll have one of my office staff run down the list. How's that?" I nodded my thanks, and Nick added, "Do you know yet who was drivin' the truck?"

I hesitated, mentally inventorying how many people were privy to this same information. I took the plunge. "Tammy Woodruff."

"Tammy? Nah. Her daddy might be rich, but he ain't going to buy her a new one every year. She just got that Ford of hers in November. I damn near had her in one of mine, but she got a close-out deal on a '93 from Artie Swanson over in Silver City." He shook his head sadly. "Drive a hundred miles to save ten bucks."

"Well, then she borrowed this one from someone."

Chavez sat back, picked up a pencil, and tapped his lower lip. "Brand-new, you say?"

"We have reason to think so."

"And maybe white."

I nodded.

"Whoever saw this truck," Nick said, and his tone was careful, as if to say that he didn't want to know, "didn't get a good look, or what?"

"What do you mean?"

150

"How come you don't know if there were any accents, or if it was an extended cab? Somebody just see the back of it?"

"That's right."

He closed his eyes. "So it could have been one, two, even more years old, then. Maybe a used truck. Maybe somebody bought themselves a cream puff."

"It could have been. But we have reason to believe that it was new, or nearly so."

Nick leaned back some more, hooked his hands behind his head, and gazed at me as if he were trying to assess just how much more I'd pay for the car of my dreams.

"What's Tammy say?"

"When I find her, I'll ask her."

"Ah . . ." Nick grimaced. "I probably don't want to know what's going on, do I?"

I grinned. "Probably not."

He pulled a pad of paper over and hastily jotted some notes. "Let me get this right. Pickup truck, any style, white-ass end, who knows what's up front. Probably new, maybe not. Sold within the past thirty days if that temp sticker is any good." He glanced up and grinned. "Remember Art Beauchamp?"

"Sure."

"He once bought a used car from me and drove for almost two years on his window sticker."

"Whatever works," I said, and got up. I don't know why I trusted Nick Chavez, but I did. Even so, I didn't want to tell him any more than he needed to know. I thrust my hands into my pockets and surveyed his office, choosing my words with care.

"Nick, we'd appreciate your help. And keep your ears open. You hear anything, you give me a call, all right?"

"You can count on it." He held the door for me. "When's the funeral?"

"Thursday at ten," I said. Nick nodded, astute enough to see that I didn't want to discuss it. I'd done my best so far not to think about that hour of misery.

22

◆◆◆

I settled into 310 and sat for a while, looking west toward where the sun sank over the flank of the San Cristobal Mountains. A couple of answers to a couple of simple questions would shuffle all the pieces into order. But the answers were elusive. I sighed. Even Estelle Reyes-Guzman's powerful intuition wasn't helping us much.

I keyed the mike. "Three oh two, this is three ten."

I hoped for an instant response, but the seconds dragged by. I almost keyed the mike again, but thought better of it. Estelle would have heard the first time if she was in the car and if the radio was on. I glanced at my watch.

"Three ten, PCS."

I lifted the mike. "Go ahead." I recognized Aggie Bishop's voice. Howard's wife, who worked occasionally as a matron for the department, had been dragged in to cover dispatch while we used part-timer Ernie Wheeler on the road. She wasn't very good at it, but she was better than a dead radio. I hoped she wasn't spreading her flu through the office.

"Three ten, Dr. Guzman called just a few minutes ago."

"Ten-four." I waited for Aggie to make up her mind about what she wanted to say. Life at the Bishop home must have been fascinating. A one paragraph conversation between Howard and Aggie would last all week.

Fifteen seconds passed, and I keyed the mike. "PCS, go ahead."

"Three ten, a Dr. Guzman called." She spaced out the words and spoke considerably louder into the radio.

"Ten-four," I said again, and chuckled in spite of myself. "What . . . does . . . he . . . want?"

"Oh. Three ten, is Estelle . . . is Detective Reyes-Guzman with you?"

"Negative."

"Ah, three ten, do you know . . ." and she stopped dead in the water, wanting to use one of those wonderful ten codes that spill from cops' lips with such abandon. But Aggie didn't have a clue. I could picture her, leaning across the desk, looking at the ten-code chart that was faded to uniform brown on top of the radio housing. "Do you know her ten-twenty location? Where she is?"

"Negative, PCS." I glanced at my watch. At 5:13, the streets of Posadas were both rolled up and blanketed in gloomy twilight. I didn't suggest that she try to call Estelle at home, since it seemed obvious to me that the good doctor would have tried that himself, first.

It took less than a minute to go around the block and pull into the hospital's parking lot. I had no intention of grilling Linda Real again that day. She had told me all she could, and probably couldn't tell me what we most urgently needed to know. And I didn't want to face another confrontation with her mother. But if Francis Guzman had important information for us, I wanted it fast and firsthand.

I hustled inside. The main hallway and lobby of the hospital was deserted. Even the reception desk, usually manned by someone from the auxiliary, was empty. I hastened down the hall past radiology, the lab, physical therapy, and all those other little smelly holes where friendly folks with million-dollar machines pry secrets out of a patient's most private corners.

When I reached the nurses' station I glanced toward the intensive care ward. Patrolman Tom Pasquale from the village depart-

153

ment was taking another turn staring at floor tiles and loving every minute of it.

"Are you lost?"

I turned. Helen Murchison had padded up behind me, and she leaned one hand on the Plexiglas shelf in front of the glass partition of the station.

"Ah, Helen. Is Francis Guzman handy?"

"He's in surgery."

"For long?"

Helen raised an eyebrow. "I don't know. The ambulance just brought in someone who tried to put an ax through his ankle."

I winced, and Helen started to smile, then thought better of it. "So he's tied up," I said.

"Yes."

"He left a message to call him."

Helen took a deep breath, signaling that she was much put upon by all this. "I believe," she said, "that he was wondering where his wife was."

"She's not home?"

"Evidently not."

A mental image of Sofia Tournál as a baby-sitter flashed through my mind. Perhaps she would start *el kid* off on Blackstone. In Spanish, of course.

"I'll run on down to the emergency room and see if I can catch the good doctor."

She shook her head. "Dr. Guzman won't be able to talk to you just now, though."

"I'll catch him when he finishes."

She nodded. "And Bill . . ."

"Yes?" I was surprised at being called anything but "sir" or "sheriff" by Helen Murchison.

"Thanks again for the help with Mrs. Real earlier." She lowered her voice to a hoarse whisper. "She's dreadful." As if that one indiscretion was all she could allow herself for that week, Helen nodded curtly and stalked off.

154

She was right, though. Francis Guzman couldn't talk to me for several minutes. I sat down outside the emergency room and waited while the physician repaired the magnificent damage that George Payson had done to himself with a camp hatchet while trying to split kindling for an evening fire.

In short order, the yellow plastic chair in which I sat metamorphosed into a lumpy rock, and my initial complacent acceptance of inconvenience drifted toward concern mixed with irritation.

Squirming didn't help, so I got up and walked to the door, looking out into the gathering darkness. An ambulance sat under the portico, its four-way flashers pulsing.

I glanced at my watch, and then walked to the pay phone beside the drinking fountain. I dialed Estelle's home phone and waited for ten rings before the receiver was lifted.

"Hello?" The voice was soft and distant.

"Señora Tournál? This is Bill Gastner."

"Ah. Good evening, señor."

"I don't mean to disturb you, but has Estelle called?"

"No, señor, I have not seen Estelle since . . . since before lunch, you know."

"The minute she comes in, would you ask her to call the sheriff's office?"

"Certainly. And señor, I believe Francisco is at the hospital." Her heavy accent stressed the last syllable, elegantly.

"I saw him," I said, not trying to explain that it had been a quick glimpse through the Plexiglas of the emergency room doors. In the background I could hear the sort of ruckus caused by a tower of wooden blocks crashing to the Guzman's living room floor, followed by a fourteen-month old's screech of delight. "You're entertaining the squirt, eh?"

She laughed. "Ah, *el kid*. He is a charmer, no?"

"Indeed. The baby-sitter had to go home?"

"Yes. She left shortly after lunch, señor. I told Francis that perhaps I could manage this one afternoon."

"Charge the good doctor a fancy dinner," I said, and Sofia chuckled. "Will you please tell Estelle to call me?"

"I will do that, señor. And perhaps later we can all meet for dinner. Everyone is so . . . *occupado*. No, you say, 'busy.' " Señora Tournál didn't sound busy—she sounded serene. Hell, one of us had to be.

After I hung up, I dug out another quarter. I suppose I could have saved a few cents by using the radio in the car, but I despised public announcements. Half the county listened to the police scanner, listened to business that was none of their own. I dropped in the quarter. Aggie Bishop answered after three rings.

"Aggie, this is Gastner again," I said. "Has Estelle checked in with you yet?"

"No sir, she sure hasn't."

"Crap," I said.

"Sir?"

"No, nothing, Aggie. Are you doing all right?"

"I guess so, sir. Gayle said she was going to come in around eight to relieve me."

"Fine. Look, I'm going to stop at Don Juan's for some food, so I'll be there for a bit. Then I'll come on down. If you need anything, ring the restaurant. All right?"

"Yes, sir."

"And Aggie . . . if Estelle calls, tell her I want to see her right away, if not before. Tell her where I am."

"I sure will."

The drive across Posadas to North Twelfth Street took only four minutes. By then, it was dark. I pulled into the parking lot of the Don Juan de Oñate Restaurant and parked beside a monstrous RV with Utah plates. That and a white school bus with Chihuahuan tags and several dozen pairs of skis in the top rack were the only vehicles. I hesitated, not sure I wanted to put up with a score of noisy adolescents inside the restaurant, all of them doubly excited to be in a foreign country and headed for the ski slopes up north.

I did go inside, though, and found myself a dark, quiet corner. I told the hostess that I was expecting a phone call and she promised not to forget me. After ordering a beef burrito plate with green chili, sour cream, beans, and rice, I settled back in the imitation leather booth with a basket of chips and a bowl of salsa. I ate two chips, then turned sideways on the seat so I could look out the window and watch what passed for traffic on Bustos Avenue.

"Tammy Woodruff," I murmured. What had Tammy Woodruff been doing out there on State Highway 56 Sunday night? She hadn't simply gone to the Broken Spur to drink with a boyfriend and had another spat. It went beyond that. Into the darkness of that desolate prairie. And down another goddamned fork in the road.

I ate another chip, the salsa dripping and running down the palm of my hand into my sleeve. Before she had that flat tire, if that was actually what had happened, was she going to turn on Country Road 14, or continue straight?

I pulled a pen out of my pocket and spread the napkin out flat. I was no artist, but the sketch gave me something to do other than spilling more salsa, and it helped organize my thoughts.

If Tammy had stayed on the state highway after she passed the Broken Spur Saloon she would have driven about fourteen miles before she reached the tiny hamlet of Regal. From there, Route 80 headed west toward Bisbee, Arizona. Eastward lay Deming, the border crossing at Columbus, or even El Paso. If Tammy had elected to go straight through Regal, she would have run into a dead end. The new border crossing was a mile beyond the ruins of the Nuestra Señora de Tres Lágrimas Mission. But it was a day entry only—at six P.M., the customs agents swung the gate shut and went home.

If she turned on County Road 14, she'd drive north through seven miles of some of the most desolate country that Posadas County had to offer, including scrambling up the face of San Patricio Mesa. After crossing County Road 27—if she planned to cross it and not turn east or west—she'd drive through the rugged canyon country for three more miles until she came to the gate of the Torrance ranch.

157

If Tammy was headed out to visit Patrick Torrance, that's where she'd turn off.

I rapped my pencil on the table and stared out the window. I had enough *if's* to keep an entire geometry class busy. But of one thing I was certain. Tammy Woodruff hadn't been headed for the Torrance ranch to see Pat. That particular cowpuncher was drinking himself sick at the Broken Spur Saloon when all those choices presented themselves to the young lady.

"Excuse me, sir." The waitress appeared with Don Juan's specialty, a mammoth platter of calories guaranteed to cure whatever was the matter with me. "Be careful, now," she said as she settled the creation in front of me. "It's hot."

The aroma from the meal drifted up to my nose just as my mental wheels kicked into gear.

Patrick Torrance must have seen Tammy Woodruff at the Broken Spur. The world was just too small for it to be any other way. I chewed the first delectable mouthful and my eyes started to water from the initial blast of chili. Tammy would have seen the young buckaroo's truck parked there and she would have stopped—and maybe later they'd had an argument and she had gone spinning gravel out of the parking lot, maybe fishtailing a little, maybe cutting a corner, maybe spiking a wheel on an old piece of rebar hiding in the grass.

All that was conjecture. But by the second bit of burrito, I realized what was *not* conjecture.

When news of the shooting spread to the bar, via a babbling Francisco Peña, the place emptied. That was the ghoul in folks. If there was a little blood, they would turn their heads and gawk. But a lot of blood was an irresistible magnet that would pry even the most dedicated barfly off his bar stool, especially since the cops—living ones, that is—hadn't arrived yet.

So the patrons of the Broken Spur had adjourned to marvel at all the holes someone had punched in Paul Enciños and Linda Real. They had watched Paul Enciños bleed to death, and were willing to do the same for Linda.

158

But Victor Sánchez and Patrick Torrance both told the same story. Patrick had not joined the crowd down at the scene of the shooting. He'd stayed at the bar, as if he knew all along what he might find down the road.

My appetite vanished as my pulse raced. If my old slow brain could figure it out, Estelle Reyes-Guzman's would have clicked hours before.

I pushed myself out of the booth, dropped a twenty-dollar bill on the table so that the waitress wouldn't think that I'd been insulted by the burrito, and hustled outside. The air was cold, with a nasty wind building from the west. If Estelle had driven out early that afternoon to talk with Pat Torrance, she was having a hell of a long conversation with a taciturn cowboy.

23

THE western side of Posadas County was split by a four-tined fork of major highways. The county couldn't have afforded to maintain two miles of any of them. The interstate slashed through the county from one side to the other, with one interchange for the village. Two of the state highways snaked into town to converge at that interchange—State 56 headed southwest to Regal and State 17 roughly paralleled the interstate.

Further to the north, State 78 entered the county from the hamlet of San Pasquale to the east, edged around the bottom of the mesa, sped by the airport, and then swung northwest.

If you imagined those highways—three state and one interstate—as the four tines of a fork, then County Road 14 was like a tangled hair connecting the tines at the midpoint.

I drove out State Highway 17, knowing that if I turned south at County Road 14, Herb Torrance's ranch would be only five miles of jouncing gravel road away. Shortly before seven, I pulled into a narrow lane that passed under an arched, wrought-iron gate. The H-bar-T spread was ten-thousand acres of grazing land leased from the Forest Service and Bureau of Land Management, tacked onto the original 160 acres Herb's father had bought in 1920.

If there was a moon that night, it was hidden behind the clouds that earlier had gathered over the San Cristobals and now fanned

160

out across the entire sky. Herb had every light in the house turned on as I approached.

The original Torrance home had burned to the ground on a summer Sunday in 1956, and Herb and his father had done the expedient thing. They'd bulldozed the ashes into a big pit, covered it with topsoil, and planted a garden. The new house, one of those things with too many tiny gables, pitches, and angles, was purchased from the Sears catalog and planted a few yards further up the slope of the mesa.

Estelle's car was not in the driveway. Herb's huge pickup, crusted with mud from front grill guard to back bumper, was angled in, crowding his wife's brown boat of a sedan against the white picket fence. If Patrick's truck was there, it was hidden out back.

I buzzed down the window and left 310 idling with the radio on when I got out. With all the mesas and canyons, radio reception on this side of the county was uniformly awful, but old habits were hard to break.

Herb had solved the reception problem. Squatting in the middle of his front yard was one of those enormous satellite dishes that allowed him access to 150 channels of what passed for entertainment. By the time I'd let myself through the small swinging gate and skirted the antenna, Herb Torrance was standing in the front doorway, framed by the light.

"Well, I'll be," he said by way of greeting. "You're just in time for some dessert."

I grunted my way up the six steps to the high front porch and shook Herb's hand. "How are you, Herb."

"Fine, fine. Come on in." He held the door for me but I shook my head.

"I can't stay. Has Detective Reyes-Guzman been by today?"

Herb frowned and then remembered. "Oh, the young gal. The one who looks like she ought to be in the movies."

"Right. Has she been by?"

Herb scratched the top of his head like his monumental memory was somehow stuck. "No, not that I know of. The wife was in town

161

most of the afternoon shopping, and I was workin' in back, in the shop. So, you know, she might have stopped and didn't think anyone was to home."

"How about the kids?"

He shook his head. "Three youngest were in school all day. Benny went over to Deming with a load of hay. Ain't seen Patrick since yesterday." He didn't sound pleased about the latter, and he carefully shut the door, as if he didn't want our words to filter into the house for the wife and kids to hear.

"What the hell happened down south, there, Bill. Where that young cop got shot."

"We don't know yet, Herb. That's why the detective wanted to talk with Patrick. He was at the Broken Spur Sunday night."

"The officers already talked to him," Torrance said. "Every which way. He's so tore up he don't know what to think."

"And I'm sure we'll have to talk with him again, Herb."

"You think it was just somebody passin' through?"

"We just don't know, Herb. Sometimes folks remember things, you know. Little things that they didn't think of right off. That's what the detective was hoping was the case with your son. That he'd remember something more. Maybe just some little thing."

"Well," Herb said, "I guess."

"But you say she hasn't been by."

"Not that I know of, no."

"Well, then I'll leave you in peace." I started down the steps and stopped halfway. "By the way, when Patrick goes down to the Broken Spur, does he go by himself, or with somebody, usually?"

"Oh, it just depends," Herb said, and he joined me as I walked back toward the patrol car. "But he sure goes there too much," he added with chagrin. "Kind of concerns his mother and me. He's got an older brother and an uncle both who can't stay away from the stuff. And Patrick's been awful moody of late."

"Moody?"

Herb waved a hand in dismissal. "Ah, you know how these young ones get." He looked at me and grinned. "I think he's got woman trouble. Mind you, the wife and I don't pry." He groped a cigarette out of his pocket and turned his back to the breeze while he lit it.

"Who's he been squiring around?" I asked pleasantly, as if it were just a passing thought.

"You name it," Herb said. "Anything with tits, at his age." He held the door of 310 while I settled into the seat. "The one he's really moonin' after at the moment is that little gal from town. The one who used to be hitched up real tight with Gus Prescott's boy?"

"Tammy Woodruff?"

"Sure," Herb said. "I guess Brett cut her loose, and now Patrick's givin' it a turn." He smiled again and patted the door of 310. "Or tryin' to. He tried once before, seems to me. Sure as hell glad I don't have to go through none of that anymore."

"Amen," I said, and pulled 310 into reverse. "But you haven't seen him today?"

Torrance ducked his head. "No. He sometimes stays with a friend, or somethin' like that. Him and Benny used to light out to Juarez once in a while, but if that's where he went, then he went by himself."

I grinned. "These kids are kind of hard to keep track of, aren't they."

"You got that right. But hell, he's on his own now. I don't pry. Long as the work gets done when he's livin' at home."

I took my foot off the brake, and 310 started to drift backward. Torrance straightened up. "If the detective does stop by later this evening, tell her to call the office, will you?" I said.

"You bet."

" 'Preciate it. You take care."

I idled the car slowly out the Torrance driveway, and as I left the circle of light from the house, the blackness was formidable. In the distance, over the mesa to the east, was the dull glow of Posadas, just enough to be noticed out of the corner of the eye. A single light flickered in the west, over where Francisco Peña and his family lived.

I drove south on County Road 14 for two miles until I reached the intersection with County Road 27, another rough gravel byway that cut through the heart of the lava flow. I continued south, idling along 14 as it zigzagged down through first one arroyo and then another.

After five miles I started up the incline of San Patricio Mesa. The road was narrow and rock-strewn, steep enough that the patrol car kicked gravel noisily, lurching now and then as the back tires scrabbled for traction. If the county had ever brought a road grader out here, it hadn't been in the past six months.

I reached the top of the mesa, and if there had been moonlight, I could have seen the graceful C-curve sweep as the road paralleled the lip of the mesa, to descend on the other side to the flat brush country that was cut by State 56.

I stopped for a moment, looking out into the blackness. If Patrick Torrance cared enough about booze that he took this road frequently to the Broken Spur, then his father had every reason to be concerned.

"Three ten, three oh two."

I damn near banged the top of my head against the roof.

"Jesus," I said, and reached for the mike. "Three oh two, go ahead."

"Are you on top of the mesa?" Estelle's voice was quiet, but I recognized the scratchy, thin quality of a handheld radio. Her broadcast wouldn't carry two miles before it would be bounced to death in the myriad canyons that cut the mesa side.

"Ten-four. Where the hell are you?"

"Sir, drive around the rim until you see my car. It's pulled way in, behind a grove of piñon. I'm down the hill from that."

"What are you doing?"

There was a moment's hesitation. "I've got a little problem, sir."

24

No lights flickered down in the black hole formed by the curve of the mesa rim. In several places the road skirted the very edge. When the road had been made in the 1930s, the dozer operators must have had fun watching the cottage-sized rocks plunge down the hill, smashing piñon and juniper, shedding chunks, and finally shattering into a million pieces.

Now and then through openings in the trees I could see two lights flickering out on the prairie, far in the distance. One was the Broken Spur to the southeast. The other was so far away I could only catch the flicker out of the corner of my eye—maybe Gus Prescott's place north of Moore.

I slowed 310 to an idle and buzzed down both front windows. The winter air was dry and cold, the wind strong and steady from the northwest.

"My car's just ahead of you, in that piñon grove to your right."

I switched my radio to the car-to-car channel so I wouldn't blast my side of our curious conversation all over the county.

"And where are you?" I asked.

"Down the hillside about a hundred yards."

"Shine your flashlight."

Silence for about six heartbeats followed, and then Estelle said, "I don't have it with me, sir."

A moonlit walk would be one thing, but the night was moon-feeble at best. With my heart driven up into my throat by apprehension, I drove 310 as close to the edge as I could and swiveled the spotlight around so the beam stabbed into the darkness. The rock slope plunged down at sixty degrees or better, a long slide of granite and steel-gray tree fragments. Fifty yards down from the road cut a spine of rock outcropping jutted from the talus slope, its form softened by a stand of ponderosa pine and scrub.

"A little to the south, sir," Estelle said. "By the trees." I drifted the beam across the slope and into the pines, then worked up toward where the spine first erupted from the slope. I saw motion at the same time that Estelle said, "Right here."

In the wash of light from the spotlight, I could make out a tiny figure. She waved a hand. I jammed the gear lever into park, stamped down the parking brake, and got out of the car for a better view. The place was enough to give me the willies in broad daylight, much less on a February night with the wind beginning to moan up through the trees.

"What have you found down there?" I asked.

"Nothing right here, sir," she said.

"Are you all right?"

The hesitation told me she wasn't, but after a moment she said, "I just sprained my ankle. It's kind of slow going."

"So you aren't all right," I muttered, and then said into the radio, "How long have you been here?"

"Since about three o'clock."

I groaned. With my flashlight in one hand and the handheld radio in the other I walked along the edge of the slope, searching for a route down through the rocks. When I was directly above Estelle's position I pointed the flashlight downhill. She was so far away the narrow beam was lost in the glare of the spotlight.

"I'm going to call rescue, Estelle. Are you going to be all right for a few more minutes?"

"Yes."

"Are you bleeding?"

Another pause, and then she said, "No. Really, I just sprained my ankle. I can't put any weight on it, so I can only come up the hill one rock at a time."

"All right, now listen," I said, as if she had much choice. "It's going to take me a while to get down there. In the meantime, just sit still. Stop trying to move. I'll radio the EMTs, so they'll be on the way."

I started back toward 310. "I don't think you should come down here, sir," Estelle radioed. I almost chuckled. Hell, I didn't think so, either. But it would be close to an hour before the EMTs could reach her. A lot could happen in an hour. She'd been stranded on that hillside for half a day. Hurt as she was, her reserves had to be about shot.

"I'll be careful," I replied.

"Sir, before you do anything, you need to make sure that the shoulder of the road is secured from the spot just south of where I've parked all the way back to where the road goes into the trees."

"We'll worry about that later, Estelle. Let me get rescue on the way."

"Sir . . ." her tone was sharp enough to stop me in my tracks.

"Go ahead."

"Sir, all the way at the bottom of this rock slide, a hundred yards below me, there's a pickup truck, or what's left of one. I don't think your light will carry far enough, but if you drive forward and park right behind my car, you may be able to catch a glimpse of it with your spotlight. Don't drive along the edge any farther, though. You'll obscure the tracks."

"A recent wreck, you mean?"

"Yes, sir. I got close enough to see that it was a late model white over blue Ford. I almost got close enough to see the license plate before I fell. I think it's Tammy Woodruff's."

I sagged against the door of 310 for a minute and cursed a long, eloquent string. Then I used the car's boosted radio to call dispatch.

Gayle Sedillos was working, so I only had to say things once. Posadas County Search and Rescue would arrive in forty minutes, close on the heels of a Posadas County EMT unit. I had asked for a silent approach, no lights, no siren. I didn't want a million extra feet trampling the evidence.

I told Gayle to dispatch Sergeant Torrez. I glanced at my watch. Even if Bob had been waiting with the nose of his patrol car pointed in the right direction, it would still take him nearly thirty minutes to reach us.

I picked up the handheld radio. "Estelle, help's on the way. How are you doing?"

"All right, sir."

She didn't sound all right. My imagination heard her voice fading and distant. I pulled the large first-aid kit from the trunk of the car and slung the strap over my shoulder. With that and a blanket tucked under my arm, I stood on the road, looking down the hill. There was no easy way.

"One rock at a time," I said aloud, and stepped off the road's crumbling shoulder.

It would have been a hell of a lot easier without so much belly preceding me. The spotlight from the patrol car created hard, razor-edged shadows. Part of the rock was illuminated as brightly as noon, while the backside, the side waiting to receive a foot or hand, was pitch black. The bottom half of my bifocals swam the shadows together until finally, with a curse of irritation, I stopped, snatched off my glasses, and stuffed them in my shirt pocket.

After fifty feet, I was breathing hard. I stopped and peered ahead. Somehow, Estelle's tiny figure, a little lump against the gray of the rocks, didn't look any closer.

I slid the radio out of my belt holster. "Be patient," I said.

"Yes, sir."

I took a deep breath and leaned against a rock, shifting with a grunt when one of its razors dug into my elbow. "How did you know it was me driving by?" I asked.

168

Even the lousy metallic filter of the radio couldn't completely wash away the soft warmth of her voice. "No one drives the way you do, sir." She didn't elaborate.

It took another twenty minutes for me to descend, one rock at a time, to within conversational distance of Estelle. I took another short breather. This time, Estelle's voice drifted over the rocks without radio delivery.

"I'm sorry for all this," she said.

"Me, too," I replied, and promptly stumbled as a small, angular rock turned under my foot. My arms flailed as I windmilled for balance and the handheld radio went flying off into the darkness. I cursed and dropped into a crouch to shift my center of balance downward. "No worry," I said, breathing in gasps. "What's an eight-hundred dollar Motorola more or less." I flipped the beam of my flashlight back and forth, but didn't see the radio.

With one hand uphill as a prop and the other clutching the first-aid kit and blanket, I stumbled the final yards to Estelle's position. She was sitting with one leg drawn up, arms clasped around her knee, and the other leg stretched out downhill.

"Jesus," I said when the beam of the light touched her face. Her left cheek, eye, and forehead were a mass of sticky, dried blood. She held up her right hand defensively as I reached out to push her hair to one side, then held still while I examined her head. "No blood, huh," I said. "That's quite a gash you've got there above your eyebrow."

"I did an Olympic-quality cartwheel," she said, and managed a lopsided grin.

"Did it knock you out?"

She shook her head once from side to side. "I wish it had. It would have hurt less. I did a pretty good job on my right ankle. That's why I fell. A rock turned, and I pitched off-balance downhill."

I swung the flashlight down. She was wearing blue jeans and a black version of the sturdy waffle-soled oxfords that nurses wear.

"Great hiking shoes, doll," I muttered.

"I didn't plan any of this, sir."

"Let me look," I said, and even a gentle touch that was only enough to move her jean cuff upward brought a flinch. I was no orthopedist, but I knew in what general direction a foot hanging off the end of an uninjured leg should point. Hers didn't.

"Nah, it's not sprained," I said, then added, "busted into a million tiny pieces, maybe. But definitely not sprained."

"That's good news."

I stood up and watched as she slowly brought her right arm back up around her knee, her hand holding her left arm just above the elbow.

"Arm, too?"

She nodded wearily. "I caught my left elbow on a rock. It's all right. Just hurts."

The EMTs were on the way, and I didn't want to make a mess for them. The only painkiller in the first-aid kit was aspirin, and Estelle was far beyond the aspirin level. After tucking the blanket around her shoulders, I sat down beside her. "The folks will be here in just a minute," I said, and even as I did I could hear the howl of a big V-8 working its way up County Road 14.

"That sounds like Bob Torrez," Estelle whispered.

"You can tell all of us by how we drive?" I put my arm around her shoulders and she leaned against me.

"You idle," she said. "I think you're the only person who's driven every road of this county at an idle."

"That's my best thinking speed," I said. I lifted my flashlight and pointed it downhill, but the trees on the rock spine blocked my view. "The truck's on the other side?"

"All the way at the bottom," Estelle said. "On its top." She tried to shift position and a little gasp escaped. "I was within fifty yards of it when I fell, sir."

I looked at Estelle in astonishment. "You managed to climb this far back up with a busted ankle, cracked head, and bent elbow?"

"I didn't want to spend the night, sir." She turned her head and looked up the hill. "Another couple of hours and I would have made it."

"Yep," I said. "That would have been a long couple of hours." I flashed my light downhill again. "You think it's Tammy's truck?"

"I'm positive, sir."

"How did you see it?"

Estelle sat forward, resting her back. "I decided I needed to talk with Pat Torrance. I was driving up the county road really slowly . . ."

"Idling?"

"Yes, sir. I saw tracks going off the shoulder of the roadway. Nothing deep. No skid marks or anything. Just straight and true." She imitated the trajectory with her right hand. "So I stopped and got out. I didn't see it right away, but when I walked along the road a bit, I could just see the glint of shiny paint. The tailgate is facing uphill."

"And so you decided to climb down and check."

"Yes, sir. At three in the afternoon, it didn't look so steep."

I took a deep breath. "Well, if she's in it . . ."

"I think she is, sir. Just before I fell, I saw what I think was a piece of colored cloth. That's when I got excited and didn't pay attention to where I was putting my feet."

"While we're sitting here waiting, here's another grim thought for you to consider. I'm here because I drove out to the Torrance ranch myself. Nobody had heard from you, and I figured that was the most likely place to look."

"That's where I was going."

"True enough. I talked to Herb Torrance. Among other things, he hasn't seen Patrick since sometime yesterday."

The rumble of Bob Torrez's patrol car bounced off the side of the mesa as the vehicle emerged from the trees and slowed to a stop in the middle of the road. He switched on the red lights briefly, creating a psychedelic pulse against the surrounding rocks and trees.

"If Pat Torrance is involved in some way," Estelle said slowly, "then the odds are good that either he put that truck down there, or . . ."

"Or he's in it," I finished for her, standing up.

Estelle thumped her right fist against the flat surface of the rock. "Damn, damn, damn . . ." she groaned, and I knew what she meant. Being left out of the chase was more painful than any fracture.

25

"Looks like one occupant." Bob Torrez's voice was matter-of-fact over the radio. He'd scrambled down the talus slope like a sure-footed youngster, checked on the two of us briefly, and then continued on.

For a few minutes we had been able to see his flashlight beam slashing this way and that as he traversed the boulder field, but then the trees hid him from view.

"Can you ID?" I asked.

"Oh, yeah," Torrez said, and I knew exactly what he was going to say before he said it. "It's Tammy Woodruff." I wasn't ready for what he said next. "And she's still alive, sir."

"Oh, my God," I breathed. That option had never occurred to me, and judging from Estelle's quick intake of breath, not to her either. "Is she conscious, sergeant?"

"Negative. Hold on a minute." As Estelle and I sat in the dark cold, we could hear vehicles coming up the county road. "Sir, she's inside what's left of the cab. It's twisted around her pretty good. It's going to take a lot of cutting to get her out of there."

"Rescue is just arriving now. They'll be down in a few minutes. Stay with her, Bob."

"Tell 'em to bring both the jaws and a saw. They're going to have to cut through a piece of frame to get to her."

173

More winking lights lined the road above us, and I stood up and waved my flashlight.

"Sheriff, what the hell are you doing down there?" Sam Gates's voice was a welcome sound as it crackled over Estelle's radio.

"Sam, we're going to need two Stokes. One where I am for a patient with multiple fractures and cuts, and one farther on down the slope. Do you see the deputy's light?"

"You're kidding."

"No. And you'll need both the jaws and a saw. There's a vehicle down there, and it's going to be a puzzle."

"Jesus," Gates said, never particularly mindful of the FCC. "Occupant's still alive?"

"Affirmative."

Bob Torrez interrupted. "Pulse is 130 and ragged. Respiration is shallow and uneven. Hustle it up, guys."

Estelle moaned a single syllable and then bit it off. I pulled part of the blanket around her shoulders and tried to pad the rest between her back and the rock against which she was leaning. "Just a bit longer," I said.

She shook her head. "They need to go on down to the truck."

"No heroics now," I said. "They know what they're doing. They'll have both of you out of here in no time."

Which, as it turned out, wasn't the case at all. Cassie Gates arrived first, breathing like a locomotive and carrying enough luggage to stay a week. "Look at this place," she said, as she searched for a level spot to spread her paraphernalia. "God, how I love it. Sweetheart, couldn't you have found a steeper cliff to dive off of? Let me see what you did, now."

I backed away, giving the EMTs room. Cassie was joined almost immediately by two members of the Search and Rescue crew, another young EMT I didn't know, and Nelson Petro. The last time Nels had been with us was when he ran the cherry picker for Estelle down on the state highway. He looked a little unsure about this mess.

I could see a flow of lights angling down the talus slope toward the wreck below. A gentle nudge from one of the EMTs pushed me farther out of the way. There was nothing I could do but shut up and watch, giving them lots of elbow room. Their efficiency left me feeling all thumbs and stupid.

Cassie had a BP cuff on Estelle, and in short order she was evaluated and immobilized on the Stokes with her lower leg and foot encased in one inflatable splint and her left arm in another. Radio reception back to Posadas was blocked by the mesa, but one of the S and R folks up on the road served as a relay.

Even Velcroed in as tight as she was, Estelle still let out a single gasp and clenched her teeth when the six men picked up the Stokes and the guide rope tightened. It was going to be a hell of a long ride to the top.

Longer still for Tammy Woodruff. By the time Estelle's litter had progressed to within fifty feet of the road, the first generator fired up. In rapid succession, 500-watt quartz floods snapped on, bathing the hillside in white light. Another generator was on its way down the hill. I watched the four men horsing it down over the rocks and felt a wave of exhaustion. I sat down on a convenient rock to catch my breath.

I heard the boots on rocks behind and above me, but ignored them, content to sit in the dark cold and watch.

"Sir, are you all right?" It was one of the EMTs. I turned my head and watched him crab across the jumble of loose, football-sized talus that twitched and turned under his boots like a living thing.

"Yeah, I'm all right."

With a cough, the second portable generator sprang into life and more light blossomed. I still couldn't see the wreck, so I gestured across the slope. "I'll make my way over that way," I said.

The EMT glued himself to my elbow, and after about the fourth assist, I felt like an old maid trying to cross a busy street.

"Shouldn't you be helping down the hill?" I said at one point as I stopped to catch my breath.

175

"I'm fine," he said.

I turned and pointed my flashlight at his name tag. "Curtis, I don't need an escort."

He grinned. Of course he wasn't short of breath. "I'd sure hate to be on this cliff by myself in the middle of the night, sir. Think of it as your escorting me." He was a foot taller than I was, fifty pounds lighter, and a century younger. He could have carried me up the hill and still had that grin on his face when he reached the top. "Cross over to those ropes and they'll be a help to the top, sir."

I had wanted to cross the talus slope for a better view of what was happening down below, not to be dragged up the hill. But I realized that what the kid said made sense. They needed me down at the wreck about as much as they needed another broken leg. I stopped and looked up the hill. Those hundred yards were leagues.

"Shit," I said. "You think they're going to call a chopper?"

"No, sir."

I leaned against a rock with my hands on my knees. "Too windy?"

"Yes, sir. For a while I thought they might, but not with the wind gusting to twenty knots. It's just too risky."

We'd progressed far enough past the spine of trees that I could see the wreck site down below. The image was surreal, with the artificial white light bathing the gnarled piñon and juniper. A cascade of sparks shot into the sky as the steel-cutting saw chewed into the pickup carcass, and I could hear the scream of it echo off the mesa wall behind us.

"She's been crushed in that thing for maybe two days, Curtis."

"That's what I heard. It's a miracle that she's alive at all. I guess that's another reason Sam won't ask for a chopper. The odds are pretty stacked against her. It doesn't make it a good gamble to risk a helicopter crew on a night like this."

I took a deep breath and pushed myself upright. "Let's get this miserable job over with, Curtis."

"Yes, sir. Are you sure you're feeling all right?"

I chuckled in spite of myself. "No, Curtis, I'm not feeling all

176

right. Just stick close." It wasn't the climb I dreaded so much. Or another sleepless night. It was facing two old friends and telling one of them that his daughter was smashed to pieces . . . and telling the other that every circumstance pointed right down his son's tracks.

26

WHEN I stepped off the last treacherous rock and onto the solid, comforting gravel of County Road 14, I would have taken a great breath and sighed with relief if I had had the energy. Instead, I settled on the convenient tailgate of one of the search and rescue trucks. I was dirty, unshaven, and had a rent in my trousers—I looked like an old derelict who didn't have the gumption to face the trash cans down the alley one more time.

The activity was a blizzard around me. I was too tired even to pretend that there was something I could do to help.

The night wind had changed direction, beginning its dawn cycle. This mesa top should have been a beautiful, quiet place. There should have been a potpourri of aromas to enjoy other than diesel and small-engine exhaust. There should have been quiet night sounds other than radios, engines, shouts, shrieks of metal-cutting blades, and the groaning of bending metal forced apart by steel jaws.

Lots of things *should* have been. Tammy Woodruff should have been home in bed, curled around a good boyfriend, not crunched up and squashed inside the grotesque wreckage of her pickup truck.

Behind me, Deputies Tom Mears and Tony Abeyta tried to make sense of the tracks left by Tammy's truck. Apparently, she had managed to drive up the winding county road without incident until she reached a point just before the road opened up on top. After rounding a tight, decreasing radius curve, the road passed between a limestone outcropping and a thick grove of scrub oak.

Sprayed gravel and a deep gouge in the trunk of one of the five-inch oaks showed that someone—probably Tammy—had lost it on that corner and strayed into the brush. She'd had time to correct and cuss a couple of times before she broke out on top.

And then, like a straight and true missile, her truck had drifted to the right, with no signs of swerving or correction, until the right front wheel dropped over the rocky edge. Even if she'd been sober, at that point there was nothing she could have done to save herself.

The gouges in the road's shoulder showed that her truck had executed a slow roll to the right, with the first flip sheering off the passenger-side mirror. Mears found the mirror lying wedged between two boulders within fifty feet of the road. After that, it was impossible to tell exactly what gyrations the vehicle had executed as it tumbled down the talus slope, shedding bits and pieces as it went.

The total distance from last contact with the county road to the truck's resting spot in the scrub trees at the bottom measured 346 yards. Three and a half football fields. And Tammy Woodruff, twenty-three years old and 105 pounds, had survived it all.

She had to know the circumstances that prompted her lonely drive up County Road 14, but maybe she wouldn't be able to remember how she'd come to drift that shiny, year-old truck too far to the right. And if she was lucky, she wouldn't remember a damn thing about that never-ending flight down the talus slope.

A dark, uniformed figure appeared at the side of the truck on which I was sitting. I turned and recognized Deke Merriam, one of the enforcement officers for the Forest Service. This mesa top was their turf, even though the tallest tree on it couldn't skin twenty feet.

"Why aren't you down there, Deke?"

He snorted. "Why aren't you?"

"I was. Well, part way. I saw enough."

He groped in his shirt pocket and pulled out cigarettes. I watched

179

him light one, and smelled the first waft of smoke that the night air thoughtfully brought to me.

Down slope, a new shower of sparks shot a dozen feet into the air. "It looks like they're going to have to cut that truck into a million pieces to get her out," Merriam said.

"Looks like," I agreed. "It's wadded up pretty good."

"What was the deal, anyway? She was speeding, or what? One of the guys said it was the Woodruff girl from town."

"It was, and we don't know. She's got a boyfriend out in these parts."

"What, on up . . ." Merriam made gestures toward the north.

I nodded. "Right. One of the Torrance boys."

"They know about this?"

"I don't think so."

"When did this happen? You figure that out?"

I shook my head and leaned an arm on the side of the truck bed. "We just don't know for sure."

"How did you happen on it?"

"One of our detectives was out this way."

Deke Merriam grinned. He knew the size of our department, and knew every soul onboard. We only had one detective. "Estelle found it?"

"Yes."

"What the hell was she doing out here in the middle of the night?"

I didn't bother to tell him that it hadn't been the middle of the night when Estelle had seen the vehicle. "She was detecting, Deke. That's what we pay her to do. Detect."

"All this is tied in with the shooting, somehow, eh?"

Deke wasn't as stupid as he liked to sound most of the time. "We think so," I said.

He carefully ground out the cigarette on the tailgate, then walked around, opened the driver's side door, and put the butt in the ashtray. Perhaps the owner wouldn't mind.

"I'm surprised she wasn't thrown out," he mused, returning to

180

lean against the truck with one boot heel hooked on the edge of the tire tread. "All that twisting and crushing is bound to spring the doors and shatter all the glass. Even the seat brackets can snap off when the cab twists. Maybe she was wearing her seat belt. But hell, even them sometimes fail."

I looked at Deke for a long moment, musing. "Let me bum one of your smokes, Deke."

"Why sure," he said, with generous alacrity. "I thought you quit."

"I did. Two years ago."

I took the book of matches he offered and thoughtfully peeled one off. The cigarette filter tasted chemical and sterile between my lips, bringing to mind the odd image of the ball of cotton a nurse uses to patch a hypodermic needle hole in a patient's arm. I lit the match, held it for an instant, then snapped it out. "Ah, maybe later," I said, and put the cigarette in my pocket.

"Tough hombre," Deke said.

"Yeah, I'm tough, all right. Thanks just the same."

Sergeant Torrez had already passed some initial information to me via the handheld. The wreckage, he said, despite the lapse of time between the crash and its discovery, still smelled like a liquor store to which someone had taken a baseball bat.

We knew something of Miss Woodruff's drinking habits. She drank until she was lit—that seemed to be the girl's standard operating procedure. If there was nothing else pressing to do, she'd drink herself unconscious.

With a grunt I reached around and slid Estelle's handheld radio out of my belt holster and keyed the switch.

"Torrez, Gastner."

I waited for ten seconds and then heard two quick bursts of squelch that told me Bob had heard me, had found a quick moment to reach around and tap his mike key a couple of times, and then had gone back to work.

"He'll respond when he can," I said, and set the radio on the tailgate beside my leg. In silence we watched, our vantage point fifty feet down the road from where the lines snaked out of the rescue truck's winch.

At 3:50, with dawn still hours away, we saw the tiny figures down the hill working around the Stokes litter. The radio beside me barked and I startled.

"This is Torrez."

"Bob, are they about to come on up?"

"Affirmative."

"How's she doing?"

"Not too good, sir. They stabilized her as best they could, but it doesn't look good."

"Not conscious?"

"No, sir."

"No sign of any other occupant of the vehicle?"

"No, sir. And if someone else was in the truck and was thrown out, they would've been found, with all the people up and down this thing."

"Ask him about the seat belt," Deke prompted me, and I frowned with irritation at being prompted.

"Bob, was she wearing her seat belt?" In the dark, on that mesa top, with the yawning talus slope in front of me, the question sounded ludicrous. If our local walkie-talkie conversation could be picked up by an avid scanner-ghoul with a humongous booster, he'd wonder about us for sure. Were we going to write the poor girl a ticket for not buckling up?

"Affirmative. One of the brackets broke sometime during the crash, but she had the belt on when she started out."

Deke Merriam nodded sagely. "Pays to buckle up," he said, with that curious graveyard humor that we all adopted at times when someone else was hurting the most—or was dead.

I keyed the radio again. "Bob, you're going to make arrangements to sift through everything down there come morning?"

"Affirmative."

"I'm going to follow the ambulance on into the hospital, then."

"Affirmative. Is Estelle all right?"

"Busted up some. She'll be okay."

The Stokes litter, with its six-man crew carrying it up behind the pull of the lead line, was already a quarter of the way up the slope.

I pushed off the tailgate and stood up. "Deke, thanks for the smoke. I'll talk with you tomorrow. We'll get all the paperwork to you just as fast as we can crank it out."

He grimaced and waved a hand.

With Tammy Woodruff on her way, I heaved a sigh of relief. Gayle Sedillos was working dispatch, and that meant the girl's parents had been notified. They'd be at the hospital, waiting. So would half of the world, probably. I wasn't in the mood to talk with any of them.

I walked—maybe shuffled would have been a better description—to 310 and edged the car out through the sea of vehicles. The ambulance carrying Estelle would be in Posadas already, but the second unit with Tammy Woodruff would be half an hour behind me. I had some time to think. I idled the patrol car down the county road, windows open.

I hadn't taken a formal survey, but I suspected that youngsters who got their kicks out of roping cattle or riding broncs, or even one-ton, evil-tempered bulls, wouldn't be too excited about strapping on a seat belt when they climbed into their mild-mannered pickup trucks.

It was hard to picture Wild Tammy carefully arranging her beer cans and whiskey bottles on the seat and floor of her truck, then diligently buckling herself in for the drive up County Road 14. Buckling herself in, guzzling all the way?

The dark mesa top didn't offer any answers. I reached the intersection with the state highway and stopped. In the five minutes I sat in the parked car, the stop sign large and gaudy in my headlights, no vehicle passed.

I knew that I needed to talk with Patrick Torrance, even though we had no direct evidence tying the young rancher with any of this mess. True enough, he'd chased after Tammy, maybe even caught her a time or two. True enough, he'd been at the Broken Spur the

183

night of the shooting, when Tammy somehow had gotten tangled in the barbed wire of her adventures. True enough, Patrick hadn't been home for a few hours, but at his age and pace, that was frequently the case.

I took a deep breath and turned out onto the state highway. Patrick Torrance was a nice enough kid. He hadn't come home last night. Most of the explanations for that were innocent enough. Most of them.

27

◆◆◆

Just west of Moore, a rough two-track road angled off to the north. Ranchers from up north used it once in a while as a shortcut to the feed store at the end of Arturo Mesa, but not often enough to discourage the sage, goat-heads, and kochia from flourishing in the center mound.

By taking the two-track, I could circle around first by the Prescott ranch and then by the Torrance ranch without driving through Posadas. I knew of one cattle gate I'd have to fuss with, where one of Gus Prescott's grazing allotments crossed the two-track. If I remembered correctly, the two-track skirted a windmill and stock tank less than a hundred yards behind Prescott's trailer.

The road would be slow going, but apparently even a broken and bruised Estelle Reyes-Guzman had noticed that idle speed was my most productive pace. The digital clock on the dashboard told me it was 4:37, still an hour and a half before dawn. A good time to go calling.

With the abandoned mercantile building looming large to my right, I turned off the state highway and bounced along for no more than a tenth of a mile before my headlights illuminated a sign that announced *End of County Maintenance.*

Dry sage rasped against the undercarriage of the patrol car, touched the hot catalytic converter, and released a pungent bouquet.

185

It was one of my favorite aromas. I had tried to explain it to Martin Holman once, but he'd just muttered something about his sinuses, looked miserable, and asked me to find some pavement.

After two miles of relatively flat prairie, the two-track plunged down into a sandy-bottomed arroyo. On occasion the Rio Salinas shared that arroyo, but not in late winter.

I stopped on the lip and turned the spotlight this way and that, convincing myself that the patrol car wouldn't high-center in the bottom of the arroyo or spin to a stop trying to climb out the other side. I shrugged. If ranchers could haul stock trailers up and out of this thing, the car wouldn't have any trouble. "Hell, why not," I said aloud, and nosed the heavy patrol car down into the arroyo.

Downhill was fine, and the two and a half car lengths across the bottom of the arroyo were almost smooth. The sedan made it halfway up the other side before I realized that idle speed wasn't going to cut it. I tapped the gas and the car slewed sideways as both back tires kicked sand and fine riverbed gravel. In an instant, instead of riding nicely on the high ground, the tires sank into the softer sandy ruts where trucks and rains had cut deep channels.

The frame whomped against something hard and the radials chuddered a burrow into the sand. The patrol car halted, skewed with its ass end pointing into space.

"Well, this is fine," I muttered, and slammed the gear lever into park. I got out and switched on my flashlight. What I saw didn't make me feel any better. If I tried to back up, there wouldn't be enough room to straighten out before the car slipped over the edge. Rocking back and forth would just bury the back tires deeper. I switched off the flashlight and sighed.

Ernie Wheeler was back on dispatch when I radioed in.

"PCS, three ten is ten-seven on Moore Road."

"Ten-four, three ten."

Wheeler had worked for us long enough to accept messages at face value, no matter how bizarre. He knew the county as well as anyone, but didn't waste time trying to figure out why I might be out of service on that ridiculous little road.

After a moment though, he did add, "Three ten, do you need assistance?"

"Negative."

I switched off the car, got out, and locked the doors. With the burbling engine killed, the night closed in silent and dark. I huffed up the last few feet out of the arroyo and plodded along the two-track, working hard to plant my feet carefully so I wouldn't crack an ankle. There was just enough light that, if I didn't look directly ahead, I could make out the road's path through what little vegetation the cattle hadn't found.

After a quarter of a mile, I pulled my jacket closer and hunched my shoulders. The night breeze was raw. Its cold seeped into the crevices, found the thin spots in my clothing, and ran up the hollow of my back.

The road skirted along the Rio Salinas's banks. Someone had tried to fence cattle out of the arroyo—God only knew why. Gus Prescott hadn't bothered to remove the old fence, worthless as it was.

A quarter mile of posts and wire meandered along the rim of the arroyo beside the road until I reached a spot where, perhaps fueled by a late summer cloudburst, the seasonal stream had gnawed out the bank and collapsed fifty yards of fence. The arroyo yawned black and bottomless to my left, and out of reflex I stepped into the opposite track of the road. If I fell into that pit, no one would ever find me . . . at least not soon enough for me to care.

A mile farther on, and just another mile south of State Highway 17, lay Gus Prescott's ranch. On a spring morning, it would have been a fifteen-minute stroll. In the heat of summer, dodging humorless rattlesnakes, maybe a ten-minute sweat. It took me half an hour that night, stumbling along like an old man with glass ankles.

Gus Prescott didn't share Herb Torrance's ranching success. He ran a small string of mongrel steers, trying to fatten them on good intentions and wishful thinking. But there simply wasn't enough water on his spread for more than his small herd. Morning and afternoon, he drove a school bus route that earned him a few extra bucks. His wife Gloria cashiered at Posadas Foodmart.

The apples of their eye were daughter Christine, who would have earned a 5.0 average if such a thing had been offered at Posadas High School and who was sailing through her second year at New Mexico State University, and her twin, Brett, a 20-year-old picture-book cowboy who'd never crossed tracks with the law. I didn't know much about him except by hearsay.

The past Friday night, Tammy Woodruff had backed her pickup into Brett's at the Broken Spur Saloon. Since Brett was under twenty-one himself, I'm sure his mama hadn't known where he was . . . or assumed that the lad was just at the saloon to drink soda pop and enjoy an NBA game on the big-screen television.

At any rate, Tammy's maneuver apparently was the end result of a tiff between the two kids. The lethal thought had been there, but she hadn't managed any damage, being too drunk to judge the speed and trajectory of her missile properly.

Sergeant Torrez had intervened, or who knew what else she might have done. The collision had apparently put the finis to Tammy and Brett's relationship, and she'd bounced on over in Pat Torrance's handsome direction.

Maybe the Torrance ranch was where she was headed, loaded down with booze, when her truck pitched over the edge of San Patricio Mesa. If so, she had decided not to wait for Patrick before beginning the party.

A fence loomed out of the darkness and I switched on my flashlight just long enough to find the closure side. I managed to open the barbed wire gate without bleeding, and just as I was closing it behind me, I heard the long, plaintive bellow of a cow calling for its calf. The windmill and stock tank were off to my left. Dark forms shifted and I veered away.

The Prescotts, either through poverty or choice, had elected not to blast their property at night with a sodium-vapor light. They preferred to take their chances with what ever illumination they were given naturally. I kept my flashlight off as I approached the mobile home, knowing full well that the fragrant, soft sand that my boots hit once in a while was not sand at all.

By the time I reached the spot where Gus Prescott's old Bronco, his wife's Pontiac, and Brett's big dualie ranch truck were parked, I could see that there was a light on somewhere in the bowels of the trailer. I breathed a sigh of relief. Something wet thrust into my hand and I jumped sideways, sucking air. One of Prescott's dogs looked up at me, wagging furiously.

"Christ," I said, and patted the Aussie sheepdog on the head. He dashed off toward the door of the trailer, ready to show me where the food was.

Gus Prescott answered my knock, his craggy face early morning puffy. He had a cup of coffee in one hand and a cigarette in the other.

"Damn," he said by way of greeting.

"Mornin', Gus," I said. He looked out past me, squinting. The first tracks of dawn were beginning to build in the east, and I pointed my flashlight out past his used car lot. "I walked," I added.

"Well, damn," he said again. He bent his lank, slightly stooped frame so that he could hold open the storm door. "From wheres?"

"Ah, I pulled a stupid and got myself stuck down in the arroyo."

He looked at me with wonder. "You walked from way down there?" I knew that walking more than two pickup truck lengths was wonderment in itself for a rancher. Two miles in the middle of the night damn near rivaled parting the Red Sea in Gus's miracle book.

"Yep. Is Brett to home? I was hoping maybe he could give me a pull with that truck of his."

"Well, sure." He beckoned me in. The sheepdog tried to follow, but Gus planted a boot in his path. The dog cringed, spun on his heels, and scampered down the steps. "He's just gettin' up. Let's get you a cup of coffee."

"I could use it," I said. I needed a tow, all right, but just as badly, I needed to talk with Brett Prescott. What I didn't need was a production. I got one anyway. And maybe it was my predawn constitutional, or maybe it was the peace and quiet of this spot of bare earth so removed from town, or maybe it was just the quiet, friendly, complete way the family included me in their morning rituals, but, whatever it was, the breakfast Gloria Prescott fed us tasted better than anything I'd eaten since God knows when.

Gloria was just as lean as her husband, her hair now steel gray. Her movements were deft and sure and graceful. The trailer was close to twenty years old, but looked like it'd been built the week before. She had kept it simple, with no taste for knickknacks or other fuss.

In one of those moments when nature works just right, Brett Prescott had inherited all the right genes from each parent. He had his mother's intense, intelligent green eyes and his father's shock of thick, reddish hair. And no amount of braces ever produced teeth as perfectly straight as his.

Once his mother had seated herself at the breakfast table, it was by some unspoken command that Brett became the waiter, refilling the coffee cups—always his mother's first—or fetching an ashtray for his father and himself. He talked just enough to be polite, and he called his father "sir." I liked the kid.

I could sense that both Gloria and Gus Prescott wanted to ask about the tragedies that were the talk of the town, but they skirted that conversation, careful to remain polite and gracious at a distance. I didn't volunteer to feed the grapevine, and I didn't tell them that we'd just pulled Tammy Woodruff's remains up a goddamned cliff.

Instead, we talked circles around all those troubles, hitting the weather past, present, and future, the condition of the range, the possibilities of the Washington folks raising the grazing fees on allotment land, even the record of the Posadas Jaguars. Eventually,

190

I wrapped my hands around a third cup of coffee, leaned my forearms on the table, and looked at Gloria Prescott.

"This was wonderful, ma'am," I said. "I haven't been able to relax like this in days. I need to get stuck more often, I can see that." I watched the smoke curl up from the tip of Gus's cigarette. His fingers were yellow from the nicotine, and between him and Brett, the ashtray was filling rapidly. "If I could talk Brett into giving me a hand for a few minutes, I'll be out of your hair."

Gus glanced at his watch. "I guess you got yourself plenty to do, sheriff." He pushed himself away from the table and got to his feet. "Brett, the chain's in the toolbox of the Bronco. I was usin' it yesterday to help Stubs move that pump."

Both husband and wife escorted me to the door of the trailer. "I banged up my hip some earlier, or I'd go on down with you," Gus said.

"No need," I replied quickly. "The car's not really stuck. I just don't have room to back up, and she'll spin herself in deeper if I go forward. A little pull is all it'll take."

"Well, have at 'er." He shook hands with me. "Old Brett there's a good hand. He'll get you squared away. And come on back when you can sit a spell." His faint smile told me that he had a good enough notion why I'd headed his way in the middle of the night, but it was plain that he trusted his boy.

"I appreciate it," I said, and the sheepdog escorted me to where Brett waited by the big pickup. We rumbled out of the yard and I started to get out when Brett stopped at the gate.

"Let me get it, sir," he said, and in a heartbeat he was out of the truck. He sprinted to the gate, snatched it open, and dove back into the truck with an alacrity that startled me. Just as quickly, he drove the truck through, stopped again, and repeated the procedure. I looked out the back window and saw the reason for his haste.

Thirty head of cattle had left the area near the stock tank and were herding toward the truck, eyes locked intently on the vehicle that they knew, deep down in their slow bovine brains, held the morning feed.

"They'll sure crowd the truck if you ain't careful," Brett said, and grinned. " 'Specially this time of day. They're smart. They don't ever bother Mom's car or even the Bronco."

We jounced across the prairie with the truck lugging along in fourth gear, valves rattling and screaming for a downshift that never came. The youngster apparently felt that once in top gear, the truck should stay there until the day's work was done. We reached the arroyo and Brett braked to a stop. He frowned.

"Well, that don't look too bad."

"It isn't," I said. "Just a little pull."

The chain was long enough to loop through the steel nerf bars on 310 that were welded to the frame under the front bumper, and Brett flipped the other end around the ball hitch of the truck. I started the patrol car, put it in drive, and breathed on the gas while the kid idled the pickup truck forward. And that's all it took.

"You going to go back the way you came, or head on up to Seventeen?"

I gestured ahead.

"Just bear left at the gate then. There ain't no bad spots to give you trouble."

I leaned against the fender of the idling patrol car. "Brett, I need to ask you a couple questions."

He reached out and put a hand on the black iron of the truck's stock rack. It was a casual thing, a "let's pass the time of day" gesture, but his face was watchful. He groped a cigarette out of his shirt pocket and lit it with an old fashioned Zippo lighter. "What about?" he said, exhaling.

"When was the last time you saw Tammy Woodruff, Brett?"

He drew hard. "Tammy?" His dark eyebrows gathered. "Friday night, I guess. When she got herself arrested."

"At the saloon?"

"Yes, sir."

192

I didn't ask what Brett had been doing there. "And that's the last time you saw her?"

"Yes, sir."

I folded my arms and settled my weight on the fender of 310. "You see much of Pat Torrance?"

Brett took a long, deep breath as he ground his unfinished cigarette out under a boot heel. I waited while he thought out what he wanted to say. Close as he was to his parents, his reticence told me he knew some things he hadn't discussed with them.

He traced a geometric doodle on the fat, fiberglass fender of the pickup. I pulled my jacket tighter and waited. He pulled out another cigarette and let it hang from his lips, unlit, as he flipped the Zippo over and over in his hand.

Finally he looked up at me, maybe checking to see if I'd left. What he saw was an old, fat, crew-cut Buddha, arms folded, sagging the car's springs, patient as all hell.

"Patrick came by Sunday night late. Mom and Dad was already in bed, but they know his truck, so they didn't say nothing."

"What time?"

"Close to midnight. He told me about the shooting and all."

"Had he been drinking?"

"Yes, sir. He was near to drunk. And scared."

"Scared? You know why?"

Brett chewed his upper lip. He was set to begin another thinking binge, and I told myself to be patient.

"He thought that maybe Tammy was involved somehow."

"In the shooting?" I tried to sound surprised, even though I knew damn well the young lady had been involved—somehow.

Brett Prescott nodded. "He said he'd seen her earlier in the evening. He said she'd stopped by the bar to show him something. They had some kind of fight and Patrick . . . he said Tammy left in a huff. Said she was in some new truck and spun gravel all the way across the parkin' lot, and damn near went into that empty field there just west of the bar."

193

It was like gluing little shards back together to reconstruct a shattered Indian pot.

"Why should all that scare Patrick?" I knew perfectly well that woman trouble could scare the most seasoned bull rider, but maybe there was something else.

"Him and Tammy had been together, and he said they'd . . . I mean that you, the police . . . he thought that you'd think he had something to do with it. Whatever trouble she was in."

"And you don't know what that trouble was?"

"No, sir, I don't."

"What did Patrick do then?"

"He just said he was goin' home, to think some."

"And you haven't seen him since?"

Brett Prescott shook his head. "Tammy neither."

I looked at the kid with sympathy. He'd find out sooner or later about his ex-girlfriend. I didn't want him thinking I'd been playing games. "Tammy's in the hospital, Brett. It doesn't look good."

He blinked rapidly. "In the hospital? For what?"

"She was in a wreck. Up on San Patricio Mesa. One of the deputies found her. They got her out sometime early this morning."

He looked at me cautiously. "Up on the mesa? She was with Patrick?"

"We don't know who she was with. Her truck went over the side. It was a long ride down, Brett. It looks like it happened sometime in the past twenty-four hours."

"She been drinkin?"

"Yes."

He took a deep breath and shook his head. "Ain't never met nobody like her, sheriff." He looked up at me. "Had to happen sometime." He retraced the figure in the dust on the truck's fender. "Does Patrick know?"

"We haven't been able to find him, Brett."

His finger stopped abruptly. "You're sayin' it was an accident, aren't you?"

"I didn't say, son. If you see Patrick before I do, tell him I'd like to talk with him. You'll do that?"

Brett Prescott nodded slowly.

I pushed myself off the fender of 310 and held out a hand. His work-rough grasp was strong. "Maybe you'll let me go on ahead. That way if I run into trouble, you'll be behind me."

"Sure thing." He didn't sound happy.

28

I knew what was going to happen long before I picked up the microphone and pushed the transmit button. Going missing for several hours wasn't going to endear me to the line of folks who were no doubt waiting to bend my ear. But the breakfast break had done me good. My head was clearer than it had been in hours.

I pulled the patrol car to a halt facing the stop sign on State 17. I flipped open my notebook, clicked my pen, and keyed the mike.

"PCS, Three ten."

"Three ten go ahead."

I glanced at my watch. Gayle Sedillos was back on the air. She was getting as little sleep as the rest of us.

"Three ten is ten-eight," I said.

She didn't ask me where I'd been, didn't ask what I'd been doing. Instead, she replied with a cryptic, "Ten-four, three ten." The radio went silent.

I closed my eyes, trying to picture Gayle sitting in front of the radio, telephone to her left, logs to her right, message file behind the microphone stand. I pictured her slender fingers rifling through the little slips of paper. I gave her to the count of ten. When I reached eight, the radio crackled and I grinned.

"Three ten, PCS."

"Three ten."

I could imagine her with a fistful of messages, considering which one to pick. Or maybe Sheriff Holman was standing at her elbow . . . or Captain Eschevera, wondering when in hell I was going to condescend to talk with him . . . or someone from the hospital . . . or . . .

"Three ten, ten-nineteen."

I sighed. "Ten-four. Ten minutes." Always politic, and always mindful of my irritation at messages that went out over the radio airwaves for anyone to hear, Gayle had taken the simple approach by shagging me back to the office where I could fight my own battles. I pulled out onto the highway and headed for Posadas.

Gayle saw me coming up the walk from the parking lot and met me at the door. She handed me half a dozen slips of paper, all with *While You Were Out* printed on the top. I reached out to take them, but Gayle held on to their collective corners until she was sure she had my attention.

"Sir, Sheriff Holman wants to see you before you do anything else. He said even before you read these." She released the messages and I fanned them out.

"Thanks," I said. "What's the word on Estelle?"

"Nasty cut on the left temple, broken bone in her ankle, and a torn left elbow tendon. She was released from the hospital just a few minutes ago. Francis took her home."

I nodded and was about to say something when Gayle added, "And she wants to talk to you." She pointed at one of the notes.

"But you weren't supposed to tell me that," I chuckled. "Thanks, Gayle. His majesty in his office?"

"Yes, sir."

I glanced at my watch. I could have counted on one hand the number of times Sheriff Martin Holman had been in his office before seven o'clock in the morning. Nine o'clock coffee with the *políticos* down at the Posadas Cafe on Third Street, yes. I pushed open the door of his office.

He was sitting behind his desk, swivel chair reared back, hands clasped behind his head, polished boots up on the corner of his desk.

His tie was pulled askew, and when he heard the door open, he opened one eye and surveyed me without moving another muscle.

I closed the door behind me.

"How do you do this?" he asked as the door latch clicked.

"Do what, sheriff?"

"How do you stay up all night long, all day long, all night long . . ." He let it drift off. I sat down in the padded leather chair in front of his bookcase.

I couldn't think of an intelligent reply, but Holman saved me the trouble. He tipped his head back and rubbed his right eye with one hand while he held his left hand straight up, as if he had just finished giving blood. "I want to go to bed," he said, and swung his feet down off the desk. The chair screeched as he leaned forward. For a minute I thought he was going to lay his head down on the desk blotter and pass out. But he stopped just short of that, hands folded in front of him.

"Tammy Woodruff died en route to Cruces," he said. "In the Medivac helicopter." He took a deep breath. "She made it for a whole goddamned day, and then couldn't hold on any longer, I guess."

"Did you talk with the family?"

Holman nodded and rubbed his eye again. "Got back about . . ." He glanced over at the wall clock. "About an hour ago, I guess. They're taking it hard. Especially the idea of an autopsy."

"Karl's aware of the law," I said.

Holman shot me a quick glance of reproof. "That doesn't make it any easier, Bill."

"I'm sure it makes it a good deal more difficult, knowing there are lots of questions about the circumstances of the girl's death."

"Francis Guzman is sure it was homicide." Holman leaned back again and folded his hands over his belly.

"I haven't had a chance to talk with him." One of the messages in my hand was from Estelle's husband.

"No," Holman said, holding up a hand. "I'm telling you. That's what he said. I talked to him at the hospital."

"What makes him think so?"

"Apparently he believes Tammy Woodruff's level of intoxication was too high for her to function in any conscious way. She could never have driven that truck. That's what he's saying."

I chewed on my lower lip, frowning. "So someone took her for a drive. Have you talked with Sergeant Torrez yet? What's he say?"

"No word yet. I sent the information out to the scene with Mears so they'd maybe have a little more direction in what to look for. I didn't want it out over the radio."

"Good." I looked down and fanned the messages. "What's Schroeder want, do you know?" The district attorney had called less than half an hour before—another banker's hours habit shot to hell.

Holman let a hand fall to the desk. "That's what I wanted to talk to you about. Listen." He sat up a little straighter and ticked off the points on his fingers. "The DA and the county attorney both want to see you about Sonny Trujillo. Eschevera wants to talk with you about Sonny Trujillo. I'm sure Trujillo's family is going to sue the county, the department, and you in particular for billions of dollars. Linda Real's mother wants to sue every one of us as well, but you in particular. More than that, of course, she wants to pin you down and waste half your day caterwauling about Linda, who's doing just fine, by the way. Except she can't remember anything else about the incident." Holman took a deep breath. "And the press, of course. Frank Dayan wants this and wants that, especially now that he figures we owe him."

"How do we owe him?"

Holman grimaced with irritation. "He turned over an entire set of photographic prints from the other night. He's been one hundred and ten percent cooperative." The sheriff waved a hand. "And this, and that. Now listen. I don't want you taking time with any of that shit."

I sat back, not bothering to hide the surprise on my face. "I wasn't planning on it, sheriff."

"No, I mean with *any* of it—not with the county attorney, not with Eschevera, not any of it. I want you full time on the Enciños case. Period. I'll run all the interference for you that you need. As far as I'm concerned, you aren't available to anyone, for anything." He leaned forward. "Estelle tells me that you all are close to this thing. That it's going to crack?"

I took a deep breath. "Martin, remember those thousand-piece jigsaw puzzles?" He nodded. "That's what we've got. It's starting to coalesce around the corners." I drew lacy curtains in the air with my fingers. "It's taking some form. But the entire middle section— the picture—is just a jumble of pieces. But one at a time. If Tammy Woodruff's death was a homicide—if we can find one little piece that tells us for sure that it was—then that's more of the puzzle."

"Gayle said you were out all night."

"Yes."

Holman waited a moment, and a smile slowly lit up his dark features. He held out a hand. "Do I get to know?"

"I was talking with Brett Prescott."

"That's the ranch out on Seventeen?"

"Yes."

"What did he have to say?" Holman prompted.

"Prescott was one of Tammy Woodruff's many flames, sheriff. But they broke up a few days ago. Remember when she backed into the Prescott kid's truck out at the Broken Spur? Well, that was the wrap-up, I guess. The girl went after Pat Torrance on the rebound. We know that young Patrick was at the Broken Spur the night of the shooting. Brett Prescott says that Patrick came to his house afterward, scared all to hell. And now it looks like a reasonable guess that Tammy was on her way to Patrick Torrance's place when her truck went over the edge of San Patricio Mesa."

"What's the Torrance kid say about that?"

"He doesn't. We don't know where he is."

Holman leaned back, his mouth snapping shut. After five squeaks of the chair, he said, "Well, I'll be damned."

"Yep."

"Have you put out a want for him?" I nodded and Holman pursed his lips and whistled a tuneless series of notes. "Why do you think she was headed that way?"

"I don't know."

"What time of day was it when she went over the edge, have you figured that out?"

"No."

Holman whistled some more, eyebrows knit. "Then Patrick Torrance is the key."

"He may be."

"Shit, Bill, we've got to have something on this. We've got to have something definite."

I shrugged. "We don't. Maybe the Torrance kid is a key, like you say. When we find him, we'll know."

"And what about the truck? The white one that Tammy was supposedly driving Sunday night. The one that Linda Real says that Tammy was driving."

"No trace."

"Maybe Linda was mistaken."

"That's possible. It's unlikely, but possible."

Holman rubbed his face with both hands as if all the cobwebs of this case were tightening around his brain. "God, I hate this," he said finally. "I feel like someone is playing games with us. Making us look stupid."

"Yep."

He shot a withering glance at me. "What's next?"

I fanned out the messages. "Before I circle back out to the Torrance ranch, I want to talk with Estelle."

"She's busted up pretty badly."

"I know. But her brain isn't. And I want to talk with Linda Real again, if I can slip into the hospital without a ruckus. And before I do that," I said, holding up one of the notes, "I'd better return this call."

The note said that Donni Weatherford had called at 4:35 A.M. That was puzzling, as was the telephone number.

"Maybe they left something behind," Holman said.

"It would have to be something mighty important to bother calling here at that hour."

"Maybe she forgot her husband."

I chuckled. "Maybe." I walked down the hall to my own office and closed the door. After dialing, I waited while circuits connected. After three rings the receiver was lifted and a cheerful young voice said, "Western Court Motel. This is Sally. How may I help you?"

"I'd like to speak with Donni Weatherford, please."

"Just one moment." I heard muffled voices and paper rustling, and then the cheerful voice said, "May I ask who's calling, please?"

"Undersheriff William Gastner, long distance from Posadas, New Mexico. I'm returning Mrs. Weatherford's call."

"Just one moment." More voices, and then the phone was passed off to someone who sounded official—and tired.

"Who's this?"

I repeated myself, and the voice said, "Give me your phone number there, sir. I'll get right back to you." I did, and broke the connection. For two minutes I sat in my silent office, listening to the tick of the gas heater over by the window. When the phone lit up I punched the line-one button.

"Gastner."

"Sheriff," the tired voice said, "this is Sergeant Stanton Judge with the Weatherford police in Weatherford, Oklahoma."

My stomach flip-flopped with apprehension. "What's up, sergeant? A Mrs. Donni Weatherford asked me to call."

"You met the Weatherfords, I understand."

"Their van tangled with an interstate guardrail down our way Sunday afternoon. The husband was the only one hurt. He spent a day in the hospital here. When he was discharged, they headed for home. Iowa, I think."

"Well, they made it as far as their favorite town. They bought a new vehicle in Posadas, is that right?"

"Yes. I don't know what financial arrangement they made, but

202

they bought a new Suburban right off the lot. Or at least made a hefty down payment. He's a lawyer."

"That's what she said."

"What happened, sergeant?"

He cleared his throat and coughed. I could picture him leaning against the check-in counter of the motel, cup of coffee on the counter and a cigarette between his fingers.

"The vehicle was stolen early this morning."

I let out a stream of pent-up air, a sigh of relief and exasperation mixed together. "The brand-new one was stolen?"

Sergeant Judge had the good grace not to say, *no, stupid, the wrecked van.* Instead he said, "Right out of the goddamned motel parking lot. Mrs. Weatherford happened to glance out the window shortly before dawn. It was missing then. So, sometime between midnight and about five-thirty."

"Christ, the original hard luck family."

Judge grunted agreement. "Yeah. She told me they always stop in Weatherford when they're traveling through. Some sort of family joke, she said. Started when the kids were little . . . told 'em that the whole town was named after them. Something like that. Anyway, we've got an all-points out. But if the thieves had a five hour head start, that's the last we'll ever see of that baby, I'll tell you that."

"No one heard or saw anything?"

"Well, maybe. Maybe not. A trucker whose rig was parked in the motel's parking lot said he heard the chirp of an auto alarm being turned off. He didn't look out of his sleeper cab or anything. Didn't check the time. He said he remembers it because it sounded so damn close. He didn't pay any attention to it beyond that. Said he heard a vehicle start shortly after."

"Where was the Suburban parked relative to his rig?"

"The width of the driveway, plus three parking slots. Close enough that it could have been the one."

"No broken glass?"

"No. And that Suburban had a hell of a burglar alarm screamer on it. The Weatherfords say they made sure it worked, too. The kids had made it holler more than once."

"And no one other than the trucker heard it?"

"That's right. So either it didn't work the one time it should have, or . . ."

"Or someone had a key."

"That's right. Or something sophisticated. Some kind of gadget."

"Is Mrs. Weatherford there?"

"She's standing right at my elbow."

When Donni Weatherford came on the line, she sounded like a good sport whose sportsmanship had been stretched to the limit.

"Sheriff? This is Donni. Can you believe this? I mean, can you believe it?" She spoke as if our acquaintance had been seasoned by years instead of hours. "I mean, I can't believe it."

"I'm certainly sorry, Mrs. Weatherford," I said lamely. I wasn't about to drive up to downtown Oklahoma to pick up the family and chauffeur them to Davenport, Iowa . . . and that's about the only offer that would have done them any good.

"Well, I just thought I should call you, sheriff. I thought maybe you might like to know. You folks were all so kind to us, and then your deputy, the one who was so helpful, was killed later that very night. Have you caught them yet?"

"No."

"This world is full of wretched people, I'll tell you that."

"Yes, ma'am. Are you absolutely certain that the alarm on the Suburban was set properly?"

"Absolutely."

After assuring Mrs. Weatherford that Sergeant Judge would take care of the family's immediate needs, and countering another round of thank-you's, I hung up. In less than a heartbeat, the line two light blossomed and the phone buzzed. With my fingers resting on the receiver, I contemplated not bothering to answer. After another two buzzes, I picked it up.

Herb Torrance's gravelly voice was loud. "Sheriff? That you?"

"Herb, how you doing?"

"Not so damn good. The wife and me are about worried sick. Listen, I just got a call from Patrick." My heart skipped a beat. "He went and got himself arrested."

"Where's he at?"

"Well, let me read it. He's . . . hold it still, Adeline . . . he's being held by the Campbell County Sheriff's Office. Now, that's in Gillette, Wyoming."

"What the hell's he doing up there?"

"Damned if I know, sheriff. He didn't want to talk over the phone too damn bad. He just wanted me and his ma to know he was all right, and we was to call you."

"Patrick said to call me?"

"That's what he said."

"All right. I'll get right back to you, Herb. Sit tight."

29

◆◆◆

I punched in the number for long distance information, listened to the robot recite the number, and then dialed the Campbell County Sheriff's Office. The circuits between Posadas and Gillette popped and clicked, and another throaty-voiced robot came on the line to patiently tell me that she was sorry, the number I had dialed was no longer in service.

I doubt that she, or it, really was sorry in the least. Annoyed, I peered more carefully through my bifocals at the number information had given me, and tried again. This time, I was rewarded with a real human, a man who sounded like he was talking between tightly clenched steel dentures.

"Campbell S.O., Whittier."

I introduced myself and then said, "I understand you may have one of our best and brightest in custody."

"Who's that?"

"A young fella named Torrance. Patrick Torrance."

"Lemme check." The line went dead and I spent several long minutes pencil shading in the square for February first on my desk calendar. A voice startled me.

"This is Lieutenant Brennen." The voice was husky and soft. I wouldn't have placed bets on gender.

"Lieutenant, this is Undersheriff William Gastner of Posadas County, New Mexico. I need to speak with someone about one of your detainees. A Patrick Torrance."

"What do you need to know, sir?"

"First of all, is he in your custody?"

"Yes, sir."

"When was he arrested?"

I heard a faint rustle of paper. "Five-thirty-six A.M."

"That's today?"

"Yes, sir."

The lad had wasted no time leaving Posadas County in his dust, and he'd flogged the horses all the way north. "What was the charge?"

"Driving while intoxicated."

"You're kidding."

"No, sir." The voice was about as flappable as the telephone company's robot.

"Apparently he telephoned his parents?"

"He did make a telephone call. Yes, sir."

"Let me tell you what we've got, lieutenant. We've had a homicide down here. One of our deputies. Did you receive the information?"

"Yes, sir. We got the teletype on the homicide earlier. The deputy who arrested Torrance remembered the name of the county and brought it to my attention. I was going to telephone your office this morning. But we had a family dispute an hour or so ago that was settled with a shotgun, so we got kinda busy ourselves."

"I think it's the moon, lieutenant. Who the hell knows? What are the chances of talking with the Torrance kid?"

"No problem, sir. Give me your number, and I'll call you back in about five minutes." I heard voices in the background, one of them loud and angry. "Make that ten minutes," the lieutenant said.

"It's urgent, if that helps."

"Isn't it always," the lieutenant said, and for the first time I could hear some humor in the voice.

While I waited, I dug out the road atlas from the overloaded bookshelf behind my chair. The tiny numbers blurred, and I ended up holding the damn thing about six inches from my nose. The red numbers said Gillette was sixty-nine miles east of Buffalo, Wyoming, on Interstate 90. Buffalo sat squarely on Interstate 25, that north-south express ribbon that connects the major cities on the east flank of the Rockies. I-25 dove all the way south through Las Cruces, east of Posadas.

I flipped pages until I found the mileage chart, its type designed to be read either through a microscope or by a ten-year-old with 20/10 vision. Las Cruces wasn't listed, but El Paso was, and I followed the column over until I was under the one for Cheyenne, Wyoming. Seven hundred and ninety-two miles. Cruces was 50 miles north of El Paso, so that made it 742. Add 60 coming in from Posadas to the west. That was 802. Cheyenne was still a far stretch from Gillette.

I flipped to the page for Wyoming. "Jesus," I said, and jotted down the 326 miles the map said it was from Cheyenne to Sheridan. Give or take 50 miles, that figure would apply to Gillette, too, if my eyes could stay focused long enough to add the tiny red numbers. The grand total was 1,128, give or take. At a steady 60 miles an hour, that was almost nineteen hours. Nobody averaged 60 over that kind of distance, no matter what they might tell you. One stop for fuel killed the average, and there were too many radar traps to allow sustained speeds to make up time.

But Patrick Torrance hadn't let the moss grow. Sometime between twenty and thirty hours before, he'd left Posadas. I glanced at my watch. He'd been arrested at five-thirty. Some eight and a half hours before, his father had mentioned to me that he hadn't seen his son since the previous day. And fourteen and a half hours before the Campbell County deputy pulled Torrance over, Estelle

Reyes-Guzman had spotted Tammy Woodruff's mangled pickup truck.

Tammy had been wadded up in the crushed cab for God knows how long—perhaps as many as twenty-four hours. I frowned and dropped my pencil on the desk. The time window was plenty wide to accommodate the young man's panic.

"Shit," I said aloud. I tossed the atlas back on the bookcase.

Seven minutes later the telephone buzzed.

"Sir, this is Lieutenant Marjory Brennen from Gillette." Marjory. I tried to form a mental picture, but her personality was perfectly guarded by that soft, neutral voice. "We're on conference."

"Patrick?" I asked. I picked up the telephone recorder and pushed in the record buttons.

"Yes, sir. I'm here." He sounded relieved.

"Patrick, this conversation is being recorded, just for the record. All right?"

"Yes, sir."

"Your dad called me a few minutes ago. Are you all right?"

"Yes, sir. I'm fine."

I didn't see any point in mincing words. "What are you doing up there, Patrick?"

There was a silence. I pictured Patrick Torrance sitting at an old oak conference table like every sheriff's department in the world has had at one time or another and staring at the dark, oiled wood in front of him as if the answers might coalesce before his eyes.

"I got scared."

"I see. Of what?"

"Of what Tammy was doing. Have you talked to her?"

I ignored his question and instead asked, "And what was she doing?" I realized then with both relief and certainty that Patrick didn't know of the girl's death.

"I ain't sure, sheriff. The night the deputy was killed, she stopped at the Broken Spur, all excited like. She came in and she was askin' me to go along with her."

209

"Go along where?"

"She didn't say. Like I said, she was all excited. Said she had the chance to make more money in one night than I'd ever see in a year."

"She didn't say how she was going to make the money?"

"No, but she wanted me to come outside with her, like maybe that might change my mind. She showed me this fancy truck she was drivin'. She said she was deliverin' it for somebody."

"Delivering it where?"

"She didn't say, but she kinda smiled in that way she has, you know. Like maybe I didn't need to know."

"What kind of truck was it?"

"Looked like a brand-new Chevy extended cab. Four-wheel drive, the works." I heard him take a deep breath. "It don't take a genius to sort out where that truck was headed, sheriff. I figured that's why she wanted me to go with her, 'cause she knew that me and my brothers go on down to Mexico all the time."

"She didn't say where she got the vehicle?"

"No, sir. But she was all excited, like it was some sort of big, important deal. Like she was doin' me some kind of favor by cuttin' me in on it."

"Then what?"

"She got all mad at me, 'cause I wouldn't go. She said all kinds of things I figured she'd forget later. She'd been drinkin' kind of heavy, too. I could smell it on her. I just had me a feelin', is all. I mean, I knew what she was doin' wasn't legit. No car dealer operates like that. The truck had to be stole."

"And then she left?"

"Yeah, she left. In an all-fired hurry, she left. Fishtailed all the way across the parkin' lot. Bounced out on the highway, and away she went."

"And you went back inside the saloon?"

"Yes, sir. And it wasn't too long after that when all the commotion started, with the deputy getting killed and all."

"Do you remember how long?"

"Maybe five, ten minutes. Fifteen at the most."

"Patrick, when the detectives talked to you the first time that night, and again on the following Monday morning, why didn't you tell them all this?"

Again a silence, and I could hear snatches of a conversation on some other circuit, the voices distant and tinny.

"I had a feelin' that Tammy was involved somehow, sheriff. I mean, she lit out in that truck and all, and just a few minutes later I hear there's a shooting. There ain't all that many cars on that road that time of night, sheriff. It's a hell of a coincidence if she didn't know anything about it."

"And so . . . ?"

"And so I tried callin' her place later that night, and the next day, and I couldn't get no answer. I was really worried, you know, 'cause if she'd gone and done something, then I hated to see her end up in jail. She's just harebrained enough not to think things through and get herself in all kinds of trouble. So I didn't say anything about her and the truck. And then I got scared, 'cause I knew that if I covered for her, that pulled me right into it, same as if I was ridin' in the jump seat."

"And so you headed out to Wyoming."

"No, sir. Not right then. I was gonna drive by her apartment around noon on Monday. Just as I was turnin' off Bustos Avenue I saw her and some other guy drive by in her truck."

"In her truck?"

"Yes, sir. I know she saw me, but she didn't wave or nothin'. They just drove on by."

"She was driving?"

"No, sir. He was."

"Did you recognize him?"

"No, sir."

"Could you identify him if you saw him again?"

"I think so."

"And then you left?"

The words came in a rush, the way people talk when what

211

they've got to say doesn't make any sense to anyone, including themselves. "Yes, sir. I just got to feelin' like I was caught up in something, you know? I didn't know what to do, and I didn't want to say nothin' about Tammy, 'cause I didn't know nothin' for sure. And then I got to thinkin' that maybe she'd be mad enough at me to say somethin' she shouldn't, and pull me in, too."

"That wasn't very bright, Patrick."

"No, sir."

"And you got yourself arrested for DWI as well."

"Yes, sir. I drove straight through, and got to this place west of Gillette where the two interstates meet . . ."

"Buffalo?"

"Yes, sir. I stopped at this little place and bought me some sandwiches and a six-pack. They didn't card me or nothin'. I was thinkin' that if I had something to eat, it'd keep me awake. I guess I drank one or two too many. The deputy stopped me and said I was speedin', and then he had me take a sobriety test, and I guess I flunked that, bein' tired and all."

"All right, Patrick, I want you to listen to me very carefully. You say you don't know who the man was with Tammy on Monday, is that right?"

"No, sir, I sure don't."

"Did he see you?"

"Sure. He looked right at me."

"Did you wave at them, or anything like that?"

"I kinda waved at Tammy, 'cause I was surprised to see her."

"And he saw you do that?"

"I suppose he did, sir."

"And you could identify him?"

"Sure. But sir, have you been able to talk with Tammy yet? I mean, what's she say?"

I told him about Tammy Woodruff. His end of the conversation went dead, and Lieutenant Brennen spoke for the first time.

"It'll be a few minutes, sheriff." While I waited for Patrick Tor-

212

rance to come to grips with the curve ball life had thrown him, I tried to figure out the fastest way to ship the boy south to Posadas. I knew, as surely as I knew anything, that if we worked the boy's memory just right, we'd have ourselves a face.

30

I sent Deputy Tom Mears to Gillette, Wyoming, to fetch Patrick Torrance. The manager of the Posadas County Airport, Jim Bergin, accepted the county contract for the charter flight with a wide grin, even though he knew damn well he wouldn't see a penny of payment for at least 90 days. I had no idea what each hour of flight time was going to cost us, but apparently he did.

What was important to me was that Bergin promised four and a half hours up and four and a half back, door to door, no waiting.

He was as good as his word. Barely ten minutes after Deputy Mears left the office, I heard the throaty moan of Bergin's Beech Baron as it cleared the mesa outside of Posadas and headed toward the north country.

Nine hours would have Patrick Torrance sitting in my office, early evening at the latest. I had dispatch pull Howard Bishop off road patrol and Tony Abeyta out of bed. While Sergeant Robert Torrez and two highway department employees continued to tear Tammy Woodruff's crushed pickup truck to pieces looking for evidence, Bishop and Abeyta began the tedious process of scouring the neighborhood around Tammy Woodruff's apartment, searching for someone who'd seen her anytime after late Sunday night.

I looked again at the assortment of messages that Gayle Sedil-

214

los had handed me earlier. Following Martin Holman's orders, all but two went in the trash.

Shortly after nine that morning, I walked in the lower service entrance of Posadas General Hospital. It sccmcd like weeks since I'd been there instead of hours. And even though I had nothing more than just a few hints, we'd made enough progress that my pulse was hammering with what I hoped was excitement and not another coronary infarction building to a head.

Helen Murchison was just leaving the auxiliary's snack bar and gift shop, blowing on the top of a fresh cup of coffee. She stopped when she saw me step into the hallway and her ice-blue eyes followed my shuffling, weary progress down the hall.

"Working on suicide, are we?" she said when I was within hearing distance of her quiet, withering reproach.

"I beg your pardon?"

She pointed with her coffee cup. "Over here for a minute."

I started to follow her to the Plexiglas enclosure where the nurses routinely planned which patients to torture next. The coffee wafted back as she walked, and it smelled pretty good.

"Let me get a cup of coffee first," I said.

"You don't need coffee," Helen said with considerable acid. "Sit down here."

I'd known Helen Murchison for twenty years. I'd survived open heart surgery and been battered into a reasonable facsimile of recuperation with the help of her efficiency and sharp tongue. Once or twice, when I'd been a particularly stellar patient, I'd been rewarded with the faint, brief lip twitch that passed for a smile on Helen's square, strong face. It was easier to cooperate than resist.

I sat. "Roll up your sleeve," she said, and I unbuttoned the left sleeve of my flannel shirt. She slapped the blood pressure cuff on and racked the Velcro strap tight, giving the unit a final, motherly pat before she started pumping the bulb.

"We've got to stop meeting this way," I said.

"Yes, we do. Shut up now," Helen replied. I watched her face

215

as she listened through the stethoscope and observed the needle jerk its way downhill.

When she finished, she took a deep breath and held it while she unplugged the stethoscope and ripped off the cuff. She sat with the gadget in her lap, those wonderful eyes of hers assessing my old tired face. She puffed her cheeks and let out her pent-up breath through clenched lips.

"When's the last time you had a full night's sleep?"

"When I was about six, I guess," I said. "What are the numbers?"

"One eighty over one ten."

I grimaced. "That's not so good."

"No, it's not. Why do you do this to yourself, sheriff?" Her tone surprised me, quiet and almost soft. I stood up and buttoned my sleeve.

"I don't have a lot of choice at the moment," I said. "Did you folks move Linda Real out of ICU?"

Helen reached for her coffee. "She's in one oh six."

"And her mother?"

"She went to Ms. Real's apartment a bit ago. She probably won't be back until this afternoon."

I stepped toward the hallway. "I need to talk with Linda again for a few minutes. Helen, thanks for the tune-up."

She shook her head in resignation. "If you're not going to take care of yourself, at least see if you can't talk some sense into the young lady's head when you go down there."

"Linda?"

"No. Estelle."

"I was told she'd gone home."

"However briefly," Helen said. "Dr. Guzman is furious. Maybe she'll listen to you."

"I'll be damned," I said, and hustled down the hall toward 106. In the hall, Tom Pasquale looked up hopefully from an old copy of *Outdoor Life*. "Hang in there," I said, and walked past him without waiting for a reply. I pushed open the door, rapping on it at the same time.

Estelle Reyes-Guzman was in a wheelchair, parked next to Linda's bed. The two women looked like members of a disaster survivors' club.

"What the hell are you doing here?" I asked.

"This is as good a place to rest as any," she said. The left side of her face was black and blue from above her eye to midcheek, with a small butterfly bandage at the end of her eyebrow. Her busted leg was propped up on the wheelchair's support, and her left arm was in a sling around her neck.

I glanced over at Linda. She was awake, her one eye watchful. I stepped over to the bed. "How are you doing, kid?"

She made a muffled sound with no vowels and reached up her right hand to take mine. Her grip was surprisingly strong.

"Look at this, sir," Estelle said, and handed me a yellow legal pad. Judging by the extent of the pencil scratching, the two had been at it for some time. "Linda remembers seeing the headlights of the other vehicle as it pulled up on the opposite shoulder of the highway. She thinks it was a pickup truck, with some kind of rack on the back. A livestock rack, maybe."

I scanned on down the page, then turned to the next. "What's this about a trailer?" I looked at Linda, and she responded with the smallest of nods.

"She's sure it was pulling a trailer as well."

"You've got to be kidding."

"She's positive, sir." Estelle shifted in her chair, and winced. "She remembers hearing it, as well, when the truck pulled up to a stop on the shoulder of the highway. She remembers it as being a long trailer, like the kind you haul livestock in."

"Not just a horse trailer?"

"No, sir."

"Linda," I said, and slid the pad under her hand. Estelle picked up the pencil and Linda took it eagerly. "Linda, when I talked to you the first time a day or so ago, you said you didn't remember anything about the vehicle that pulled up on the other side of the road. Now you're saying you remember that it was a truck, with a rack, and a trailer?"   ❧

Yes. All I've been doing is thinking and remembering. I smiled and said nothing, just gazed at her face. With a little imagination, I could see determination behind that dark brown eye, maybe even some defiance. I saw a tiny crinkle form at the corner of her eye and she wrote, *I'm not petrified anymore. Just scared.*

I reached out and squeezed her hand. "Do you remember anything about the truck other than that it was pulling a trailer?"

I think it was dirty, she wrote quickly. *Muddy, maybe.*

"New or old?"

No.

"And you don't remember the make?"

No. The pencil hesitated. *Sorry.*

I closed my eyes, trying to picture the scenario. "I really don't understand this," I said finally. "Tammy Woodruff is on one side of the road in a new pickup that doesn't belong to her, and then the killer stops . . . and he's driving a rig with a livestock trailer."

"Rustling livestock is not a new occupation, sir," Estelle said.

"You think that's what the deputy and Linda stumbled on to?"

"I don't know, sir. It's possible."

"None of that fits what Patrick Torrance told me earlier this morning," I said, and I repeated our telephone conversation. "He was afraid that either he'd implicate Tammy in something, or that he'd be blamed. He says that's why he took off."

"He also drives a pickup and pulls a trailer half the time," Estelle observed.

"He had nothing to do with the shooting, Estelle. I'm as sure of that as I am of anything."

"But you think he knows who did?"

"All I know is that he may be able to recognize the man he saw with Tammy Woodruff earlier. That may take us somewhere." I shrugged. "Or it may not. But right now, it's the first solid lead we've had." I looked hard at Estelle. "Helen tells me that Dr. Guzman isn't entirely happy with you."

Estelle smiled. "A busted ankle is not the end of the world, sir."

"And a conked head. And broken elbow."

"Not broken. Just bent."

"Whatever. I was told you went home."

"I did, sir. *Tía* Sofia and I talked. She said that Linda would remember more and more as she regains her strength. I just thought it might be restful for both of us if I spent some time here, with her. Someone for her to talk to." She glanced at Linda. "Someone to write to."

"You were home for at least an hour, then," I said.

"At least." Estelle laughed and shrugged.

"How'd you get back here?"

"Sofia drove me. There was some shopping she wanted to do anyway. She took el kid."

"Brave woman," I said, and was about to say something else when the small pager on my belt chirped. "Don't go anywhere," I said, and left the room. The nearest phone was at the nurses' station, and when I dialed the Sheriff's Department, Gayle Sedillos answered on the second ring.

"Sir, Nick Chavez asked that you stop by as soon as you can. He says it's urgent."

"At the dealership?"

"Yes, sir."

"I'll go over right now. Any other messages that can't wait?"

"No, sir."

"Thanks, Gayle." I hung up and sat for a minute, deep in thought. After a moment I realized I was being watched, and looked up to see Francis Guzman leaning against the fiberglass window frame. He was wearing his quiet, long-suffering doctor's face, a little bemused, a little preoccupied, a little concerned.

He didn't say anything as I leaned back in Helen Murchison's chair and rubbed both eyes. "I saw Estelle. Do you want me to take her home?"

The young physician grinned with resignation. "It wouldn't do

219

any good. She'd probably walk back. *Es una aguila descalza,* as my Aunt Sofie would say."

"Meaning?"

"It's an old Mexican expression. Roughly translates that she knows what she's doing."

"Yes, she does. And she'll be all right." I heaved myself to my feet, saw Francis's brow furrow with concern, and held up an index finger. "Don't you start."

His frown stayed put. "You be careful, sir."

I nodded and slipped past him. "How do things look for Linda?"

"She's a fighter."

I stopped and looked sharply at Francis. "That's not really an answer, doctor."

He looked down at the floor. "I guess I was just thinking of what she's still facing down the road. She's lost an eye and suffered nerve damage to some of the centers that control gross body motion."

"She's paralyzed, you mean?"

"She's going to have difficulty walking, yes. And she's going to face a series of operations to reconstruct the bones of her left jaw and the left side of her face. Like I said . . . it's a long road."

"She'll make it." I glanced down the hall and saw one of the nurses enter 106. "And we're going to catch the son of a bitch who's responsible for all this, too."

After telling Estelle that I'd stop back around noon, I drove around the block and down Bustos Avenue to Chavez Chevrolet-Oldsmobile. He'd told Gayle it was urgent, but to Nick, everything was urgent. Selecting a luncheon guest for Rotary Club was urgent. Selling me a new truck was urgent. As I pulled into the parking area in front of the small showroom, I was planning to allot him about thirty seconds of my time.

I got out of the car and he met me at the door. One look at his face told me that he was going to need a hell of a lot more than thirty seconds.

220

31

Nɪᴄᴋ Chavez painted on his glad salesman's face and ushered me across the showroom floor. We had to skirt a new addition—a brand-new Blazer. Nick patted it affectionately on the hood and at the same time hooked his arm through mine as if we were the oldest of buddies.

"Have I got a deal for you, Bill," he said. "Come on in here and let me show you some figures." One of the other salesmen looked up from his desk and grinned at me—much the same grin a hungry cat might give his still-kicking dinner.

"I don't think I have time for this," I said without much conviction. Nick was smiling his best salesman's smile from the nose down. His eyes gave him away. I followed him into his office like a docile, committed customer, and he closed the door behind me.

"Sit, sit," he said, and beckoned me toward his own swivel chair behind the desk. I started to move toward one of the others, and he motioned with considerable impatience. I shrugged and took his chair, commanding a nice view of the showroom, the other salesmen's desks, and the parking lot outside.

Nick sat down in the customer's chair, his back to the world. He ran a hand through his hair, keeping his eyes closed. One hand closed around a pencil, and the point hovered over a salesman's work sheet. He looked for all the world like a salesman who had negotiated all night, and was now at the point of splitting his commission with the customer just to nail down the sale.

"I'm really pissed, Bill." He opened his eyes, but he wouldn't meet my gaze.

I leaned forward and rested my hands on the desk like a helpful father confessor. "What's the problem, Nick."

He was one of those people who talked with his eyes closed, as if he were reading a script etched on the inside of his eyelids. "Look, I don't know why I checked. After you and me talked yesterday, or whenever the hell it was, I got to thinkin', you know. And the thing that bothered me the most was . . . ah, to hell with that."

I leaned back, unsure of where this interesting flow of disconnected thoughts was leading him.

"Look at this." He pulled a bound pad of forms out of a folder and slid it across the desk toward me. "Temporaries."

"I see that," I said. Anyone who purchased a vehicle in New Mexico had seen them—approximately half the size of a standard sheet of typing paper, the temporary permit was filled out by the dealer and taped in the back window of the vehicle until plates could be issued by the Department of Motor Vehicles.

"Now look here," Nick said, and leaned forward. He kept his voice low and pointed with the pencil. "Each one of them has a serial number. See that?"

"Yes."

"Consecutive, the whole pad. We buy the pad, and issue the temporaries one at a time."

I nodded.

"So, the numbers should match, right?"

"Should match what?" I asked.

Nick frowned with impatience. "If we sell ten cars in a week—and wouldn't it be goddamned nice if we did that—then we should use ten of these."

"All right."

"So we're missing some."

"Someone took some, you mean?"

Nick shrugged. "Maybe."

"I don't understand the 'maybe.' It seems a pretty simple inventory problem."

Nick ducked his head. "Sure. That's what's so goddamned embarrassing. And that's one of the things that's got me so pissed. I mean, we aren't required to keep some kind of careful record of these things, you know. I mean, I don't know anyone who does. We stick one copy in the back window, stick the back copy in the file, and that's it. Who the hell's going to spend all day long checking those kinds of goddamned things." His voice had risen, and he suddenly checked himself. He continued in a near-whisper.

"And I guess that's kind of dumb, when you consider that these things are the equivalent of a free license plate for thirty days," he said.

"So you think that you're missing some temps, and you don't know for sure how many. That's it?"

Nick nodded. He turned and reached into the folder again. "The past two months I can account for. Why? Because it's been slow, and just by chance we've been workin' off this one pad. And I used the first one. I remember havin' to go get it out of the file." He slid a piece of paper across and I tilted my head so my bifocals could focus on the neat rows of numbers. "That number there on my list corresponds to this number on the temp." He tapped the printed number on the first permit of the pad.

"All right," I said.

"Now, from here, count backward," and his pencil moved up his handwritten list. "If we sold sixteen cars since this pad was new, which we did, then the first number of the pad would be this one." He circled the top number of the list.

"And it doesn't come out," I said.

"Right. It don't come out. And for another thing, look here." He leaned across and with his pencil eraser drove through what little was left of the pad, rapidly lifting each permit in turn. He stopped and pointed. "See that number?"

"Uh-huh."

"Check this out." He turned to the next permit. "What do you see?"

"They skipped a number."

Nick nodded. "I mean, who's gonna notice, huh?"

"You did."

"Only 'cause you got me thinkin'." He sat back with one hand resting on the folder. "And that ain't all." He pulled out a second pad of permits. "Brand-new pack." He tossed them in front of me. "Twenty-five temps there, with copies. Check it out, about a third of the way through the pad."

"And there are supposed to be twenty-five here?"

"Twenty-five. That's what we pay for, and that's what shows in the number series."

I rifled the pad, watching the serial numbers tick by. "There's one," I said, as the digit 4, the last digit in the long state number, was followed by a number ending in a 6. I looked up at Nick. "How many missing from this pack?"

"Two."

I looked at the neat bundle and frowned. "So two missing here, and one or two from the other pack."

"That's right. And these goddamned things are registered with the DMV when you buy 'em. I mean, the serial numbers are recorded by the state against my dealer number."

"I can buy one of these myself, can't I?"

Nick Chavez nodded. "Sure, one at a time."

"And when I do, the DMV takes down all the transfer information."

"Right."

"I remember. I once gave one of my sons an old truck that didn't have a plate, and we had to go through the whole rigmarole. Why else would someone steal one?"

"Hell, I don't know. So they could drive a vehicle on the highway without goin' through the DMV, I guess. You tell me." He paused to take a breath. "You'd stop a vehicle on the highway if it didn't have no license plate, right?"

"Sure."

"What about if it had one of these?"

I held up my hands. "Not unless there was a traffic violation of some sort, or some other reason to be suspicious."

"Right."

"Nick, who has access to these temps?"

He snorted and thumped his fist on the arm of his chair. "Every goddamned person in the building, one way or another. I mean, they aren't kept in a vault or anything. Shit, most of the time, they're lying right here." He tossed the pad of permits across to the narrow bookcase that rested against the wall beside his desk.

"And your office isn't locked?"

He made a snort of derision that I took as a "no."

"You know, you were tellin' me that the deputies stopped a late-model pickup truck. And your gal, there, the one who got all mucked up . . ."

"Linda Real."

"Yeah. She recalls seeing a temporary in the back window. Now, is that permit going to be mine? When you and your posse haul somebody's ass in for that shooting, is the whole world going to come down on me? God, that pisses me off."

I ducked his questions, since he knew the answers as well as I did. "Who buys these things for you?"

"What do you mean?"

"Who actually goes over to the DMV office and picks up the new permits. The new pack. Or packs. Whatever."

"Well, hell, whoever is free. Me, Rusty, Manny, Carlos. Becky goes down sometimes. You know. Whoever. It's not like going to Fort Knox or anything. It's just another one of those goddamned errands. Paper, paper, paper. Remember when you could just give a man his money and walk off with the car?"

I laughed gently. "Now they just walk off with the car."

"Shit. That ain't funny."

"We'll look into it, Nick. I don't know what to tell you, unless we get lucky." I removed a page from the legal pad and jotted down the missing numbers. "If these show up somewhere, we've got a starting point. We'll get 'em on NCIC."

"Do you want me to kind of snoop around here? See what I can find out? I mean hell," and he leaned forward and dropped his voice to a whisper, "I ain't got that many employees. I ought to be able to turn something."

I held up a hand. "Not yet. Don't do anything." I had a mental picture of Nick pulling a tremendous magnifying glass out of his coat pocket as he sifted through his building. "Don't talk to anyone about this at all." This time, I lowered my own voice. "And I mean *no one*, Nick. Let us try and fit it all together." I stood up and folded the piece of paper with the temp numbers. "And by the way, in the small world department, remember the Weatherfords?"

"How could anyone forget. I thought those noisy kids of theirs were going to camp out in my showroom."

"They got as far as Weatherford, Oklahoma."

"The first day? That ain't bad."

"No. To Weatherford, period. Their new Suburban was stolen right out of the motel parking lot."

I don't know what reaction I expected from Nick Chavez, but it wasn't the one I got. He froze in his seat, and then his eyes narrowed ever so slowly. He leaned one elbow on the edge of the desk and cupped his jaw in his hand with his fingers covering his mouth. I suppose it was one of those gestures with which a psychiatrist would have a heyday.

"What?" I asked.

"You know," he said through his fingers, "I saw that Suburban."

My pulse kicked up ten notches, booting my already impressive blood pressure skyward. "When?"

"Goddamn, I saw it." He lowered his hands and sat up straight.

"I thought I was crazy, and didn't think much about it earlier. But goddamn it, I saw it."

"When?"

"I was coming to work, and I saw it go through the intersection of Grande and MacArthur. I was startled, see, 'cause this one was absolutely identical to the one the Weatherfords bought here. I mean absolutely. It even had the goddamned temporary tag in the back window, because I looked in my rearview mirror and saw it. And I remember thinkin' to myself, 'I thought they left, but maybe not.' Maybe they decided to stay another day. Except she wasn't drivin' it."

"Who was?"

"Beats me. I didn't get enough of a look."

"What time, Nick?"

He closed his eyes. "I got here at five minutes before eight. I looked, 'cause I needed to talk to the service manager, and he always walks through the door at eight sharp, like he's some kind of digital freak. So, subtract from there. MacArthur up to here is about a minute and a half, give or take. So, seven minutes before eight, maybe."

I did some mental calculations. If the thieves had taken the Suburban at midnight, eight hours averaging fifty miles an hour would see four hundred miles—and that wouldn't see them to Posadas. But if they took the lightly traveled back roads, like Route 70 across the Texas panhandle, they could average much faster with ease. It was possible.

"You really think it could have been their truck?"

Nick shrugged. "How many can there be with a paint job like that in this area?"

"Why . . ." and I stopped. I had planned to ask why the car thieves would bother bringing the unit back to Posadas, but the pieces of the puzzle were beginning to tumble together.

"Nick," I said, rising from his comfortable seat, "you're going to be here all day?"

"Sure."

"Keep this conversation to yourself, all right?"

"Goddamn right."

"If this works out the way I think it will, I'll buy that," and I pointed at the Blazer on the showroom floor.

32

VICTOR Sánchez watched me pull into the parking lot of the Broken Spur, but he didn't stand on ceremony. He walked inside using the side door and let it slam shut in my face.

I followed him into the utility room beside the kitchen.

"What do you want?" he asked.

"You snakebit or something?" I said. The utility room was neater than the last time I'd seen it. Victor continued unloading the sacks of paper products that he'd brought in from his truck.

"I'm busy," he said, his back still turned to me.

"Then I'll wait until you've got a minute," I said pleasantly. I leaned against the edge of one of the prep sinks and crossed my arms over my stomach. Victor ignored me. While he muttered and arranged—and rearranged—his dry goods, my eyes drifted around the room.

There was nothing unusual, nor did I expect there to be. That's why what was obviously a rifle barrel arrested my gaze. The gun stood behind the back door, in company with several old brooms and a squeegee-mop. I pushed away from the sink, walked over, and hefted the antique. It was an old junker, one of those single-shot break-open things that cost about $49.95 when they're new.

I pushed the lever and the breach opened. It was loaded. I slipped the little .22 shell out and turned it this way and that in my hands.

229

It would do to kill a jackrabbit who made the mistake of holding still, or maybe a rattler by the back door.

"That ain't the gun that killed the deputy," Victor said.

I turned and looked at him, the shell in one hand, gun in the other.

"I can see that," I said.

"Leave it loaded."

I put the cartridge back in the gun and set the weapon down in the corner.

"I got five minutes," Victor said. "What do you want? Where's the girl?"

"The girl?"

"The one who works for you. The detective. Reuben's niece."

"She's in the hospital with a broken leg."

"That's too bad," Victor said—and he said it about the same way he'd say, "cut up this bunch of celery."

"I wanted to ask you about someone else," I said, and walked back to my leaning spot against the sink.

"Don't you ever get tired of stickin' your nose in other people's business? I've got a business to run here. I ain't got the time."

"Victor, you've got all the time in the world."

He glanced over at me, his ugly round face framing unblinking eyes. No doubt Victor was a real charmer as a bartender. I could imagine a disconsolate traveling salesman pouring out his heart and soul to Victor during a Christmas Eve drinking binge at the Broken Spur. Right at the climax of the salesman's sob story, just before he rose from his stool to walk into the restroom to blow his brains out, Victor would say, "Look, you want any carrot sticks or not?"

"I oughta just throw you out." He said it without much conviction.

I shrugged. "You could do that, I guess. Hell, old and fat as I am, it wouldn't take much."

"You people are bad for business." He gestured toward the parking lot. "That car out there . . . ain't nobody going to stop while it's

230

here. If it ain't parked there, then you guys sit down at the windmill."

"Help me put somebody in jail, and we'll leave you alone," I said.

"Who are you talking about?"

"I want to know about Tammy Woodruff."

He laughed a short, harsh bark. "What you think, you're going to put Tammy in jail, now?"

"I didn't say that. I just want to know a little more about her."

"So would every other *tachón* in the county," Sánchez snorted.

"I know she was a little wild, Victor. That's why it's important. She may have known something about the other night," I said. "Give me five minutes."

"You could write a book about that *ramerita*." He pushed a six-pack of paper towels into perfect alignment on the shelf, then stood facing the shelves with his hands on his hips. I didn't say anything, and finally he turned around and regarded me. "You want some coffee?"

"Sure."

He walked through the swinging door to the kitchen and I followed. The coffee was a lot fresher and more fragrant than I was used to and I didn't bother drowning it with milk and sugar.

Cup in hand, he beckoned me out toward one of the dining rooms off the main barroom. We sat down at a chrome-edged table, Victor turning his chair sideways so he could lean against the wall. I turned mine so my belly wouldn't crowd the table.

"What's she done now?" Victor asked.

"We're trying to find one of her boyfriends."

Victor almost smiled. "You got a good cutting horse? It's a big herd."

"So I'm beginning to understand."

"What's his name?"

"We don't know."

He regarded me with interest. "Not such a good time for you, eh?"

I thought about the last week. Victor was right. "No. Not such a good time."

He took a sip of his coffee and then lit a cigarette. "Why don't you ask her?"

"We can't. She's dead."

The coffee cup had gotten halfway to Victor's mouth before his hand stopped. He didn't say anything for a long time. I didn't break the silence. Without taking a sip, he set the cup back down. "How did she die?"

"We think she was murdered, Victor. Up on San Patricio Mesa." He knew who lived near the mesa as well as anyone.

He frowned and looked off into the distance. Then, so softly I could hardly hear him, he said, "This is bad."

"Yes, it is."

"Did you talk with the Torrance boy?"

"Yes."

"He followed after her with his tongue down to here," Victor said, and dropped his hand to his crotch. "But that's not so strange. At one time or another, I think she gave a turn to everyone in the county, except maybe old Francisco Peña."

"Brett Prescott?"

"Sure."

"Who was she with Sunday night?"

"I didn't see her Sunday night."

"Patrick Torrance was in here then?"

"I already told you he was."

"And you didn't see her come in that night? The boy told me that she did."

Sánchez shrugged. "If she did, it was when I was in back. You could ask my son. Maybe he saw her. She even made a pass at him one time. I told him to mind his own business. He's too stupid to know any better."

"Who was tending bar that night?"

"I was."

"And you didn't see her?"

He looked at me with remarkable patience considering his temperament, but he didn't bother answering the repeat question.

"Do you know who drives an older model pickup truck with a wrought-iron stock rack on the back? Pulls a big stock trailer once in a while? Whole rig covered with mud?"

"Half the ranchers in the county, maybe. You want more coffee?"

"No thanks. No one in particular?"

He shrugged. "If I saw the vehicle standing in front of me, maybe I could tell you. Otherwise . . ." He ground out his cigarette.

"Did you think there was anything unusual about the way Patrick Torrance was acting Sunday night?"

"I didn't notice." He looked at his watch. "You know, I got concerns of my own. I don't pay any attention."

I didn't pursue the questions any further. Being the "see nothing, hear nothing" bartender that he was, nothing I could say was likely to jar Victor loose. He could sit on a keg of gunpowder, and when it exploded, he'd say, "You know, I might have heard something, but I couldn't be sure. I was too busy."

I left the bar feeling better, though. Victor hadn't told me not to come back. That was a start.

I pulled out on the state highway from the parking lot and drove south, passing the turnoff to County Road 14. I stayed on the highway as it curved up through the western pass of the San Cristobal Mountains. On the south slope, after a series of switchbacks guaranteed to keep drivers of huge, clumsy RVs alert, the highway swept down through the intersection with State 80 running east and west and finally past the ancient village of Regal.

That settlement, counting twenty-five people on a good day, was a quarter mile off the highway, and the dirt approach road was hard-packed clay and stone. It wound across an arroyo and passed within ten feet of the carved front doors of the Iglésia de Nuestra Madre. The year 1849 was carved in the cornerstone of the mission, the second oldest structure in the village. An even older mission, now in ruins, lay half a mile to the east, it was part of one of the least visited historical monuments in the state.

233

Like so many ancient Mexican settlements, the streets of Regal were sunken dirt channels that meandered from yard to yard, with the adobe houses fronting immediately on the byways. If I wasn't careful, I could catch the front fender of 310 on someone's porch swing.

As many houses were abandoned as occupied, and they varied from neat, tidy little four-room adobes with steeply pitched metal roofs and brightly painted window trim to crumbling piles of rain-melted adobe blocks with broken windows, shattered door casements, and junk-strewn yards.

I idled up one nameless pathway after another, threading the patrol car right through yards and winter-dormant gardens. And one dog after another joined the chase, escorting me through town.

What few names were posted either above doorways, on long-abandoned mailboxes, or in the small yards were musical and familiar, Martinez, Sánchez, Chavez, Misquez, Hernandez. As I drove by one small house with M. Esquibel on the bent peeling mailbox, I saw an old man making his way one shaking step at a time around the side of his home, eyes glued to the ground, cane placed carefully for each step. In one arm he carried half a dozen sticks of firewood.

He ignored me, perhaps not even hearing the quiet idle of my car's engine, or perhaps not seeing well enough to catch the motion.

Around the other side of the house was a small adobe barn, remodeled sometime during the current century to serve as a garage. The wooden door was down, making the structure unique. It was the only outbuilding I'd seen in the village whose contents weren't both visible and spilling out far beyond the confines of the original structure. But it fitted the rest of the yard, neat and tidy.

I watched Señor Esquibel disappear into his house. I didn't know him, but I was willing to bet he'd been born within a hundred yards of where he now labored to stoke his wood-burning stove.

Parked next to the garage was his wood supply, a stock trailer a quarter filled with split piñon and juniper.

I spent another fifteen minutes in Regal. I didn't drive over to the border crossing gate less than a mile away. Deputy Howard Bishop had already talked to the officers there, with little success. It was a day crossing area only, with the gates locked at night and no officers on duty after six. The border patrol had the same details on our case as anyone else. They'd be watchful and even helpful when they could.

Easing 310 back out on the paved road, I glanced at the dash clock. Jim Bergin's Beech Baron would be approaching Gillette, and in another four and a half hours Patrick Torrance would be back in Posadas. Then we'd start constructing a face.

33

DEPUTY Bishop winked the lights of his patrol car at me as we passed on Bustos Avenue. I turned into the small parking lot of Kenny Pace's Western Wear and waited while Bishop swung around and pulled in behind me.

Howard Bishop was one of those big, sleepy-eyed characters, loose-jointed and tending toward flab. The two major loves of his life were his wife, Aggie, and collegiate football. He'd married Aggie right after the two of them had graduated from Posadas High School. The closest he'd ever come to collegiate football was watching it on television.

"Howard may look like he's slow, but he's got a mind like a banana slug," Sheriff Holman had once said in a rare moment of amused pique. That description was both unkind and untrue. Bishop had an exasperating allergy to paperwork, but generally was an intelligent, honest, fair cop.

He adjusted his Stetson and folded his dark glasses into his shirt pocket before getting out of the car. I walked back and leaned against the front fender of 307.

"Sir, I talked to twelve different people about Tammy Woodruff."

"Anything of interest?"

Bishop laid his clipboard on the hood of the car and ran his fin-

236

ger down a neatly printed list of names. "These here are the people I talked to. Neighbors, mostly. Seems like Tammy didn't have too many close friends. Except whatever cowpoke she was going out with at the moment."

"Who are the boyfriends?"

"Torrance and Prescott most recently. But Jane Ross—Tammy's boss when she was working at Ross Realty?—Mrs. Ross says that Tammy talked a lot about some guy she'd met down in Cruces during the half year she spent at the university."

"That's not surprising. And she was in Cruces more than two years ago." I knew that Tammy Woodruff's work and school record had been as checkered as her romance list. She'd briefly tried a dozen or more occupations before evidently deciding that the best career for her was living off her father's incomprehensibly soft heart—at least until a suitable, deep-walleted boyfriend could be found. "Who were Tammy's girlfriends?"

Deputy Bishop looked puzzled. "She was spending all her time chasin' the boys, sir."

"She has to have a girl friend, Howard. Someone for girl talk. We know that wasn't her mother. And the odds are good that if she does have a best friend—girl friend—then there's a well of information there."

"I don't know," he said dubiously.

"Start with the high school yearbook for the year they graduated. Look at the pictures in the activity section. Maybe rodeo club. Who the hell knows. Talk to Glen Archer. He's been at the school ten years or more, so he was principal the year Tammy graduated. See who her girl pals were. And then see if she was still hanging out with one or more of 'em."

I silently cursed the bad luck that had put Estelle Reyes-Guzman in a wheelchair. She could talk information out of a stone, and in a tenth of the time it would take the other deputies. As I watched Howard Bishop ease his county car back out onto Bustos Avenue, I wondered if I had been focusing on the right set of tracks. I sat in

310 with the door open for a few minutes, watching the light traffic of Posadas.

Sheriff Martin Holman had talked to the Woodruffs the night of Tammy's transfer from crushed truck to ambulance to helicopter, as had Sergeant Torrez. The couple had been hit hard by their daughter's death, and since those terrible moments had been holed up in their Posadas Heights home.

A scant twelve hours had passed since the first rap on their front door by Martin Holman. Twelve hours wasn't enough time to think about the healing process—that would take months, even years. But Karl and Bea Woodruff might be able to think again, if someone with a light touch talked to them.

I closed the door of 310 and headed for the hospital. When I arrived, Estelle Reyes-Guzman was helping Linda Real deal with the reporter's bizarre mother. Mrs. Real had decided it was an appropriate time to visit and complain. She glared balefully at me, but didn't repeat her earlier litigious threats.

Estelle agreed with my suggestion, and Robert Bales, the hospital administrator, suggested we use his office. I went home, showered, shaved, and donned a fresh uniform. And then I drove across town to Karl Woodruff's home.

I hadn't seen Woodruff since the two of us had talked in his drugstore Monday. When he opened the door, he looked like his own father. Dark circles under red eyes, drawn cheeks, blotchy, pale complexion—even his hair looked more heavily streaked with gray.

"Bill," he said, and held open the storm door.

"Can you give me a few minutes, Karl?"

"Of course." He beckoned me inside.

After he had shut the door, I put my hand on his shoulder. "Karl, is Bea here?"

"She's resting."

"It's really important that we talk with you both, Karl."

His brow furrowed and he looked at his watch. "We're expecting some relatives from out of town before long." He managed a smile. "You picked the one time when the place hasn't been full of neighbors. I had to shag everyone out so Bea could have some peace and quiet."

"I understand. And I know it's not a good time for me to be here, either. I wouldn't be bothering you folks if I didn't think this was important. What we really need is to talk with both you and Bea. Detective Reyes-Guzman and I."

"Oh," Karl said, and it came out as more of a groan, the kind of noise he might have made as he pulled out a really deep sliver.

"We have an office we can use at the hospital, if you would."

"The hospital?"

"The detective was injured last night. She's in a wheelchair and can't travel yet."

Woodruff frowned and looked at the floor. After a moment, he shook his head and half turned away. "Give me a few minutes," he said, and walked across the living room toward the hallway.

Five minutes turned into ten, and just about the time I was looking about for a comfortable chair, Woodruff reappeared.

"Can we meet you there in twenty minutes?"

"Fine," I said. "I'll be happy to drive you down there and back."

He smiled faintly. "That won't be necessary."

The couple had their own private sense of time, because it was more than an hour later when Karl and Bea Woodruff settled into the leather chairs in Robert Bales's office. Estelle Reyes-Guzman had drawn her wheelchair up near one of the large brown hassocks and propped her leg cast up. That and having a checkered afghan loaned by the hospital auxiliary draped around her shoulders made her look frail and vulnerable.

Bea Woodruff winced as she looked at Estelle's plasterwork, arm sling, and forehead stitchery. "You should be home in bed," she said. I saw her back straighten a little as she focused on someone else's troubles.

Estelle smiled and reached out a hand, taking Bea Woodruff's in hers. "I'm fine," she said. "Really." She leaned forward in the wheelchair, still holding Bea's hand. "Mr. and Mrs. Woodruff, we

have reason to believe that your daughter's death was not acci-
dental." The room fell silent and Karl and Bea's eyes were locked
on Estelle. Tears flowed down Bea's cheeks, but she ignored them,
letting them drip off to make tiny dark blotches on her blue linen
dress.

"We feel that there is no way, no physical way, that Tammy
could have driven up that road as far as she did, given the level of
intoxication in her blood that the medical examiners believe existed."

Again, the couple remained silent. "Mr. and Mrs. Woodruff," Estelle said, "we believe someone was with your daughter Sunday
night and again on Monday. Someone she knows. Perhaps someone she had come to trust."

"What can we tell you?" Karl Woodruff asked. "I mean, who
would do such a thing?"

"That's what we need to know, sir," Estelle said. "Do you know
Patrick Torrance?" Estelle's voice was almost a whisper.

The Woodruffs nodded, and Karl started to say, "But he's . . ."

"We don't believe Patrick Torrance had anything to do with
your daughter's death, Mr. Woodruff. I know it looks that way, with
the crash happening on County Road 14 on the way to the Torrance
ranch. But the evidence just isn't there. We also have heard that
Tammy had been seeing Brett Prescott."

Karl Woodruff nodded. "We thought well of him, too. And I've
known the family for years. Surely . . ."

"Can you think of anyone else she was seeing?"

Bea Woodruff leaned back into the dark leather and rested her
head, eyes closed. Karl sat hunched, his hands covering his face.

"I hadn't seen my daughter for three weeks," Bea Woodruff said
finally. She rocked her head from side to side. "Three weeks. We
had some stupid . . . some stupid little argument, and she wouldn't
come over to the house." The woman groped toward her purse, and
Estelle leaned over with a box of tissues.

"What was the argument about?"

Bea Woodruff honked, dabbed her eyes, and waved a hand in

240

dismissal. "You know. One of those silly things. I had talked to Jane Ross—she and I are such good friends—and Jane agreed to offer Tammy another chance at the realty. You know, I always thought that Tammy would be so good at that. She's so good with people, you know." She leaned her head back again and closed her eyes. "I just mentioned it to Tammy, and she exploded. Such a temper she's always had. Told me to stop meddling. That she didn't want to earn a living 'selling land to fat, rich Texans.' Those were her exact words."

"And that was three weeks ago?"

The woman nodded. Estelle looked at Karl. He was working his hands as if he had a ball of putty between them.

"Sir, do you know anyone else with whom she may have been associating?"

Karl shook his head. "I learned a long time ago that Tammy and I could stay on the best of terms if I didn't pry," he said softly.

Estelle shifted in the wheelchair, moved her leg a fraction, and then cradled her face against a fold of the afghan in her right hand. She looked like a little kid.

"Who was Tammy's best friend?" Estelle asked. Both of the Woodruffs looked puzzled. "Her very best friend."

"You mean, like a girlfriend?" Bea asked, and Estelle nodded.

"During high school, for example. I know she was popular, but most youngsters have got one person as a friend who's special above all the others."

Bea almost managed a smile. "Oh, she and Elena Muñoz were inseparable since ninth grade. And oh, that Elena. Do you know her?" She looked at Estelle. "I think her parents are from Mexico."

"I know her parents," I said, and both of the Woodruffs snapped around as if they were surprised to discover that I was in the room.

"Well," Bea said, "she was a wild one, I guess. You'd never guess it to look at her. Little slip of a thing. Beautiful hair down to her waist. Face like an angel. But she hated school, my goodness how she hated school. She skipped so much during her sophomore year that they finally suspended her."

241

"That makes sense," I said.

"Doesn't it, though," Bea replied. "And she never went back. Then Tammy started to skip. Half the time she was with Elena, and who knows what troubles the two of them together could concoct."

"And after Tammy graduated?" Estelle asked.

"No one, really. Not that I'm aware of," Bea said. "I know she still spends time with Elena. I saw them coming out of one of the clothing stores a week or so ago as I was driving by. They had their heads together, giggling like a couple of little kids. I remember because I'd been feeling so badly for her . . . for Tammy, I mean. I so wanted her to be happy. And I saw her that day, and she looked so carefree, so radiant." Bea leaned her head to one side, eyebrows arched as she reminisced. "Packages in one hand, arm-in-arm with a friend."

Mrs. Woodruff began to cry again, and Estelle covered the woman's left hand with her own, and a handy tissue. I shifted in my chair, uncomfortable with this recitation of the Woodruff family scrapbook. Estelle caught the agitation and shot me a quick look of impatience. I folded my hands on my lap.

"Do you know where Elena Muñoz works now?"

Bea shook her head, but Karl Woodruff replied, "She works at the Laundromat on Bustos and Second."

"We may want to talk with her at some time," Estelle said. "Had Tammy been drinking more recently?"

The abrupt change of subject startled Bea Woodruff and she glanced over at her husband. His eyes remained locked on the parquet floor tile.

"I don't think more . . ." she started to say, but Karl interrupted.

"A *lot* more," he murmured.

"How do you know?" Estelle asked, and somehow she kept any accusatory tone out of her voice.

"I could smell it from time to time, on her breath. When she came into the pharmacy. I saw an open bottle once in her truck." He shrugged helplessly. "Of course, I should have said something."

242

"What did she drink, mostly. Beer? Hard liquor? Maybe scotch, vodka, things like that?"

Woodruff nodded. "What difference does it make now? Beer, wine. She was particularly fond of rye whiskey." He snorted. "The cowpuncher's drink, I guess. I don't know for sure what she liked or didn't like other than that." He looked up at Estelle, into those wonderful dark eyes. "She drank to excess. We know that. And it killed her. We know that, too."

"Sir, would you look at this list? These are the items that were found in the cab of her truck at the accident scene. Either in the cab or in the immediate area." She slipped a single sheet of paper out of her leather folder and handed it to Karl Woodruff.

He read the list and grimaced, then made a little whimpering noise as he looked away. "Jesus," he said, and handed the list to his wife.

Bea Woodruff read the list and I saw her jaw quiver.

Estelle leaned forward. "Sir, we know that there is no way that Tammy was able to consume all that alcohol and still operate a motor vehicle. She would have been unconscious." She reached over and indicated one of the items on the list. "A couple of six-packs, maybe. A few shots of rye, as you say, maybe at the Broken Spur on the way. But half a quart of vodka on top of everything else? Not someone her size. It would have put her in a coma."

I saw the muscles of Karl Woodruff's jaw clench. "She wouldn't have drunk that stuff, anyway."

"Sir?"

"She couldn't stand vodka, officer." He reached up and touched his own forehead between his eyes. "It gave her an instant headache, right here. Made her sick."

Estelle leaned back. "Then someone else was either drinking with her at the time, or Tammy was planning to join someone and knew what his . . . or her . . . favorite drink was."

Karl went back to kneading his invisible ball of putty. "I wish to hell I could believe that in a few minutes I was going to wake up," he said. "Goddamned nightmare. I realize, sitting here, that my daughter is dead, and I can't tell you people one thing about her life the past couple years. I don't know who her circle of friends is. Hell, I don't even know if she *had* a circle of friends. I don't know what she was doing. I don't know how she was spending her time. Or what trouble she was in." He looked across at me, his eyes tortured. "And now she's gone."

"I'm sorry, Karl," I said.

"And I can't help her."

"I'm sorry," I repeated. I didn't know what else to say.

34

An impossibly fat woman looked me up and down, one hand on her hip, the other resting on the lid of a commercial washing machine.

"She called in sick today," she said. "She ain't here."

"She's home, then?"

"If she's sick, that's likely," the woman said. "Her gal friend died, you know."

"You don't say," I replied. "I'll check her house. Thanks for your time."

The fat woman watched without shifting position as I walked out of the Laundromat. As I pulled 310 away from the curb, she was still standing, watching.

The telephone book listed Elena Muñoz at 223 Garfield, a little dead-end street that angled off of Pershing, two blocks east of the hospital. The address was a cinder-block house that had been a rental unit for twenty years.

I stood on the concrete step and waited. The doorbell button lit when I pushed it, but I heard nothing. After a minute, I rapped hard on the door. While I waited, I turned and looked at the older model Ford Escort in the driveway. The tires were bald, and one taillight unit had been replaced with red plastic and duct tape. Life at the Laundromat wasn't making Elena Muñoz rich.

The door opened against the security chain, and I could see about two-thirds of Elena's pretty face. Her hair was a mess, and the makeup around her eyes had blurred and run, no longer covering up the red from crying. She lifted her chin a little when she saw me, and said, "I wondered when you'd show up."

Elena Muñoz didn't look like she needed threatening just then, so I smiled and thrust a hand in one of my pockets, trying to look a little more casual—like maybe I'd just stopped by on a lark.

"Me in particular, or just the cops?" I asked.

She looked past me at the Sheriff's Department patrol car parked at the curb. "I thought maybe Bobby would stop by."

"Bobby?"

"Bob Torrez. He's my cousin."

"No kidding?"

"Well, sort of." She slipped the chain and opened the door. "More like third or fourth cousin. Come on in."

"Do you have a few minutes?"

Elena turned and smiled, lighting up the tear stains a little. "I got nothing but time, mister."

"Why didn't you call us?"

"Why should I?"

"You don't have any idea who killed Tammy Woodruff?"

Her lower lip jutted out like a second grader deprived of morning milk break. I thought for a minute that she was going to start crying again. A box of tissues sat on a small coffee table, and I pulled one out and handed it to her. She waved it away and sat down on the sofa with a thump, hands folded between her legs.

I sat in a fake leather monstrosity opposite and waited.

"Sure, I got an idea," she said.

"Who?"

"Well, it happened up on Fourteen, didn't it?" She shrugged and turned away as if that were all the answer I needed.

"Yes, it did."

"Well?"

"Well, what?"

She turned her head and glared at me through eyes brimming with tears. "So he lives up there. That's what."

"Who lives up there?"

"Torrance. That son of a bitch."

"Patrick Torrance, you mean?" I asked, and she nodded. "You think he killed Tammy?" She nodded again. "Why would he do that?"

For a long time, she looked off to her right, eyes locked on something far beyond the cinder-block walls, beyond the yard outside, beyond Posadas.

"I just think he did."

"Why?"

"She said he threatened her."

"She told you that?" Elena nodded. "Why would he threaten her?"

After taking a deep breath and wiping a drop off the end of her nose with the back of her hand, Elena said, "Because she was through with him."

"Come on, Elena. Tammy didn't make a hobby out of monogamous relationships. We both know that. She'd broken up with him before. She left Brett Prescott and went back to Patrick. He knew what to expect."

"She was pregnant. She just found out."

"So what?" My response jarred her, and her mouth opened as if to say something. Nothing came out. "She was twenty-three years old, Elena. There's no mystery about a pregnancy. It's not like she was a twelve-year-old midschooler." She looked down at the floor and her forehead furrowed. I continued, "Was it Patrick Torrance's child? Did she say?"

"She didn't say."

"Who was she seeing this weekend, then? If she'd broken up with Patrick, who was she seeing?"

Elena Muñoz frowned again, as if all the pieces of the puzzle were floating around in her brain, refusing to fall into place or pattern.

"Tammy's mother said she saw the two of you last week, coming out of one of the stores."

"So?"

"And all the time you were with her last week, she never said who she was seeing?"

"Sure, she talked about it."

I spread my hands, waiting.

"She was all excited."

"About what?"

"She said she had a chance to make all this money."

"The last thing Tammy Woodruff needed was money," I said, and instantly regretted it.

"Her own money," Elena said with considerable acid.

"How was she going to do that?"

"That's what she said . . . that no one really thought she was much good for anything. This was her chance."

"What was she going to do?"

"She didn't say. It was some big secret."

"She never told you?"

Elena Muñoz shook her head. "But she kind of had this crazy glint in her eyes, you know? Like it was something she'd never done before? Or even thought about?"

"On Sunday night, Elena, we have evidence that Tammy was the driver of a truck that one of our deputies stopped to assist on State Highway Fifty-six." The girl blinked but said nothing. "Patrick Torrance told me that he saw Tammy Woodruff driving her own pickup truck around noon on Monday. And there was another man with her." Again Elena said nothing, and I added, "No one saw her alive after that, Elena. Patrick got scared and ran off to Wyoming."

Elena looked incredulous. "Wyoming?"

I shrugged. "He has relatives up there. He got scared. For Tammy and for himself."

"That does a lot of good, the dumb fuck," she muttered.

"Maybe, maybe not. If you know who she was seeing, we'd like to know. Before anyone else gets hurt."

248

"She wouldn't tell me his name. She said she didn't want her father to find out."

"Why is that?"

Elena looked at me defiantly. "Because she said he was a Mexican."

I frowned, puzzled. "So?"

"So the Woodruffs don't like Mexicans. He doesn't like me. His wife doesn't like me. That's why Tammy and I aren't sharing an apartment. He wouldn't let her."

"How could he not let her?" I said, puzzled. "She was over twenty-one. She could live where she wanted . . . and live with whomever she pleased."

She made a face and dismissed that remark without comment. "I still found out who she was seeing, though. I saw them Sunday. I saw them drive by. I was working, and Tammy looked right at me and smiled this great big old smile like she had it all over everybody."

"Who was with her?"

This time she didn't hesitate. "Carlos. Carlos Sánchez." She mistook the expression on my face for a blank brain, and added, "His father owns the Broken Spur Saloon."

35

I borrowed Bob Torrez's pickup truck, a ridiculous old Chevy with chrome running boards, twin spotlights, toolbox snuggled in between wrought-iron curlicues in the bed—even one of those web tailgates that's supposed to boost mileage from ten to twelve. The truck was painted mostly semigloss black, a good grade of house paint slathered on with a high-quality nylon bristle brush.

Everyone in the county who cared about such things knew that it was Bob's truck, and that was just fine. What I didn't want was a police car.

I cruised down Bustos Avenue, feeling the throb of the powerful 454 V-8 under the hood and smelling the waft of exhaust fumes from a leaky manifold mixed with the aroma of roasted corn chips long forgotten in a corner between windshield and dashboard.

More expensive than the pickup truck was the small cellular phone unit that rested in the middle of the seat. It, like the ones in my Blazer and Estelle's little sedan, belonged to Posadas County. If the carbon monoxide didn't get me, the truck would suit my purposes.

As I passed Nick Chavez's dealership, I scanned the vehicles parked behind the main building. They ranged from derelict parts cars to vehicles owned by employees—and right smack in the middle, sandwiched between a bent Volvo station wagon and the Weatherford's crumpled van, was an older model pickup. I couldn't see much of it as I passed, but I did see the stock racks in the back. I hoped for mud as well, but the truck glinted in the early afternoon sunshine, clean as a whistle, the miracle of a modern drive-thru carwash.

I turned left on MacArthur, gathering a back view of the dealership. At the fork of MacArthur and Camino del Sol, I swung around and headed back. The dealership wasn't crawling with people, but there were enough—one salesman talking with an elderly couple outside, one of the servicemen half under a van with out-of-state plates, and Nick Chavez down on the new-car line, talking to a kid who would have traded his little sister for the sleek coupe parked in the end slot. No one paid any mind to the old rattletrap that idled into the lot, around the back of the service building, and out the other side.

As I passed the pickup with the stock rack, I jotted down the license plate number. The plate itself was ancient and hard to read, the corners folded and the letters marred from countless strikes by hay bales, firewood, old car parts, and whatever else twenty years use and abuse had inflicted.

Pulling out onto Bustos again, I pulled the microphone off the dashboard hook and turned up the volume of Bob's cheap discount radio. I was about to call the plate into dispatch, and then thought better of it. There were too many overeager ears. I drove back to the Sheriff's Department and ran the plate in person.

The NCIC information came back with no wants or warrants, and that didn't surprise me. The vehicle, listed as a 1978 Ford three-quarter ton, was registered to Mateo Esquibel, d.o.b. April 6, 1903. Señor Esquibel, if he could still walk that far, picked up his mail from P O Box 6, Regal, New Mexico.

"You slimy son of a bitch," I said aloud, and Gayle Sedillos turned in her chair.

251

"Sir?"

"Nothing, Gayle. I'm not here."

"Yes, sir."

I closed my office door and locked it, and sat down at my desk. After a minute's thought, I picked up the phone. Victor Sánchez answered on the tenth ring with a curt "Yeah."

"Victor, this is Gastner at the sheriff's office. I've got one more question to ask you if you've got a minute." Sánchez said nothing, but he didn't hang up. "Does Mateo Esquibel still drive?"

After another long silence, Victor managed a single word. "What?"

"Mateo Esquibel? You know? Down in Regal. He's some relation to you, isn't he?"

"You mean the old man?"

"Yes."

"You want to talk to him, you're going to have to drive down there. He's got a phone, but he don't use it. He's deaf now."

"Oh. No wonder," I said.

"What do you want with him?"

"Me? Nothing. One of my deputies wanted to buy his truck or something like that. I said I'd ask you about it."

The line fell dead again. "Thanks a lot," I said.

"Yeah."

I telephoned the hospital next, knowing I shouldn't, but wanting Estelle's advice. She agreed with everything I wanted to do except my plan for leaving her sitting right where she was. But she had no choice.

In an hour, I felt confident that I had all bases covered. Bob Torrez had changed into civilian clothes, taken his leaky truck back to Chavez's dealership, and purchased a set of exhaust manifold gaskets from the parts department. On the way out, a casual glance into the business office of the dealership had confirmed that Carlos Sánchez was there and busy with a stack of paperwork.

Bob parked behind his aunt's house on MacArthur, pushed up the hood of the pickup, and settled down to enjoy the clear, thousand-yard view of the dealership's two driveways.

Tony Abeyta took 306 and began regular patrol of the county. When he reached the end of a shift at four that afternoon, Tom Mears would relieve him. At midnight, Howard Bishop would take over. All three were instructed to avoid getting themselves tangled in something that couldn't be dropped at an instant's notice. All three were told to stay central in the county; to make no effort to avoid State Highway 56, but to give the highway no special attention.

And Gayle Sedillos, caught in the trap of being efficient, smart, and quick-witted, planned to camp out for the duration at dispatch. She kept tabs on the deputies as the day wore on, making sure that their location in the county at any given time was no mystery.

If Carlos Sánchez made any kind of move, he'd know as well as I did exactly where the working deputies were. And that's what I wanted.

At 5:05, Carlos Sánchez left the dealership driving old man Esquibel's truck. He drove directly to his apartment at 131 MacArthur Terrace, a short cul-de-sac off the main street. He drove right by Carmine Torrez's house on MacArthur Street, and if he'd looked to his right, he would have seen Bob Torrez under the hood of the old Chevy, portable radio propped up on one fender, grease up to his elbows.

At five-thirty, I heard the moan of Jim Bergin's Beech Baron as it circled the village and lined up for final approach. I was at the airport waiting, and I hustled Patrick Torrance into one of the small pilot's conference rooms in the FBO Building. Without giving either his mind or his stomach time to stop spinning from the trip, I spread out a series of photographs on the table. Several of the photos were meaningless, dug out of files at random.

One photo was a clipping of Nick Chavez's Christmas advertisement, with all the employees of the dealership gathered in front of the showroom, holding a large wreath.

"Take your time," I said to the youth. "Examine the faces."

Patrick sat down, taking each photograph in turn. He hesitated quite a while at one picture taken of Sheriff Martin Holman on the capitol steps with one of our state's senators. Eventually he put that photo down and picked up the group shot of Nick Chavez's gang. His forehead furrowed.

"I have a magnifying glass out in the car if you need it," I said. At the same time I placed my small cassette recorder on the table in front of him and switched it on.

Patrick shook his head. "No." He drew the photo up close to his nose, squinting. "That's him, right there." He picked up a pencil and pointed with the tip. Carlos Sánchez was in front, kneeling at one side of the wreath, looking pleasant and professional.

For the benefit of the tape recorder, I said, "Patrick, you're pointing at Carlos Sánchez. Are you sure that's the man that you saw in the pickup truck Monday with Tammy Woodruff?"

"Yes, sir. I am."

"You'll testify to that?"

Patrick's eyes opened wider, but he didn't protest. He nodded slightly and looked back at the photograph. "I'm sure that's him."

I reached over and turned off the recorder. "Then that's all we need, son. I'd like to ask that you go home and stay there until I call you."

Patrick nodded, and then said, "Do you want me to call my dad?"

"From here? There's no need. Just go on home."

He smiled for what I guessed was the first time in many days. "Sir, my truck is in Wyoming. It's a long walk out to the ranch."

"Ah," I said. "I'll drop you off. When you take the bus back to Gillette to get your truck, save the bills. The county will reimburse you." I patted him on the shoulder. "Bus, Patrick. Baggage class."

I didn't take time to chat when I left Patrick at the driveway of

254

the Torrance ranch. It was already dark when I pulled back out onto the state highway and headed my old Blazer south toward Regal. I was after one final piece of the puzzle, and I knew exactly where to look.

36

FROM the pass above Regal, I could count the lights, a sparse scattering of a dozen spots of yellow. Farther to the south and east, I could see the bright glare of the sodium-vapor lights at the border crossing. The gate would be locked, the officers gone for the day.

With the windows down, I drove through the narrow dirt lanes, keeping a sedate speed neither too fast nor too slow to attract attention. A single bulb burned somewhere in the bowels of Mateo Esquibel's little house, the light faded to little more than a candle's worth by the time it washed up against the lace curtains.

No lights were on at the ancient building next door. More than sixty feet long and only twelve or fourteen feet wide, it might have been a mercantile or feed store at one time. A portion of the roof had collapsed, and the three elm trees in the yard were dead. I stopped the Blazer near the end of the building, pushed off the lights, switched off the engine, and got out.

For February, the night was mild with just the faintest breeze stirring the tall grass along the old building's foundation. But I wasn't interested in history. I pushed the truck's door closed just enough to turn off the dome light and skirted the old store, heading toward the back of Mateo Esquibel's property.

If the old man had a dog, it was inside. I moved slowly, keeping my flashlight off. I didn't remember any fences in my path, just an open side yard strewn with rocks and cacti.

I reached the trailer where the old man kept his wood supply, and bent down to look at the hitch that rested on a stout chunk of railroad tie. If it had been used recently, fresh steel-against-steel contact marks would show on the bottom of the housing that covered the ball. I was about to attempt an impossible position so that I could see the hitch when the dog began barking.

From inside the house came the insistent, rhythmic yapping and I froze in place, flashlight switched off. For the better part of five minutes I stood there while the mutt ran through its entire repertoire of canine noises. No one came to either door or window, and eventually the dog gave up. For another five minutes I stood still, giving the animal time to lose interest.

Moving cautiously, I backed up and made my way around the back side of the trailer, and then to the back wall of the garage. A side window had been boarded up years ago, the nails rusting and sending streaks of black down the wooden walls.

At the front corner I hesitated, listening for the dog. Then I eased around to the doorway. It was secured with an old iron hasp and an enormous brass padlock. Any shine the brass may have had when it was new had given way to a dull patina decades before. By placing a single finger between the two sides, I tried to pry the doors open. They didn't move a fraction of an inch. Whoever had hung the door had been an expert.

I made my way around the east side of the garage. Another window was covered, this time with a combination of boards and cardboard. One of the eight panes of glass had been hit in the corner with a small projectile—no doubt a neighbor kid's rock from a slingshot. The pane hadn't shattered, but by working my pocketknife into the hole I could pry loose a small wedge of glass.

I did so, and then pushed the cardboard that had covered the inside of the window to one side—just an inch or less, but enough for the beam of the flashlight to lance into the garage. I squinted and sucked in my breath. The beam bounced off chrome and fancy paint.

With care, I went to work with the pocketknife again, enlarging the hole by prying out another sliver of glass.

This time, when I looked, I could see the bright colors clearly, the trade name on the fender, and, as I swept the beam back, the fancy gas cap, air dam, and roof rack. The Weatherfords' Suburban had survived its high-speed trip from Oklahoma no worse for wear.

I took a deep breath and snapped off the flashlight, standing quietly with my back to the garage.

Now that the pieces were drifting into place, it all made perfect sense. Carlos Sánchez had himself an effortless pipeline for prize vehicles, straight to Mexico. He could make copies of the keys at leisure; he could lift an extra temporary sticker and fill in appropriate names. It wouldn't be hard to find willing drivers—both for the excitement and the money. And either explained how Tammy Woodruff had gotten sucked in.

A dozen questions still circled in my mind like hungry vultures over a carcass. It made no sense that Carlos Sánchez would let this vehicle sit in a garage a rifle shot from the border. No matter how innocent the garage appeared, every minute the stolen truck stayed on the U.S. side of the line, the risk increased. That meant that all we had to do was wait.

I made my way back to the Blazer, climbed in, and released the clutch, allowing the vehicle to roll forward down the slight incline. When the road forked, I turned left, started the engine, and drove out of the village as casually as if I lived there.

The last dirt road turned off the pavement just before the first switchback. I followed it, winding up the hillside toward the enormous white water-storage tank that had been installed with monies from a federal grant five years before. The tank provided ample and dependable storage, and its broad, smooth sides provided local spray-can artists with an open canvas.

I drove around the back side of the tank and parked under two-foot high letters that proclaimed *Esmarelda y Paco, '93*. The bulk of the tank shaded me from the vapor light. From there, I com-

258

manded a view of the entire valley. I could clearly see the patch of black behind Mateo Esquibel's house where the garage stood.

I turned the volume of the radio up just enough that I could hear the broadcasts, but kept the windows of the truck closed.

The night closed in, broken only by an occasional jet high overhead or a coyote somewhere in the hills behind me. Shortly after eight o'clock, a car engine started somewhere down in the village. A moment later headlights flicked on near a house a hundred yards west of Esquibel's. I watched as the vehicle oozed out of one driveway, traveled down the road a stone's throw, and pulled into another. A porch light went on, remained bright for a couple of minutes, and then went out.

The folks of Regal weren't into rompin' and stompin', at least not on a Wednesday night. I looked across to the hillside on the east where the small church stood, but if the Catholics had planned a Wednesday night service, they hadn't showed.

All evening long, I'd listened to Gayle Sedillos working dispatch, her voice caught by the repeater on Regal Peak. At 9:17, she came on the air, and I could hear a slight edge to her voice, a slight tremor of excitement.

"Three oh seven, PCS."

"Three oh seven, go ahead." Tommy Mears sounded bored. He was a good actor.

"Three oh seven, ten-twenty?" She had asked the deputy where he was less than twenty minutes before, and at that time he'd been at the airport, talking with manager Jim Bergin.

Now, he replied, "Three oh seven is two miles west, on the interstate."

"Ten-four, three oh seven. If you get a chance, would you swing by the hospital and pick up a folder from Detective Reyes-Guzman? She said it's at the information desk."

"Ten-four."

I smiled in the dark and my pulse clicked up about thirty notches. The message meant that Carlos Sánchez had left his house. Estelle Reyes-Guzman had no folder for anyone, but Carlos Sánchez, if

259

he was listening to the police scanner, had no way of knowing that. Gayle had managed the complex and dull alert message without a hitch.

The cellular phone on the seat beside me chirped, and I picked up the receiver. Bob Torrez's voice was distant.

"Sir, he's heading west on State Fifty-six."

"All right. Don't let him pick up your headlights coming out of town."

"I'll stay back. What about Tomás?"

I glanced out across the sleepy village toward the border crossing. "No sign of him. But he said he'd be there."

"I'd sure hate to see this guy slip through."

"He's not going to do that, Robert. Mears should be a minute or so behind you."

"I can see him right now. He's at the filling station on Grande."

"Don't let him get itchy. I want to see how Sánchez plays his game. Remember, if he stops at the bar, get to Gayle in a hurry. You go on past, and make sure Mears turns up Fourteen."

"Yes, sir."

The inside of my mouth was dry as I sat in the dark, trying to picture the flow of traffic southwest on 56. Carlos Sánchez had to be feeling confident. If he didn't have a scanner, he was stupid. If he did have one, all he knew was that Deputy Mears was tied up at the hospital. There had been no word on the movements of anyone else. The night was ordinary.

I took a deep breath and settled back in the seat.

Eleven minutes later, the telephone chirped and I startled so hard that I almost hit my head on the roof.

"What?"

"I think he stopped at the bar, sir, but if he did, it was just for a minute. No more than that. I didn't have time to go on by. He's headed south."

"All right. Stay back. Remember the scenic pull-out halfway down on this side. That's where you stop." Off in the distance to the south, I saw a single flash of light, as if someone had swept a

260

spotlight in a circle, shooting the beam up into the night. "And Tomás is in place," I said, hoping it wasn't wishful thinking.

At 9:38, I saw the headlights high up on the switchbacks from Regal pass. They descended sedately, almost poking along.

"Come on, you son of a bitch," I muttered. All I could see were the lights, but I could picture the old truck putting along, inconspicuous and legal as all hell. A rancher going home after checking the cattle, or a kid out in his daddy's truck, going home nice and early just like he was supposed to. There were no state police on this section of highway, and Carlos Sánchez knew—and I hoped he was gloating—exactly where the deputies were.

The truck passed the turnoff to the water tank and kept going. If Sergeant Torrez had crested the pass, he'd dumped his lights, because the mountain behind us was black.

Like a homing pigeon, Mateo Esquibel's old truck idled into the village, turning first this way and that, finally backing right into the old man's yard, back bumper crowding the hitch of the wood-laden trailer. Resting the binoculars on the steering wheel, I watched the figure get out of the truck, illuminated by the faint rays cast by the dome light.

Sánchez was a believer in taking time with his cover, apparently. If he'd allowed Tammy Woodruff to drive a stolen truck to the border, he'd used the old man's truck, hooked to the trailer, when he'd driven back up the highway to check on her, knowing that no one would give him a second glance.

From where I sat behind the water tank to Mateo Esquibel's old adobe was at most 300 yards. But even with the binoculars, the figure was nothing more than a vague, drifting shadow.

Somewhere off in the distance a dog barked; it was soon joined in chorus by half a dozen others. The dogs didn't know what the hell was going on, and neither did I. My telephone chirped again, and when I answered Bob Torrez said, "I'm at the pull-out."

"All right. Sit tight and stay on the line," I said, laying the receiver on the seat. I didn't know what to think, since I assumed Carlos Sánchez would be meeting someone at the border . . . someone

261

who would collect the vehicle and, I thought, hand over a lump of cash—perhaps ten, maybe fifteen thousand for such a vehicle.

But as yet, I saw no clear way for Sánchez to return to Posadas once the deal was made. Maybe that was his plan. Maybe this time he was headed south along with the Suburban. Two murder raps made for powerful motivation.

Down below, a blast of light illuminated the area around the garage. The backup lights of the Suburban were bright, and for a moment, perfectly clearly, I could see the wooden doors, open wide. Sánchez pulled out of the garage, stopped to get out and close the doors, and then drove out of Mateo Esquibel's yard. I tracked the Suburban as it drove through the village and reached the pavement. "Turn right to Mexico," I said, and as if he heard me, the vehicle turned toward the border. I started the Blazer and pulled out, lights off. By the time I reached the pavement, I could see the brake lights of the Suburban flash as Sánchez braked for the tight curve just before the customs' gate. I accelerated hard, wanting to narrow the distance while the slight rise of hill separated us.

As I approached the curve, I shoved the gear lever into neutral and clicked off the engine. I wanted to roll to a stop just as I crested the hill, so that when Carlos Sánchez got out of the truck, he wouldn't hear the engine or tire noise of my old Blazer.

At the same time, hidden behind a hillock on the Mexican side of the border, Captain Tomás Naranjo of the Federales had promised that he'd wait for my signal before making a move—in case our quarry somehow slipped through the gate.

Our timing was perfect. Our luck could have been better.

CARLOS Sánchez never looked back. If he had, he'd have seen the silhouette of my vehicle a hundred yards away, squatting in the middle of the road. He got out of the Suburban, walked to the border gate, and unlocked it. Simple as that. As Nick Chavez had once said, theft was simplest if the thief had a key. I wondered who Carlos Sánchez had bribed for that useful copy.

He reached for the top bar and started to swing the heavy welded pole gate toward the American side.

I started the engine of the Blazer with one hand and barked into the cellular phone, "Move it, Robert." At the same time, a light show erupted from south of the border as two vehicles exploded from behind a long creosote-bush-studded sand dune.

Sergeant Torrez had not waited at the turnout. When he'd seen the Suburban pull out of the village, he'd coasted down the hill and now was less than two hundred yards behind me.

I saw the flashing lights across the border; the Blazer's back tires chirped as I floored the accelerator.

Carlos Sánchez froze in his tracks for only a heartbeat as lights converged from both directions. With a lunge, he pushed the gate away and sprang toward the Suburban. Just as Tomás Naranjo's jeep slid to a stop in a cloud of dust and sand thirty feet from the gate, Sánchez accelerated hard, all four massive tires chewing sand

and gravel. The Suburban spun to the west, its shiny back bumper narrowly missing the gate as it turned.

I yanked the wheel to the right, thinking to block Sánchez, but back up the highway was not where he had in mind. The Suburban shot off the side of the road and bounced across the ditch, paralleling the border fence. For two hundred yards, the fence was high and solid, welded rails and wire. But farther on in both directions, it shrank to nothing more than six strands of barbed wire.

If Sánchez was headed up the line, where he could drive the vehicle right through in a tangle of posts and snapped wire, he'd face two squads of eager Federales, itching for some excitement to cap their day.

Even as I swung off the pavement in pursuit, I saw Bob Torrez's old pickup truck slide in a circle and catapult off into the sand and bushes.

But the border wasn't what Carlos Sánchez had in mind, either. His truck thundered along the rough fence access road, dove down through an arroyo, and, as it crested the other side, swung back to the north.

If I had had the speed, I could have cut him off when he turned across my path. But I hadn't engaged the front hubs of the Blazer, and was caught off guard. Now, stuck in two-wheel drive, I couldn't keep up, as my back tires churned and spun in the soft sand. Bob Torrez guessed Sánchez's route back toward the village, and angled to intercept him.

I saw his pickup hit a hummock of grass and go airborne, shedding its spare tire, oil cans, tools, and part of the right taillight assembly. In between bounces, I grabbed the police radio microphone off the dash.

"Three oh seven, make sure that highway's blocked," I shouted. "Take it at the first switchback." Mears wouldn't have any trouble putting a cork in the highway. All he had to do was park sideways at the turn. The steep mesa face would take care of the rest.

As we approached the south side of the village I could see two sets of red lights coming down the hillside as Mears and Bishop cut off Carlos Sánchez's escape to the north.

Ahead of me, the lights of the Suburban disappeared as the vehicle plunged down into the main arroyo that split the village in half. I turned away from the edge, knowing that it was a sure trap for two-wheel drive. Bob Torrez spun north, and just as the Suburban roared up and out on the west side of the arroyo he reached the dirt path that was Regal's southernmost main street.

Sánchez didn't flinch as Torrez's old truck plunged into his path. The two vehicles met with a crash, the impact spinning the pickup around so that it faced back the way it had come. With a scream of bent metal against rubber, Sánchez flogged the battered Suburban into one of the side lanes.

By then I had worked my way north along the arroyo to the lane, and when I reached the crumpled pickup I paused just long enough for Torrez to dive in, shotgun in hand.

"He can't go anywhere," I said, and even as I spoke we saw the Suburban pull into Mateo Esquibel's side yard.

"Howard, we're going to need you down here at the house," I said into the mike. "Tom, stay up on the highway."

I approached Esquibel's tiny adobe slowly. The Suburban sat in the driveway, door ajar, dome light on.

"You think he slipped out the back?" Torrez breathed.

"Be careful," I said, and he was out of the Blazer like a shot, weapon at high port. I slid the truck into gear, turned off the lights, and got out.

I knew Carlos Sánchez had not slipped out the back. I couldn't imagine that walking was his style, especially in this country. His return to the house could have been for only one reason. He had to figure that Mateo Esquibel was his ticket to Mexico.

I stepped forward and shut the door of the stolen Suburban, and the yard was plunged into darkness. The dog inside was yapping, and I could see only one light. It was so faint it would have frustrated the most dedicated Peeping Tom.

265

"Sánchez!" I shouted. "Come on out."

Other than the old dog, there was no response from the house.

"We don't want to hurt either you or the old man. Come on out." Still no response. I cursed and turned as Howard Bishop's patrol car idled into the yard. He started to get out of the car, but I waved a hand as I walked over. "Stay in the car and keep on the radio," I said. "Bob's around back. I don't think our man is going anywhere."

I turned back and walked toward the front door. Just in front of the small front stoop I stopped, hands on my hips. "Carlos! I want to come in." The damn dog started yapping again, and I heard a dull thud, like furniture being moved. "I'm at the front door," I shouted. "Don't do anything stupid." Going through the door wasn't one of the brighter things I'd ever done, but I was in no mood to stand out in the dark, trying to negotiate with silence.

Carlos Sánchez had to know as well as I did that other deputies waited outside. I was counting on him understanding that shooting one old fat officer wouldn't do him any good.

The doorknob turned and I pushed open the front door. The light came from a little burlap-shaded lamp that sat on a low table on the west wall, two paces from the woodstove. A doorway led to the back of the house, where I supposed the kitchen and bathroom to be. Mateo Esquibel was sitting in a deep, old chair. The blanket that covered it had long shed its color and was now soft from dust and dog hair.

Mateo looked at me as I stood a pace away from the door on the stoop. His face was expressionless, heavy-lidded eyes just watching. The dog sat in his lap, and yapped once more before falling silent.

Behind the old man's chair stood Carlos Sánchez, his back to the thick, impregnable adobe wall. He held a short pump shotgun, and rested the weight of the gun on the wing of the chair. The muzzle looked as big as a howitzer.

"Can I come in?" I asked.

Carlos raised his head a fraction, twitching his jaw. "Drop your gun outside," he said softly.

"No," I said genially. "You're holding that thing, and my gun's buried under my coat. I'm no quick-draw artist. Just relax."

A loud thump came from behind the house and Sanchez's eyes flickered.

"Can I walk over to the doorway there? I'll tell 'em to back off."

Sánchez nodded, and the shotgun muzzle followed me as I walked past them to the doorway leading to bed and bath.

"Robert!" I shouted. "Forget it. Go round front and keep Howard company. Everything's fine in here."

I turned and looked at Sánchez. He was smaller than I had remembered, slender and dark, with none of the bulk or coarseness of his father.

"You see? It's easy. Now, what do you want?"

"Over there," he said, and motioned to the still open front door.

"All right," I said affably. I kept my hands in plain view. "You want me to close it?" I did so without waiting for a response.

The old man raised a hand and rubbed the left side of his face. He was missing three fingers, probably lost half a century before Carlos Sánchez was born.

"Are you all right?" I asked.

"He's fine," Sánchez snapped.

"Then what do you want?"

"I think that's pretty obvious."

"What do you think is going to happen to you once you're across the border?"

"I'll take my chances with that," Sánchez said.

"Well, we're not going to let you do that," I said. "The best thing you can do for all concerned is put that damn shotgun down before anyone else gets hurt." Sánchez's eyes darted to one side, toward the side window. He shifted position slightly, putting the old man squarely between himself and the opening. "You had quite a deal going for yourself," I said, but he ignored me. Carlos Sánchez wasn't about to lapse into a long session of storytelling or explanation. "Back outside," he said, and hefted the shotgun. With the other hand, he grasped Mateo Esquibel by the elbow and urged him to his feet. The old man looked confused and frowned.

When he looked at me, I said slowly and distinctly, "Do exactly what he asks." If he read lips, he read Spanish, not English. He glanced at Carlos Sánchez, and the younger man said something in Spanish. The old man nodded.

Sánchez escorted the old man across the floor toward the front door. "You go back outside. Tell them to back off. Way off. Leave your truck."

"The keys are in it," I said. "But this isn't going to work, Carlos. You've got to know that."

"It'll work if you use your head, sheriff. Now do like I said."

I didn't move for a long moment. If Sánchez did make it to a border crossing, either by way of crashing through the fence or bribing the right person, I had no guarantee that Tomás Naranjo and his troops would feel especially motivated to fight our war for us. Sánchez had committed no crime in Mexico, beyond the sale of a few stolen vehicles—and that was damn near a national pastime across the border.

Much as I wanted the son of a bitch, I didn't want the old man hurt. If he had known what Carlos Sánchez had been up to, he was technically as guilty as the man who held the shotgun. But I found his complicity unlikely. He was going to be a sad old man now, knowing that Sánchez hadn't been visiting him out of respect for the aging.

I backed up, filling the doorway. "Carlos . . ." I started to say, but he interrupted me with an impatient wave of the shotgun.

"Call them off."

With a deep breath, I turned to shout at Torrez, who crouched behind the bulk of the truck.

Behind him, I saw more lights turned on as the tiny village gradually awoke to the ruckus in Mateo Esquibel's front yard. The old man's dog ran out of the house and made a beeline for Bob Torrez, stopping a dozen feet from the deputy to bark frantically.

I heard the guttural squelch of Howard Bishop's radio, and then the deputy slithered out of the car and crouched by the front fender. "Sir!" he shouted. "Mears just let Victor Sánchez through. He's coming in."

I stopped in my tracks and looked to the east, toward the main road. A vehicle was just pulling into Regal, going much too fast and fishtailing in the dirt.

Turning to Carlos, I said, "Is this the rescue you were hoping for?"

But to my surprise, he jerked Mateo Esquibel closer and rested the muzzle of the shotgun on the old man's shoulder. "Get him out of here." The urgency in Sánchez's voice surprised me. I waited, framed in the doorway, knowing that more confusion might work in our favor, providing a safe opening.

If Carlos Sánchez let down his guard for an instant, I could grab the barrel of the pump shotgun, wresting it away from the old man's head. Failing that, I knew exactly how Sergeant Robert Torrez operated. Even as he moved into position behind the Suburban, I'd caught the glint of light off the barrel of his .308 deer rifle. One opening was all he would need.

Victor Sánchez's fat pale-green Continental slithered into the yard, almost taking off the door of Howard Bishop's county car.

He jerked open the door and stalked toward us, reaching the back of the Suburban before Torrez blocked his way.

"Let him come through," I shouted, and I saw Carlos Sánchez duck his head. He fidgeted and backed around the old man until their two heads merged as one. He pulled Mateo Esquibel a step back into the living room. When Victor Sánchez reached the stoop, I held up a hand.

"You'd better stop there," I said.

"I don't have to talk to you!" Carlos shouted at his father, and for the first time there was a crack in the younger man's voice.

Victor's face bulged with fury as he looked at me. "What do you think you're doing here?" he whispered.

"Your son's holding Mr. Esquibel, Victor. That Suburban's stolen. He was trying to slip across the border."

Victor's eyes narrowed. When he spoke, he had to force the words out through clenched teeth.

"Carlos! Get out here!"

"Be careful," I said. "He's got a shotgun."

Victor's head snapped around like I'd jerked it with a chain. "He's wanted in connection with two murders, Victor. Deputy Enciños and Tammy Woodruff. He's not just going to let you walk in there."

I turned slightly in the doorway so Victor could see past me.

Carlos saw his father and shouted, "Get him out of here! I mean it."

"Carlos, don't do anything stupid," I said. Victor Sánchez started to push past me, but I blocked the doorway with one arm. Without taking his eyes off his son, Sánchez said, "Get out of my way." He stood patiently, waiting for me to weigh the options. Finally I dropped my arm. Victor stepped forward into the living room, standing between me and his son.

I saw no weapon in Victor's hands, and I was banking on Carlos being incapable of swinging the shotgun without having to twist away from the old man. That would give me room for a clear shot, and I edged my hand back toward my holstered revolver.

But Victor Sánchez had a different agenda. I don't know what he knew, or what he had been able to piece together. But right then, his small, hard eyes were focused on the shotgun and the old man.

He stood facing his son, hands clenched at his sides.

"¿Cómo podrias hacer este?" he whispered. "How could you do this?"

"Get out of my way, Papa," Carlos snarled. His feet shifted and I could see the knuckles of his right hand turn white.

Victor stood stock-still, his eyes unblinking. "Is it true?"

Carlos's feet danced another nervous little two-step, and the muzzle of the shotgun dipped.

"Is it true?" Victor said again, and the words were no louder than a soft puff of night air.

I edged farther into the room, two paces behind Victor's broad back. Carlos saw me, and this time there was almost a note of pleading in his voice. "Get him out of here!"

Victor had read all the answer he needed in his son's panic. "How could you do it?" he said again, this time in English. He shook his head slowly and spoke as if he were talking to himself. *"Por nada . . . y con el viejo. ¿Por un poquito dinero, tú amagas tú abuelo propio?* Your own grandfather?"

Carlos lifted the shotgun, almost resting it on the ancient man's shoulder. Its black muzzle pointed directly at Victor Sánchez's face.

"Dos personas," Victor said. *"¿Y cómo podrias robar de me? ¿Cómo podrias hacerlo?"*

"Papa . . ." Carlos started to say, and he sounded like a child.

"No creo que . . ." Victor said, but it was his hand I was watching. His right hand had drifted around behind him, slipping under the bulky jacket he wore. Even as he pulled out the small revolver, he moved as quickly and gracefully as a dancer. Lashing out with his left hand, he pushed the shotgun muzzle away from the old man's head, at the same time driving his right hand out like a prize-fighter.

The explosion of the revolver was loud in the confines of the room, and Carlos Sánchez staggered backward with a cry. Victor pushed after him, wresting the shotgun out of his grasp. The weapon thudded to the floor as Victor drove his son toward the back wall of the living room. Mateo Esquibel, looking puzzled, rubbed his face.

The two bodies crashed into the wall, and a small framed portrait of Christ dropped to the floor, its glass shattering.

Jerking the handcuffs off my belt, I lunged across the room to where Victor held his son against the wall. Carlos's eyes drifted past the purple, enraged face of his father to my own.

"He shot me," he said simply.

"Victor, give me the gun!" I shouted, and even as I did so, the revolver thudded to the floor.

"He shot me," Carlos said again, and started to sag sideways. Victor held him by his jacket until the younger man's weight was too much to support. Then he lowered his son to the dusty floor of the living room. I kicked the short-barreled .38 away and held up a hand to stop Torrez and Bishop as they charged up the front steps.

"Take care of him," I said, pointing at Mateo Esquibel.

I knelt beside Victor Sánchez, and I could smell the onions, and the fried chicken, and the beer that he served at the Broken Spur Saloon. He said nothing, but his eyes were locked on his son's face. The rage was gone, replaced by quiet desperation.

"I can't . . ." Carlos Sánchez said clearly, and stopped.

"Lie still, son." I turned to issue orders, but Deputy Bishop was ahead of me. He slipped out the door and I heard his boots thudding across the yard toward his car.

"Papa," Carlos Sánchez whispered. "It hurts." Blood was beginning to leak through the jacket, and Carlos made a strangled, choking sound, at the same time that he tried to push himself up to a sitting position. And then his eyes glazed and lost focus. "Papa," he said one more time, and died.

I rocked back on my haunches and watched as Victor released his hold on his son. Victor never took his eyes off his son's face, but he spoke in English. "How could he kill like that? And he stole from his own father. How could he do that? He just ran inside and took the money. How could he do that?"

I didn't reply as I stood up. Victor looked up at me. "Was he trying to leave the country?"

"We think so."

"He didn't even have a word to say to me."

I walked out of the adobe, leaving the two of them alone.

Bishop came trotting back, his service automatic in his hand. "The ambulance is on the way," he said.

272

"And put that thing away," I answered. I leaned against the Blazer's rusted fender and looked out across the little village.

"You want him cuffed?" Bishop asked.

I shook my head and pushed my own set back through my belt. "He's not going anywhere. Just go in and gather up all the goddamned artillery."

"No, I meant Victor. You want him in custody?"

I looked at Howard. "Where's he going to go in this world, Howard? He just shot his own son. Leave him alone until the ambulance gets here."

38

THE Posadas County Sheriff's Office filed no charges against Victor Sánchez. Over the next several days, we were able to piece together a version of what his son had done that satisfied us. We might have been wrong in a detail or two, but only time and a few lucky breaks would ever provide the answers.

We found the police scanner stowed under the seat of Mateo Esquibel's old truck; it was the type of radio unit with a power jack that plugged into the cigarette lighter. If Carlos Sánchez had overheard Deputy Enciños respond to the radio call about a possible disturbance on East Bustos Avenue that Sunday night, he may well have gotten nervous.

We didn't know yet where in the state the stolen truck had come from, but odds were good that it had ended up being parked for a short while among the many vehicles behind Nick's dealership. If Tammy Woodruff had had the key to the stolen pickup, and all she had had to do was start the truck and drive off to Mexico, it should have been a slick deal. But Tammy was Tammy.

Waiting in Regal, Carlos had made the decision to drive back toward Posadas, using the old man's truck. The trailer hitched on behind was a typical Carlos Sánchez touch. The rig would look as innocent as the old man. He would have seen the stolen truck parked along the highway, and he would have seen the patrol car behind it, emergency lights flashing. And that had to have been when Carlos took the step to bail Tammy out of trouble, knowing full well that she probably wouldn't have been able to keep her mouth shut. She'd sealed her own fate, of course, when Carlos realized what a liability she really was.

The state crime lab provided a match between the firing pin impression of Carlos Sánchez's pump shotgun and the impression struck in the primer of the single fired shell casing that he'd pumped into the grass along State 56 that Sunday night.

And Sergeant Torrez demonstrated to us how Carlos could have driven Tammy Woodruff's truck over the edge of San Patricio Mesa. It didn't take a gymnast to stand on the chrome running board with the driver's door open, since the vehicle could go over the edge at an idle and gravity would still get the job done. From there, it was a simple hitchhike back to town.

Nick Chavez closed the auto dealership for two days while we went through the building one shelf, one drawer, one file, even one toolbox at a time . . . including Nick's own office. Two days of patient searching gave us one answer that didn't surprise me. Carlos Sánchez had kept no records. Not at the dealership, not in his apartment, not in the bank safe-deposit box that we opened on court order.

There was no magic little book that listed who his drivers were, who his contacts were in other dealerships around the state or in adjoining states, or who his Mexican contacts had been. When his father put a bullet through his son's heart, he effectively erased all of that information.

There was no doubt that Carlos Sánchez had known where his father kept cash receipts at the saloon, and that his father had the bad habit of letting receipts accumulate. In one swift grab, Carlos Sánchez had been able to take nearly three-thousand dollars from his father—additional insurance for his trip south that night.

I wondered what had stung Victor Sánchez more—knowing that

his son had committed the murder of Paul Enciños and Tammy Woodruff, or knowing that Carlos had stolen from him.

I stood in Linda Real's hospital room Friday morning, feeling emotionally drained after the Thursday morning service for Paul Enciños and the two days of fruitless searching at the dealership and Carlos Sánchez's apartment. Linda had accepted the news of Carlos Sánchez's death with a tiny, resigned nod.

"I was going to stop by Estelle's place for a few minutes to pick up some paperwork. Any messages?"

Linda's good eye winked at me, and she said, "Nhhhh."

The legal pad was on the bedside table, and I slid it under her hand, and handed her a pen.

Ask her if she'll stop by once in a while, she wrote. I twisted my head and looked at the message. Linda's handwriting was getting stronger and faster.

"I'll do that," I said.

You have all the answers now?

"I wish we did, Linda. Some things we may never know."

She quickly penned, *??*

I smiled. "Am I off the record?"

What record?

I patted her hand. "Lots and lots of things we don't know, Linda."

The biggest and juiciest?

I laughed. "Now you sound like a reporter, young lady."

It'll give me something to think about.

"All right. We don't know how Tammy Woodruff got linked up with Carlos in the first place. I suppose there's no magic in that—they could have met in a bar, almost anywhere. But we don't know why Tammy agreed to drive one of the trucks for Sánchez. We don't know why she allowed herself to get involved."

Linda's pen hovered over the page, and I could see the portion of her forehead that wasn't covered in bandages furrow.

Excitement, she finally wrote.

"Maybe. And why would he talk to her about what he'd done?"

276

HEY—boys show off for girls!!!
"You think it's that simple?" She winked at me. "Maybe so. Is there anything I can get for you while I'm here?"
No. By the way, I told Mom that if she made trouble for you people, I'd never speak to her again.
"That's nice to hear."
Her pen made little circling motions before she wrote, *Sonny Trujillo? What will happen?*
"I don't know, Linda." I took a deep breath. "It'll depend on how good the lawyers are. They'll get rich, that's for sure."
A nurse wheeling a heavily laden cart pushed through the door, and Linda hastily wrote, *You'll ask Estelle to visit when she can?*
"Yes, I will. And I'll drop by now and again." I patted her hand again, put the pad back on the table, and shoved the pen in my pocket. I put the palm of my hand on her forehead. "Thanks for everything," I said, and she winked.

Pellets of snow drove down from the north, bouncing off the hood and windshield of 310 as I pulled into the Guzman's driveway on South Twelfth Street. I gathered up half a dozen folders of paperwork that needed the signature of our chief of detectives—our only detective—and shoved them under my coat so the three-carbons wouldn't water spot.

Dr. Guzman opened the door for me. "I was just on my way to the hospital," he said. "Did you stop and see Linda?"

"Yes, I did. She's doing fine, all things considered. Is Swan Diver here?"

Francis grinned. "She's in the study with my aunt."

I followed him through the living room debris produced by the cyclone of a small child and into what had been the master bedroom. The year before, Francis had hired contractors to gut the place, turning it into a book-lined office.

Estelle was parked in a recliner, her crutches lying on the floor beside her. Sofia Tournál, looking for all the world like the attorney that she was with her dark tailored suit and severe white blouse, sat in the leather chair behind the desk. She nodded pleasantly at me. I wondered what she really thought about the first bizarre week of her visit.

I greeted them both with a tired smile and then said, "Work," holding out the folders. "Do something constructive." Estelle accepted the folders and hefted them. "All the unanswered questions," I added.

"Fewer and fewer," Estelle replied. She lay the folders carefully on the edge of the desk. "Did Gayle Sedillos get a hold of you?"

"No. I was at the hospital. What did she want?"

"The Albuquerque PD called. A certain young lady"—she opened the leatherette folder that was resting in her lap—"a Carlita Nolan, one of the office staff of Todd Svenson Motors in Albuquerque? She turned herself in to the PD this morning. She says she worked with Carlos Sánchez. And she says she knows several others who did, too."

"She managed to hold out for two days, huh?"

Estelle grimaced. "She was, or thought she was, making progress toward being Carlos's girlfriend. A little posthumous revenge, perhaps, for his dalliance with Tammy." She smiled grimly.

"One more question down," I said.

I looked at Sofia Tournál. She had a pad in front of her, and all I could see was that it was two columns of hen-scratching.

"And are you still finding life in Posadas to be the pastoral, peaceful vacation time that you expected?"

Sofia smiled and leaned back in her chair. "All we need do," she said slowly, choosing her English words with care, "is break a leg." She gestured toward Estelle. "Then we have time to visit."

"You know," Estelle said, "you never did answer my question."

"Question?" I asked.

"Remember last Sunday night? At dinner?"

"Last Sunday is a lifetime ago, Estelle. What did you ask me?" I knew damn well what she had asked me.

I saw Sofia smile and push the pad she'd been writing on toward Estelle. "You see?" she said to Estelle, and turned her smile on me.

"What question?"

"I asked what you thought about me running for sheriff."

I shook my head. "No, you didn't. You told me you were thinking of running. You didn't ask me what I thought."

"Hmmm," Estelle said, and frowned. "Well?"

"What do I think?"

"Yes."

I ran my fingers around the rim of my Stetson, forehead furrowed in the deepest of concentration. Estelle waited patiently. Finally, I looked up at Sofia and gestured at the pad. "Are those all the pros and cons? Is that what you two were talking about?"

Sofia nodded, and Estelle said seriously, "It's not such an easy decision to make, I've discovered."

"Well," I said, and Estelle looked up expectantly. She looked younger than my youngest daughter. "I'm probably the wrong person to ask, sweetheart. If you lose the election, you'll be disappointed, of course. And I don't know if Marty Holman has a vindictive streak. And if he loses the election . . ." I hesitated and then grinned. "Then I lose a decent administrator on the one hand and my chief of detectives on the other. You're the one then who would always be tied up in endless county commission meetings." I held up my hands. "Lose, lose. It's a tough choice."

I knew it wasn't the answer that Estelle had wanted to hear, but that was politics. I turned to Sofia Tournál. "Have you had dinner out since you arrived here? I mean, other than in fits and snatches, or out of a bag?"

She looked mildly surprised. "No. I haven't."

"Well, then," I said, "how would you like to have dinner with me this evening, just you and me, and we will discuss this young lady's political future. No interruptions. No telephones. No radios. No fried chicken in a cardboard box. And no baby-sitting."

"Sir . . ." Estelle said.

"About seven?" I asked, and Sofia nodded demurely.

Estelle took a deep breath and then let it out slowly as she broke into a grin. I turned to go and gestured at the two-column list. "Keep working," I said.